E.L. BATES

Death by Disguise

Whitney & Davies Book 3

STARDANCE PRESS

Contents

Acknowledgments

Here it is at last! My thanks to all the fans of Whitney & Davies who have so patiently waited for this next installment of their adventures. I am grateful to you for sticking around this long in between books. Take heart—I have begun work on Book 4 already!

Thanks are also due to A.M. Offenwanger, editor extraordinaire, for her eagle eye and wise comments. I am also grateful to Carl Ayers for his Latin translations, proofreading, and willingness to listen to me verbally wrestle through issues in a story. I am deeply grateful to Amanda McCrina for taking time out of her overwhelmingly busy schedule to design the gorgeous cover—as always, I am blown away by her work.

I could have not written this story were it not for the year and a half I lived in Cambridge. Saint Dorothea's is inspired by and exists on the location of Newnham College, Cambridge—I hope they don't object to my appropriating it for this story. I loved my time in that beautiful and ancient city, and this story is in many ways my love letter to it.

* * *

Chapter 1

Lennox Davies was thoroughly happy with life. He was as far from the stultifying life of a country gentleman as he could be without actually renouncing his family name. He lived in a superbly comfortable flat in London, had his whims catered to and anticipated by a friend and manservant whose worth was above rubies, was engaged in work that was both satisfying and meaningful, and he spent nearly every day with a woman whose very existence filled him with delight.

Now that his magic, drained out of him entirely last April, was getting stronger every day, Len couldn't think of a single thing that would make life better. He grinned as he sorted through the post Becket had brought him alongside his breakfast, stifling the temptation to break into song.

Zest for living was all very well and good, but accompanying one's eggs and bacon with *tra-la-la-ing* was carrying things a bit too far.

He tossed his tailor's bill to one side and picked up the next letter, addressed in his mother's distinctive hand. What was the mater up to now? She did not generally write without a reason.

Len neatly slit open the envelope and pulled out the missive, hearing in his mind his mother's crisp tones with their Scottish lilt as his eyes skimmed over the black, decisive loops and swirls of her script.

My dear Lennox,

I trust you are well and that your work as a private detective is satisfying your ever-present urge for adventure and other similar foolishness. Some mothers might have expected their sons to have grown out of such desires by now, but I have always known your 'satiable curtiosity was here to stay. Had you been born a hundred years earlier you likely would have been an explorer of the turbid Amazon or a howling desert or an uninhabited island on the shores of the Red Sea, so I suppose I should be thankful you have taken up something as relatively harmless as detecting.

So. I shall be traveling to Stirling shortly to visit Pippa and Cameron and my new grandson, and I have a mind to come first to London to do some shopping—linens and teaspoons and such, you know. Would it put Becket to too much work if I were to stay at the flat? I will arrive Thursday 8th October, and leave the following morning. If this is inconvenient for you, you have only to write and tell me so. I can always stay at my club.

I have an ulterior motive for wanting to see you, besides Becket's incomparable muffins and an old woman's natural desire to spend time with her only son. I am not at all easy in my mind about young Charles Norris. He is not half the man his father was, and I fear that letting him take over the lease of Glyn Manor after old Mr. Norris passed was a mistake. He has fired Mackenzie for some trifling reason and hired a new steward, a Mr. Ames who slouches about and knows nothing at all about draining fields or rotating crops—and seemingly cares less. I myself have spoken to Mr. Ames about his management of the estate and received nothing but a sneer for my pains. There are also rumors that Norris is turning off some of the workers, and even talking about making some of the cottagers leave so he can put in people of his own choosing.

I do try not to interfere with the managing of the estate, and I would not dream of mentioning this to you were it not for the fact that you have not visited us in well over a year and therefore can only know what is happening here when someone else informs you of it. Mackenzie would not think it his place to write to you, I know, and I am sure Norris hasn't seen fit to tell you of any of these changes, so the unpleasant task is left to me.

If you have anything you wish me to carry to Pippa or your new nephew, have it ready by my arrival and I will be happy to take it with me so long as it is nothing unreasonably large, such as a rocking horse or a life-sized toy cannon or any of the other ridiculous things doting uncles seem to find necessary to shower on helpless babes. Until then, I remain,
Your loving,
Mother.

Much of Len's sense of wellbeing had drained away during the course of the letter. Not so much his mother's thinly-veiled disapproval of his lifestyle: she might wish he would settle down in his father's place at Glyn Manor, the Davies family estate for countless generations, but she had always understood his need for broader pastures, and even encouraged him to stretch his wings. Nor did he mind her jab about the inconvenience of putting her up for a night—that was her way of making a joke, as was referring to herself as an old woman.

No, it was her comments on Norris that concerned him. When old Mr. Norris died, it seemed the easiest thing in the world to allow his son to take over the tenancy agreement and continue to run the place. Mother was settled for life in the Dowager House by the manor gates and could keep an eye on things from there, and Len had no reason to mistrust Charles.

But this business of firing Mackenzie and hiring a new steward without even telling Len about it … no, he did not like the sounds of that. Mackenzie was a good, solid man—he had been the steward for as long as Len could remember, and the estate had always thrived under his care.

Nor did Len like the rumors of workers turned off the estate and cottagers thrown out of their homes. By thunder, that wouldn't do at all! He frowned. No good writing to Norris until he had more than the mater's word to go on. While Len trusted her wholly, it would be too easy for Norris to dismiss her concerns as those of a foolish old woman clinging to the old ways. Ridiculous—Mother was one of the most forward-minded women he knew—but best not to give Norris even that much of a leg to stand on if he chose to argue the matter.

He would write to Mackenzie, Len decided, as well as to old Amos Greer, the former head groom, given one of their finest cottages upon his getting too old to keep working with the horses. Once he had their responses, he would know better how to approach the matter with Norris.

First, though, would be to reassure Mother.

Len cleared his throat. "Oh Becket," he called.

His manservant popped out of the small kitchenette, drying his hands on a spotlessly white towel as he did. "Sir?"

"Would you be so kind as to fetch me my writing gear? Oh, and m'mother will be here next Thursday."

"Very good, sir. I will make sure to air the good linens for the spare bed on Wednesday."

"She's dropped a few hints about your muffins as well."

"I would be disappointed if she hadn't, sir."

After Becket set his stationery before him, Len thought for a few moments before picking up the fountain pen. His mother wasn't difficult, but she did require … careful handling. Finally, he filled the pen from the inkwell, set nib to paper, and began to write.

Dearest Mamma,

Of course you may come to us on the 8th—what's more, I'll come to Piccadilly Station myself to collect you while Becket bakes up a batch of the freshest muffins possible with which to greet you. Which is more than he ever does for me when I've been away, let me tell you.

Here Len paused. What next? He decided to skip entirely the conversation about his detective work, as he could not think of any way to respond to her comments without sounding defensive or overly frivolous. Let Mother make of his silence on the topic what she may.

I am much obliged to you for the information about Charles Norris, especially when it comes to firing Mackenzie. He'd better have a thundering good explanation for doing so without telling me! I have been shockingly lax in my visits to the old place, I know, but it is easy to let matters slide when I have you there to keep me up-to date on all the happenings.

Did that sound too much like flattery? He read it over and decided that it did sound like flattery, but as it was the plain truth, it would have to stay.

Still, that's no excuse. I am writing to Mackenzie as well, and you may be certain I shall overwhelm Norris with my wrath once I've heard old Mac's side of the story. And here's a promise for you: if need be, I'll come down there myself and straighten matters out. There now! I can't say fairer than that.

Len shuddered. The last thing he wanted to do was leave London even for a few days to return to the dreariness of the family estate, but duty was duty. He hoped he would not be called upon to make good his promise.

You can carry my love to Pippa and Cam when you go, and I suppose I shall have to find some bauble or other to go to my nephew. Pity Pippa didn't inherit our other sense; a color-changing ball would be just the thing. Alas, I shall have to pick up something more mundane.

Len wondered if the newest Cameron would grow up to show any magical abilities. It did not usually happen that a youngster developed the talent when neither of his parents had it, but magic was strong on his mother's side of the family, and it was just possible it might have skipped Pippa and gone right to her son. That was how it had worked for Maia, after all.

Len grinned foolishly, thinking of the other half of the Whitney and Davies detecting agency, with her tall stature, her reddish-brown hair with that hint of curl, her wide, well-formed mouth and determined chin, her eyes that looked either green or blue depending on her mood, her rich laughter and keen mind ...

He wrenched himself back to the business at hand.

I remain, as ever, your devoted son,
  Lennox.

He blew on the ink to dry it, folded the letter, and slid it into the envelope, picking up a wafer of wax to seal it the old-fashioned way.

He held his breath for a moment. Despite the nearly six months since he had, with Maia's help, regained the use of his magic, he still felt a *frisson* of doubt every time he prepared a spell. What if it didn't work? What if the only reason it had been working all along was because Maia had lent him some of her magic to begin with? What if that was used up now? What if …

He shook his head, impatient with himself. Though he still couldn't do big magic, or several small spells in a row, his magic was getting stronger every day, just as an injured limb regained its strength through regular, cautious exercise after the initial wound had healed. He might never regain fully his old strength, but there was no reason to fear it would be gone again for no reason.

"*Califace cera,*" he said, his voice a bass rumble.

The wax promptly softened into a warm puddle on the envelope. Len grinned and combed his fingers back through his hair. Ha, see, he knew he could still do it. No need to fear at all.

Before the wax could harden and he needed to go through it all over again—this time with less power at his command, as it would take some time to recover even from that small use—he twisted his signet ring around and pressed it into the wax, leaving behind the clear imprint of an ear of wheat inside a three-cornered shield.

While he had his stationery to hand, he might as well get the other letters written and out of the way as well. If by some miracle a cracking good case had come to Maia or Gwen overnight, he didn't want to have any unpleasant personal tasks hanging over his head and preventing him from investigating fully.

Stifling a sigh, he picked up a fresh piece of stationery and began the next letter.

* * *

The instant Len walked through the door of The Glass Spoon, he knew something had changed. Maia was, as usual, sitting at the small corner table they had come to think of as "theirs," but unlike most days, when her face was set in lines of patience and a frustration she wouldn't allow herself to feel, today her eyes sparkled greenly and her wide, generous mouth was smiling.

Len crossed the floor and nodded a greeting to the proprietor—Albert Weatherby, a minor magician who specialized in kitchen magic. His small restaurant was a favored haunt of most of London's magicians, and Len and Maia had taken to meeting there at least twice a week to discuss if any possible cases had turned up for them.

Len seated himself casually in the chair across from Maia, and smiled into her eyes. He had known from the start this would be a good day!

"Let me guess: we have a client."

Maia nodded. "We do indeed."

"Murder?" Len asked, trying not to sound too hopeful. Murder was dreadful, of course, but far more interesting than hunting down lost dogs or finding missing jewelry for too-rich society ladies.

"Not yet," Maia said. "I'll let our client give you the details. Here she comes now."

Len slid around in his chair to see a petite Anglo-Chinese woman entering the restaurant.

"*Gwen?*" he said, frozen in the automatic act of rising to his feet.

Gwen Zhang was the third member of their small detective agency. Once a junior member of Domestic Protection, England's magical police force, Gwen had happily exchanged the promise of a dull career of writing up minor magical infractions for something more exciting and active when Maia had proposed the switch to her. During this six-month stretch where they had had so few cases, she had been starting to show signs of restlessness. Len was hoping that a properly juicy case would help settle her back down. He hadn't expected her to be the one bringing the case.

"On behalf of Saint Dorothea's," Gwen said, sitting in the third chair at the table that Len pulled out for her and smoothing her rose-pink skirt over her knees.

Now Len was truly startled. He reseated himself thoughtfully. Saint Dorothea's, or more properly The Scholars of the College of the Blessed Saint Dorothea, was an experiment that seemed to be succeeding, despite the doubts of more traditional magicians in England. It was a college for up-and-coming magicians, hidden inside the larger Cambridge University. Len didn't pretend to understand how it worked, but somehow it did. Gwen had been a member of its first graduating class two years ago. If she was a sample of the magicians Saint Dorothea's was turning out, Len thought the college had a fine chance of holding its own well into the future. He couldn't imagine why they would need the help of Whitney and Davies.

"A few days ago, Gwen received a letter from a fellow former student at Saint Dorothea's," Maia said, then nodded to Gwen for the young woman to pick up the tale.

"Charlotte was at Saint Dot's with me," Gwen repeated. "She was training to be a healer, while I, as you know, wanted to join magical law enforcement. We had some supervisions together, and became friends. After we were graduated, I started work for Domestic Protection and then for you. Lottie didn't make it as a healer; instead she stayed at Saint Dot's, working in administration. I haven't heard from her since I left Cambridge, until she sent me this letter two days ago."

She cleared her throat and began to read.

"Dear Gwen,

"So you've moved from public work to the private sector, have you? Well done! We all knew you were too good for Deep. Has the detection business proven glamorous? Lots of adventurers and handsome lords coming to beg your aid?

"Betty and Sarah have become governesses to two wealthy families with magical brats. Too ghastly, but really, with their abilities, what more could they hope for? Charles has started out in the lowest level of the Circle and talks as though he were part of the inner ring already, poor thing. I suppose it's too much to ask him to recognize that he can't possibly hope to ever achieve more than what he has now. Wait and see, in a few years time all we'll hear from him is how nobody recognizes his great talent and if it weren't for the jealousy of other magicians he'd be much higher in rank. Pathetic, but what can one expect? Babs has managed to wheedle her way

into a position as assistant to the Governor of Dorset! She always was good at sucking up. She is no end puffed up about it all, it's disgusting to hear her talk.

"As for little old me, I'm still here at dear old Saint Dot's. Administrative work sounds dull, but the amount of work it takes to keep the only magical college in England operating smoothly while still hiding it from the university itself ... well, my dear, be thankful detectives don't have to keep up with the amount of paperwork I go through on a daily basis! Not that our status depends on me alone, of course, I'm not like Babs or Charles, thinking I'm the most important magician in England, but still: even the littlest cogs in the wheel are necessary to keep it turning, and despite what Pelham—she's too good for "Jenny" these days, it's Pelham or Miss Pelham, thank you very much—seems to think, even silly old Charlotte has her uses.

"And don't think my life is devoid of excitement and danger, either! There's been a rash of thefts here at the school—nothing of mine has been stolen, of course, I've always been so careful of my belongings—but others have lost items. I've told the victims they should report it to the Magistra—surely this is a matter for Deep—but so far everyone is too afraid of 'causing unpleasantness' to do anything about it. I wish someone would do something, though. So uncomfortable, wondering if the person you work next to on a daily basis is really a THIEF.

"Still, I've kept my head down and tried to carry on as usual, but then I started receiving the most disgusting anonymous threats in the post—trash, but too creepy for words. I was going to report them to the Magistra myself, but everyone in the office laughed at me when I suggested it, and said I was blowing things out of proportion. I never want to cause trouble, as you know, so I decided to keep it to myself. I wouldn't want Doctor Bingham thinking I was putting

myself forward in any way.

"Then last night, as I walked to the school from my lodgings—a mere worker bee like myself doesn't qualify for rooms in the college itself, you know, so I board in a dreadfully small and dingy place, with a horrid old nosy landlady, but what else can one afford on my salary?—I crossed the bridge and paused for a moment to admire the River Cam, as I always do, and would you believe it, someone shoved me in the back so hard I went right through the railings—they were old and rotten anyway—and landed in the river!

"Oh, I was in no danger of drowning, as the water levels are so low in that spot, but I confess I was unnerved. Humiliated and angry, as well. I had to go to work sopping wet or risk a scolding from Pelham. She has no sympathy whatsoever toward other people's troubles! No one there seemed to think it was an incident even worth noting—I heard some of the other girls giggling about it in the cloakroom at dinner—but I can't help but feel uneasy. As luck would have it, no one else had been near the bridge at the time—my path to and from home and college isn't one of the more attractive ones, so it is sparsely traversed at the best of times—so I have no idea who could have done such a thing.

"Now, who do you suppose would want to do harm to harmless old Charlotte? Or am I exaggerating things? You know I'm not imaginative, not like Sarah and her flights of fancy (one does hope she doesn't start imagining herself a Jane Eyre or something of the sort at her new post). Perhaps I am making too much of it, but still, it's the sort of thing that does make one nervous.

"I shall have to learn some defensive spells if this goes on! I don't suppose you know any good ones?

"Ta, darling,

"Lottie."

"Curious," Len said.

"That's only the start," Maia said.

Gwen re-folded the letter and replaced it in her handbag. "I wasn't sure whether to worry or not when I received this—I couldn't imagine something truly sinister going on at Saint Dot's, not without the Magistra knowing about it and putting a stop to it—but I thought that since we didn't have any cases on hand at the moment, I might take a couple of days to visit Lottie and make sure she was all right. I sent her a note that evening, through magical means so it would arrive immediately, but I didn't hear anything back. When there was still no response by teatime yesterday, I started to feel nervous, so I contacted the college to ask to speak to her directly." Gwen leaned forward in her chair. "They couldn't find her anywhere in the buildings or the grounds, and neither the front nor the back gate porter had let her out. Several people had seen her arrive, but then sometime between the start of the day and when I contacted them, she had vanished."

"And there's no other way out of the college except through the gates?" Len asked.

Gwen shook her head. "No, not even a convenient tree near the wall." She dimpled unexpectedly, her smile mischievous. "Trust me, I would know."

Len drummed his fingers on the table. "Curious," he said a second time.

They were interrupted then by Albert bringing over their coffee and a plate of shortbread.

"Did I hear you talking about Saint Dot's?" he said, his accent pure Cockney to match his sharp-featured face. "Me cousin thought about attending there when she finished 'er apprenticeship, but blimey, no one in our family has ever gone to university, and 'ow would me auntie explain that to the neighbors? Save the college for folk like you, that's what I say, and us common folk'll stick with the old ways."

Gwen's smile faded as Bert favored them with a cheery nod and went on his way. "That's just the trouble, the lower classes think uni is too posh for them, and the upper classes think a departure from tradition is too risky, and so how can Saint Dot's thrive?"

Len cleared his throat. "Very true."

Gwen blinked, shook her head, and added some milk to her coffee. "Sorry. No one was too concerned about Lottie, and Jenny—Jenny Pelham, who is the head secretary—was inclined to dismiss it all as nonsense even after they searched the college twice and couldn't find her, but the Magistra said it was peculiar enough that she would appreciate it if we would make the trip to Cambridge to see if we could decipher the puzzle. I didn't think either of you would object, so I said yes."

Len began to understand why Maia's eyes were sparkling. "A veritable locked room mystery," he said softly. How could a woman disappear from within the walls of a magical college? Not only that, but this was an excuse to visit Saint Dorothea's, and learn more about how it worked. So long as he was back in time for his mother's visit, he was pleased to exchange the dreariness of London in October for the charm of Cambridge.

He looked across the table to meet Maia's gaze. "When do we leave?"

"As soon as Becket can pack your bags," she answered. "I've secured us four tickets for the afternoon train."

"Jolly good," Len said, finishing his coffee at one gulp. "To Cambridge we shall go, then."

Chapter 2

The afternoon train from London to Cambridge was not crowded, and Maia was pleased when the four of them were able to claim an otherwise unoccupied first class carriage for themselves. Not only would it make the journey far more comfortable and mean that Becket could ride with them without raising eyebrows, it allowed them to discuss the case—and any other matters that might arise—without fear of listening ears. Maia had been a magician for just over four years now, and she had yet to master the art of publicly discussing magic in such a way as to sound innocuous to anyone within earshot. She could cast a spell to make their voices sound like buzzing to listening ears, but that only worked if the listeners were at sufficient distance that they wouldn't expect to hear a conversation clearly.

Len, of course, was an expert at saying one thing and meaning another, but that was only to be expected given his former line of work. When they had first met, Maia had believed him entirely frivolous and insincere, but it hadn't taken long before she started appreciating the depth of character he hid beneath that flippant exterior. By now, she had come to think of him as one of the finest men she knew—though she did still sometimes wish he would be a touch more transparent. Four years was not quite long enough to allow her to read what he was truly thinking and feeling under his "jolly good show" attitude. She could guess, but there was still an element of doubt, and it did occasionally make her more reticent to speak of her own deeper thoughts.

Not that either of them were particularly given to heartfelt speeches to begin with. They were, after all, English. Maia sometimes envied the American soldiers and nurses she had met during the war, both for their ease of communication and their "can-do" mindset. Not that she wanted to be American, naturally not … but there were times when she wished she could throw off the weight of convention and speak her mind—and heart—freely.

For example, all this talk of Saint Dorothea's had stirred up the faintest breath of regret in her heart. Oh, she didn't regret her apprenticeship to Aunt Amelia, who, if stubborn, sarcastic, and set in her ways, was still one of England's finest magicians, and had given Maia a firm grounding in the basics of magic. Nor did she regret choosing a less-than-conventional path for a journeyman magician. Rather than setting her ambition high, to become an administrator of the magicians in a county or even to join the Circle, the governing body of magicians for the British Isles, Maia had decided to use her abilities to help those who were most often overlooked by society, both magical and not. Becoming a private detective had seemed, at the time, the best way to achieve that goal.

Aunt Amelia had been thoroughly disgusted by her niece choosing such a pedestrian career and the idea of Maia becoming a "general magician" rather than specializing, but at the time, Maia had had no doubts as to the rightness of her choice.

There were days, especially recently, however, when she did wonder. So few cases had come to them over the last six months that Maia was beginning to wonder if there really was such a burning need for their particular brand of justice after all. And now, learning about the opportunities she might have had if she had chosen to attend Saint Dorothea's after completing her apprenticeship … there was a seed of doubt. She would have appreciated talking it out with Len, but that would involve more raw honesty than Maia was entirely comfortable with, plus what if he thought that meant she was regretting their partnership? No, it would never do.

Besides, she didn't really regret her choice. Especially now, with what seemed like a perfectly smashing puzzle awaiting them at the end of their train journey.

"Tell us more about Miss Carlyle," Len invited Gwen. "And more about how Saint Dorothea's operates. It is as well to go in prepared," he added, bringing a deliberate pomposity to his voice.

Gwen chuckled obligingly, then began. "Lottie, like me, was one of the first graduates from Saint Dot's." Her face changed, becoming animated as she switched tracks. "Did you know that in 1919, for the first time ever in our history, Britain was faced with the reality of more apprentices than there were masters to train them? The War changed life for all of us in England. So many master magicians were killed during the war, along with many journeymen who might have gone on to achieve mastery. Doctor Bingham had been pushing for a school like Saint Dot's for years, but it was that crisis that forced the Circle to accept that they needed to look at new ways of training and accepting magicians." Her dark eyes sparkled as she tucked an errant lock of hair back under her hat.

"The magic and creativity that went into starting up a brand-new college within the university system, one that is only discoverable by magically adept prospective students yet is still a functioning part of Cambridge itself, was phenomenal. It would have made Dr. Bingham a master magician if she hadn't already been one. To attend Saint Dot's is to be a Cambridge student, yet no one who is not a magician is aware of the college. I can say to another Cambridgian, 'Oh, I went to Saint Dot's,' the way someone else might say they were at King's, or St John's, and even though they don't specifically know the college they know that it's part of the university. It's *fascinating*."

Fascinating indeed. Maia could not fathom the knowledge that went into those spells. It served to remind her that despite her recent advances in the world of spells and sorcery, she was still very, very new to all this.

"And you and Miss Carlyle were among the first to be part of that," Len prompted.

Gwen nodded. "We were the experimental ones, the students who were willing to try something few others would. There were only a dozen of us, and mostly female—and didn't that cause a rumpus throughout the university, a co-ed college where women were awarded degrees! Only the fact that they couldn't put their finger on what exact college we were prevented them from banning us altogether. The whole thing gave us all an extra bond of friendship, even the men, whether our personalities were compatible or not."

"Are you saying you and Miss Carlyle wouldn't have been friends under normal circumstances?" Len asked, his eyes shrewd.

Gwen picked at the pleats of the skirt of her fashionable

dove-grey traveling suit, spread neatly across the blue plush of the seat. "Lottie is a lovely person, really. She is diligent, hard-working …"

"She was a nice, bright girl with no men friends," Len murmured softly. "Gwen, we need more than what people tell the newspapers about a missing person. What is Charlotte Carlyle really like?"

Gwen sighed. "She *is* diligent and hard-working, but … not much else. You must have gathered from the letter, she doesn't have strong friendships with anyone, nor even strong enmities, and she has always found it difficult to get people to take her seriously. She wanted to be a healer and settled for a glorified secretary, and even now she's clinging to the past—dredging up all our college chums and their lives—than moving forward. I think she stayed at Saint Dot's because she was too afraid to move on."

"A complaining plodder, eh?" Len asked.

Gwen winced, but nodded. "That does sum her up rather well."

"She can't be that much of a plodder if she was willing to go for something as new and different as Saint Dorothea's," Maia said, surprised at the sharpness in her own tone. Why should she feel so irritated and—yes, defensive, that was the emotion poking her—at that simple description of a woman she'd never met?

She felt more than saw Len glance quickly at her, but Gwen seemed oblivious to the edge in Maia's words.

"That's a good point," the younger woman said, tilting her head as she considered it. "I think, though … I rather think she came to Saint Dot's because she felt she might have more of a chance to distinguish herself through a new path rather than the traditional one, except she found it was more difficult than she anticipated. She was always ready to try something new, Lottie was, but whatever she tried, there was always some excuse for why she failed at it."

Maia's opened her mouth for another sharp remark, then closed it through sheer force of will. There was no reason, absolutely none, for snapping at Gwen. Whatever was causing Maia to feel so defensive about a stranger, it wasn't Gwen's fault. To keep her tongue still, she focused her attention on the scenery flashing past the window, the fields yellow with harvested stubble and the trees beginning to change color and shed their leaves.

With another side glance at Maia, Len smoothly picked up the conversation. "So Miss Carlyle has remained at Saint Dorothea's as a secretary, and within the last month or so became concerned about a rash of petty thefts at the college, which led to some minor attacks on her person, followed by her complete disappearance in an impossible fashion yesterday. Well, well, well. A very pretty case." He leaned back against the train seat, tapping his fingertips together in the approved Sherlock Holmes fashion.

"Why, does it make sense to you?" Maia asked as she turned from the window, amused despite herself.

Len smiled at her. "Not in the least. That's what makes it so pretty."

Maia stifled an unladylike snort. When Len started talking like a book detective, there was no hope of getting any more sense out of him.

That might have been the end of the conversation, but Becket surprised them all by speaking up next.

"It would seem that the thefts must have been more important than they first appeared, or else why would the thief go to such lengths to silence Miss Carlyle? Perhaps there was some sinister purpose behind them, one which we currently cannot comprehend."

"You think her disappearance a result of the theft, then?" Len said, dropping his affected mannerisms and giving his manservant full attention.

"That does seem indicated," Becket said, inclining his head modestly. "It could, of course, be the result of something else of which we are not aware, but that does seem too strong of a coincidence."

"The other question is, did she disappear of her own free will, to protect herself from this thief, or was she kidnapped?" Len mused.

Or murdered, was the chilling thought in Maia's mind, but out of deference for Gwen, she didn't say it aloud. She caught Len's eye and knew he was thinking the same.

"Surely not of her own free will," Gwen protested. "Not when she knew I was coming, and she would have help and protection. She must have let something slip to the thief without realizing who it was, something about a detective coming to look into things, and so they kidnapped her to …" She trailed off, clearly unsure of what kidnapping Charlotte Carlyle would do with a detective already on the way.

"Distract us, perhaps," Maia said. "We investigate the disappearance rather than the thefts. Or else it's possible that the thief accidentally revealed him- or herself to Miss Carlyle and then had to make sure she wouldn't be able to tell you their identity. Or—well, there are many reasons. All this is sheer speculation. We won't be able to make reasonable deduction until we've arrived and begun questioning people."

"Yes, and about that," Len said. "How shall we go about the questioning? Becket, old boy, I suppose you'll want to tackle the porter, the kitchen staff, the cleaners, all that sort?"

"If you would be so good as to leave them to me, yes sir. I believe I might be able to establish a better rapport with them than the rest of you."

"And Gwen, of course you must introduce us to the Magistra right away, since she is the one who requested our presence," Len continued. "But I'd most like to question the people who worked with Miss Carlyle. The other secretaries."

Gwen nodded. "Yes, of course. I can introduce you to Jenny—Miss Pelham, the head secretary. She was also part of our graduating class." She wrinkled her nose. "She isn't always the most pleasant individual, but *most* efficient."

"And I would like to speak with the teaching staff and students, to see if they have noticed anything odd lately," Maia added.

"Oh, and of course we must also investigate Miss Carlyle's rooms. Even though she didn't disappear from them, they might still hold some clues for us. We also ought to see what sort of spells are layered around the college grounds, to see if there's been any tampering with the official magic that might cause a person to vanish."

"Secret doors," Becket offered.

"Hidden passageways," Maia said.

Gwen frowned, then offered a tentative contribution. "Disguising a person in plain sight, like Len's favorite chameleon spell?"

Len smiled broadly. "Well, this seems a promising start. Now we have only to wait for this infernal train to get there. You know, Maia, if you'd let me drive us—"

"We'd be broken down on the side of the road somewhere and we wouldn't reach Cambridge until next week," Maia broke in.

Len tried for an injured look, but the twitching of his lips gave him away. Even he had to admit his automobile spent more time in the garage than on the road.

* * *

Gwen had said someone from the college would meet them at the station, and sure enough, there was a bright-faced young man—too young to have fought in the War, Maia's brain automatically assessed, as it always did in the almost-seven years since the War's end—awaiting them as they disembarked the train and exited the station through the yellow brick arches into the fresh air of Cambridge.

"Hullo, Miss Gwen," he said, stepping forward and touching his hand to his cap.

"Hullo, Tom," Gwen said, smiling at him and allowing him to take her valise. "It's good to see you again. Are you our chauffeur today?"

"Yes Miss, Dr. Bingham, she told me to bring the auto and collect you and your friends, so here I am. Good afternoon, miss, sirs," he said, looking over Gwen's shoulder.

"Oh, sorry," Gwen said. "Maia, Len, Becket—this is Tom Wright, junior porter at Saint Dot's, chauffeur on the rare occasions one is called for, and general aid to students in a scrape." She flashed another grin at him. "Tom, this is Maia Whitney, Len Davies, and, er, Mr. Becket." Neither Maia nor Gwen had yet managed to learn Becket's proper name, despite

23

their best efforts. Len claimed even he didn't know it, but Maia suspected otherwise.

Tom touched his cap again. "Pleasure, I'm sure. Welcome to Cambridge. Can I take your bag, miss?"

He took Maia's small carrying case in his free hand and led the way to a shining red tourer sitting in a long line of black cabs across the street from the station.

"Golly," Gwen said. "This is new."

"It's Dr. Bingham's pride and joy," Tom said, opening the boot for the luggage. "She doesn't half get nervous when I take it out! It'd be more than my life is worth to bring it back with a scratch. She must be pleased to have you back for a visit, Miss Gwen, or else I'd have been bringing your luggage in a handcart and you lot would have been walking!"

He winked and swung himself into the driver's seat. Without a word, Becket slid in beside him, and the other three climbed in the back.

"I almost wish our Gwen weren't valued so highly," Maia said *sotto voce* to Len, beside her, as they began their drive. "I think I'd enjoy the walk. I had no idea Cambridge was such a beautiful city."

Not that she'd seen much of it so far, but the trees lining the streets even this close to the rail station, and the beautiful Victorian and Georgian architecture she could see in the houses tucked away behind stone walls, were enough to strike a chord in her soul.

"Once we get this cleared up, we can toddle all around the old place," Len said. "Did you notice something interesting, though? The Magistra—Dr. Bingham—sends her precious auto for us so we arrive quickly, but she hasn't spread around the reason for our arrival."

"At least, not to the staff." Maia thought for a moment, then corrected herself. "No, not at all. If it was known at all, the porters would be aware of it." Servants generally had their fingers on the pulse of a place, and Maia could only imagine college porters even more so.

"Exactly. So she's nervous, but still striving for discretion."

"Not much discreet about this auto," Maia said dryly.

"I suppose not," Len grinned. He looked around him, then leaned toward Gwen. "Not that I'm complaining, but aren't we headed in the wrong direction? I've not been to Cambridge in a donkey's age, but I'm fairly certain the colleges are that way." He waved a hand.

Maia's eyes followed the sweep of his hand, turning her gaze north. Barely visible over the hedges and houses that lined the road, hints of grey and golden stone were sun-limned against the cerulean sky.

Gwen shook her head. "Saint Dot's isn't in the heart of the city. It would be too difficult to keep it hidden from students and tourists if it were. It's on the outskirts, still easy to walk to and from, but not as noticeable."

"That does make sense," Maia conceded.

She had never visited Cambridge before, never had a reason to. She hadn't expected to find it resembling a country village so much, but she decided she quite liked all the trees and green grass, and even the cows that stood blocking the footpaths, chewing their cuds while placidly watching cyclists and walkers alike veer around them. She liked the small shop on the corner of the road, the friendly-appearing pub a few blocks down, and the bakery Gwen pointed out as having the best pastries in the city. Above all, she relished the sense of peace and calm that pervaded the city, even to their loud motorcar.

Briefly, Maia had a vision of herself living and studying in this town—evenings arguing magical theory with her fellow students in the pub, afternoons spent strolling along the river with a sandwich in her pocket, wrestling with a recalcitrant spell, pastries and coffee in the mornings at the bakery, laughing and chatting about the day's plans with Len ...

She blinked as the motorcar purred to a stop before a high brick wall covered in ivy. This was no time for dreaming—they had a missing woman to find and a case to solve.

Maia could just see the tops of some red brick buildings on the other side of the wall, but there was little to distinguish them from the other houses and buildings along the road. A modest brass plaque affixed to the wall beside the stately wrought iron gate stated "Saint Dorothea's" with no other description.

Tom exited the driver's seat and opened the door for the rest of them. "Do you want to bring your friends inside, Miss Gwen, or should I do the honors?"

"I'll do it, thanks, Tom," Gwen said. She looked over her shoulder to make sure the others were watching, then passed her hand over the plaque. Its surface shifted from solid brass to translucent pearl and back again, and on the other side of the wall, a small man with a bowler hat and twinkling eyes popped out of the building closest to them and approached the gate, swinging a length of polished blackthorn that was clearly more decorative than necessary, as he walked jauntily without it once touching the ground.

"Hullo!" he said, unlocking the gates and opening them wide. "Welcome to—well, bless my soul, if it isn't Miss Gwen. Your train must have made good time, you're here earlier than we were expecting."

Back at the auto, Tom called out, "I'll put the car away in its shed and bring the bags in. Dr. Bingham has arranged rooms for you all."

"Mind you watch how you back that machine in, young Wright," the porter at the gate growled at him. "You nearly scratched the fender last time."

"Nearly only means it wasn't actually scratched," Tom cheekily responded. "Besides, I'd like to see the person who could back it in without coming close to disaster—the stalls were made for horses, not for autos." He released the brake and drove off, turning at the corner, before the other porter could reply.

"Impertinent cub," the porter said. "I don't know why the Magistra don't sack him. Welcome, sirs and miss, to Saint Dorothea's. Any friend of Miss Gwen's is a friend of ours."

Gwen repeated the introductions she had given Tom. "This is Appleby, our senior porter," she concluded. "What he doesn't know about Saint Dot's isn't worth knowing."

"I wouldn't go that far, Miss Gwen, but it's true I've been here from the beginning, longer than anyone else but Dr. Bingham and Miss Archer," Appleby replied, beaming at her. "But come in, do! Dr. Bingham said to let her know as soon as you arrived, and bring to her study for tea."

"Ooh, lovely," Gwen said with a sigh. Maia couldn't agree more. The train ride had left her weary and dry-mouthed, and tea sounded splendid right now. Still, she didn't want to let this opportunity slip.

"Thank you very much, Mr. Appleby, you are kind," she said, crossing the threshold of the college grounds. Once inside the gate, they stood in an open vestibule of sorts, with a roof overhead connecting the porter's lodge on one side and another brick building on the other. Maia longed to explore further, but she controlled her impulse and turned to Gwen, resigning herself to a small deception in order to gain information in an unsuspicious fashion.

"Gwen, you were hoping to see your friend Charlotte Carlyle while here, weren't you? Is she available, do you know, Mr. Appleby?"

"It's funny you should ask that, miss," Appleby said. "Dr. Bingham was looking for her just yesterday, and we couldn't find her then, either. It's a peculiar thing, that—I saw her come in to work yesterday morning, said good morning as usual, but then she didn't leave with everyone else at the end of the day, or at any time prior, for that matter. And I haven't seen her at all today, neither. Nor did she leave by the back gate—Tom or I have the only key to that, you know, and she didn't ask me for it at all, and he says she didn't ask him neither."

Hidden by a glamour, perhaps? Though that was risky— she would be running the chance that Appleby would either stop her as a stranger, or think he saw her pass through twice, depending on whether she glamoured herself to look like one of her colleagues or simply used it to disguise her own features, without modeling it on anyone in particular. Still, it was a possibility.

"Did anyone else ask you to lend them the key?" Len asked, keeping his tone lightly casual, as though he were only mildly interested.

Appleby shook his head. "Not a soul. We don't use the back gate much anyway."

"Oh well," Gwen said, trying to match Len's casual tone, though the wrinkle between her brows gave away her worry for anyone looking closely. "Perhaps she felt unwell and so spent the night in the infirmary."

The four of them knew that wasn't true, as the Magistra would certainly have checked there and told Gwen if Charlotte Carlyle was indeed there, but it served to clear up the confusion that had descended on Mr. Appleby's face.

"Of course! That must be it. Strange, though—everyone knows Miss Charlotte hates sleeping anywhere but in her own bed. Why, during that storm this past spring—it came up out of nowhere, it did, fine and sunny one moment and then raining and hail the next—she insisted on walking back to her boarding house rather than staying over like the rest of the secretaries and other staff—said she'd rather half-drown than sleep in a college bed again. Still, if she fell ill during the day, she wouldn't have had much choice." He rubbed his chin. "Odd, though, that the Magistra would come asking me if I'd seen her leave—you'd think Dr. Bingham would've known that she was in the infirmary, if anyone did."

"I'm sure she'll have a good explanation for it," Maia said. "Thank you, Mr. Appleby. I apologize for taking up so much of your time."

"Not at all, miss, not at all. That's what I'm here for. Enjoy your visit."

Gwen led them out from under the arched roof and paused for a moment so they could take in the college grounds.

Gardens drew the eye immediately, clearly a riot of color in spring and summer but subdued in shades of muted gold and crimson now in October, with neat paths cut through them and a fountain made of weathered grey stone taking pride of place in the center. By a clever spell, the water spouting from the fountain appeared to be liquid light, a color between golden and silver and shimmering to the point of blinding the eye if one stared at it too long. It looked affected to Maia, but she recalled the college motto—*Discere et esse lux*, or "To Learn and be a Light," and decided it made a bit more sense in that context. It wasn't merely showing off.

There were two other buildings inside the walls in addition to the lodge and the long, low building mirroring the lodge on the other side of the gate. On Maia's right hand was a tall, brick building with white window frames and trim, and on her left was likewise a tall brick building, this one with a rotunda in in the front. The far side of the gardens extended beyond the ends of the buildings and themselves ended in high hedges which met the brick walls that surrounded the other three sides. There was one small door, painted white, built into the hedge on the other side, but even from here Maia could see the massive iron lock in the center.

"This is where the secretaries work and where the Magistra has her office," Gwen said, indicating the building attached to the entryway. This building," pointing to the building on the right, "is lecture rooms and laboratories on the ground floor and ladies' dormitories on the first and second floors. The other one," waving at the building with the rotunda, "is the dining hall and library on the ground floor, and men's quarters above that. We haven't got a chapel yet, but that's next on the list, as soon as there's enough funding. We also want more laboratories, a separate building for the library, and eventually more student accommodations, but considering how young we are, we think we've done rather well."

"I am already impressed," said Maia, and meant it. This was a beautiful spot, striking in its serenity for all that it was so young and untried. She noted a few students wearing undergraduate robes crossing from one building to another, chatting together and laughing, or with noses buried in books.

"And now," Gwen said, the worried wrinkle returning to her brow to replace the pride with which she displayed the college, "We will visit the Magistra."

Chapter 3

Following courteously after Maia and Gwen, with Becket half a step behind him and to his left as usual, Len tried to pinpoint the cause of his faint stirrings of unease. The train ride had been fine—he'd still felt on top of the world then. The automobile ride from the station to the college was fine, save for a few heart-pangs at how smoothly the Bentley 3-Litre ran in comparison to his auto. He wasn't generally given to envy, but by George! That *was* a motorcar. He could understand the Magistra's pride in it.

No, his discomfort had to have begun here, at the college. When talking to Appleby? No, not quite there. When they had stepped into the ground? Yes—yes, that was it. Now, what was it that had caused him to suddenly feel—not afraid, no, but slightly alarmed?

Nothing about the students passing, nor Gwen's description of the building, nor the sight of the gate, nor Maia—ah. Yes. It *was* Maia. Or rather, something related to Maia.

Wrestling with this, Len barely noticed his surroundings as he followed the ladies into the secretarial building and up the flight of narrow steps until Gwen stopped in a first floor corridor filled with late afternoon sunlight pouring through the west-facing windows, and knocked on a white door.

A small woman in a neat cap and apron promptly opened the door, stepped back, and bobbed a quick curtsey.

"It's Miss Gwen and her friends, ma'am," she said over her shoulder. "Come in," she said to them. "The Magistra's been expecting you."

"Thank you, Betsy," Gwen said, stepping into the room, followed by the rest of them.

Len set his unease aside for now in order to focus wholly on the task ahead. There would be time later to pinpoint the cause—and decide on a course of action.

Dr. Bingham, the Magistra of Saint Dorothea's, was exactly as Len had pictured her: tall, straight, austere, dark hair frosted with gray cropped neatly into a tidy bob, perfectly properly attired in a simple dark suit beneath her magistra's gown, and with spectacles that in no way softened the sharpness of her blue eyes. She smiled graciously on them as she received them in her small study with windows overlooking the golden fountain surrounded by sleeping rosebushes.

"Miss Whitney, Mr. Davies, and Mr. Becket, I presume," she said, her voice crisp and her words precise. "Gwen, my dear, so pleasant to see you again. I only wish it hadn't taken this odd little mix-up to bring you back."

Gwen looked guilty. "I had intended to return this summer for a few days, but I was so busy with other things ..."

The Magistra waved a hand. "Of course, my dear, I do understand. Your work, of course. If it weren't for my concern over Miss Carlyle's inexplicable absence, I would almost be happy to have a mystery here to give us an excuse to beg your return." She then turned to the others. "Won't you all be seated? I believe Betsy has the tea ready for us. It is so good of you to come here so promptly in response to our dilemma."

They obediently seated themselves in the wingback chairs set invitingly close to the tea table, though Becket remained on his feet.

"If you would all excuse me, I will go see if there is any way I can assist Miss Elizabeth," he said, giving a brief bow and leaving the study in the same direction as the maidservant.

Dr. Bingham looked mildly nonplussed at his exit. "It's Becket's way, don't you know," Len explained. "He prefers working with the staff to being served with the nobs. He gets on better terms with them that way, and finds out information we wouldn't learn otherwise."

"I see," said the Magistra. Whether she did or not, that comment was enough to move the conversation forward.

Betsy brought out a plate of toasted and buttered crumpets, followed by Becket bearing the heavy tea tray. He set the tray on the table, the Magistra poured and passed around the delicate china cups, Betsy handed around the crumpets, and then Betsy and Becket both discreetly withdrew and the conversation turned from weather and the appalling train service between London and Cambridge these days to the reason for the detectives' arrival.

"From what Gwen told me yesterday in our communication, I understand Charlotte wrote her a letter expressing concern for her own safety, as she had received threatening letters in response to her concerns over a strain of petty thefts happening here in the college, and even what she believed to be a deliberate attack on her own person. When Gwen offered to come investigate—perhaps a touch impulsive, Gwen dear, but so like your warm-hearted self—she received no response, and the next day Charlotte vanished from within the college grounds themselves."

Gwen, usually so poised, practically squirmed at the Magistra's aside to her. Len hastily spoke to cover her embarrassment.

"That is our understanding of where things stand, Dr. Bingham. And—I realize this is a foolish question, but one must be certain—you are sure that Miss Carlyle has vanished? She is not in the infirmary, or staying with a friend here at the college? And there's no way she could have left without Appleby noticing, not even if she was in a crowd?"

The Magistra began shaking her head even before he finished asking his questions. "I have searched the college myself, both physically and magically, and there is no sign of Charlotte. And no, there is no chance she could have left without Appleby seeing her. His days are uneventful—we being a hidden college to everyone except magic-users, we don't get many visitors or tradespeople or anyone except staff and students entering and leaving daily, and so he takes special note of everyone. I believe he even has a ledger in the lodge where he jots down everyone's habits. No, even if Charlotte had left for lunch with a group of the other secretaries, Appleby would have noticed her."

Len immediately resolved to have Becket wheedle that ledger out of Appleby—that would at the very least give them confirmation, and might even give a clue, depending on who was entering or leaving that day between the time Miss Carlyle entered and when she vanished.

"Has anyone spoken with her landlady or her fellow boarders?" Maia asked now, wiping melted butter off her fingers with a linen napkin.

Again, the Magistra shook her head. "No, when Gwen said she would come and bring you all, I thought that was best left to you." She hesitated. "I did wonder if we should inform the authorities that she is missing, but it is rather complicated. One does not want to bring in the ordinary police to this college, after all—our misdirection spells would not stand up to policemen actually within our walls and investigating our existence. Nor does this seem a matter for Domestic Protection, as no magical laws have been broken that we know of. In short, having Gwen suggest you investigate seemed the perfect solution."

"And we are happy to be able to help," Len said. Jolly glad, in fact, though he didn't want to sound too enthusiastic lest Dr. Bingham think he was callous toward poor Miss Carlyle. He wasn't, but if she had to go missing, he was glad they were the ones who got to investigate.

He rather suspected that the Magistra would have hesitated to call Deep in even if a magical law or two had been broken—there was still a great deal of skepticism regarding Saint Dorothea's in the Circle and among the more traditional English magicians. A scandal involving Deep would badly damage their already fragile reputation. Private detectives had the advantage of being much more discreet.

"I assume you'll want to meet the staff and students," Dr. Bingham said. "Most of our teaching staff dines at the college regularly, and I invite you to be our guests tonight, and to join us in the senior common room after for drinks and, perhaps, a more frank discussion of the trouble here than one would wish to engage in during the meal."

"Splendid," Len said promptly. "Though it might be a good idea to spread ourselves out a bit, eh? Becket can dine with the kitchen staff, and some of us should eat with the students while someone else is at the high table."

"Gwen for the high table," Maia said without even pausing to think about it. "As a returning student, it would look odd for her to not be honored by a seat at the high table. But you and I …we could present ourselves as interested in the college for ourselves, or for someone we know, and therefore it would make sense for us to sit with the students."

"I can be looking into it on behalf of Susan," Len said, naming a young magician he was acting as a sort of mentor to, as nobody else in her family had any magical ability whatsoever, leaving her without much help as she strove to control her magic. In fact, now that he thought about it, Saint Dorothea's might just be the perfect place for her, so it wouldn't even be a pretense.

"And I can be considering it for myself, as an alternative to being a traditional journeyman," Maia said with a wry twist to her lips that he couldn't quite understand.

"Excellent," Dr. Bingham said. "I can see you won't need many suggestions from me as to how you can discreetly conduct your investigations. I am most obliged to you all." She inclined her head graciously.

"Out of curiosity, Magistra, what would you do if there should be a genuine crime here?" Len asked, trying not to be rankled by her queenly condescension toward them. Dash it, if anyone had a right to be condescending, it was the woman before him.

That didn't mean he had to like it.

"A non-magical crime," he added for clarification.

Dr. Bingham sighed and took another sip of tea. "That has been a fear in the back of my mind since we began this college," she said. "Thankfully, we might have a solution now, though I would still rather not test it. A colleague of mine, intrigued by the spells we used to hide Saint Dorothea's within Cambridge University, asked if he could adapt those spells to begin a secret magical crime division within the Cambridge City Police. Thus, if we were to have a crime here, theoretically, we could contact the police and be automatically transferred to the magical CID rather than the ordinary. Though, as I say, it is only theoretical at this point. Thank heavens, we haven't needed to test it yet, and I frankly would rather not."

Maia leaned forward, her teacup forgotten, her eyes alight. "But how remarkable! Magistra, think how that could reshape the very fabric of magical society in Britain. Rather than having entirely separate bodies to govern magicians and enforce our magical laws, we could eventually see magic integrated naturally into every part of British life. Magicians in Parliament rather than the Circle. Magicians in the Special Branch of the police force, rather than Magical Intelligence."

"Magical prep schools," Gwen piped up, nearly forgotten in her corner as the others conversed. "Or magical teachers within ordinary prep schools," she considered.

Dr. Bingham nodded and smiled, though this time her air was less patronizing. Len wondered if she was seeing Maia as a kindred spirit. "Exactly, Miss Whitney! That is my dream, that in time Saint Dorothea's will be remembered merely as the first institution of this sort to work, not as a unique oddity."

"No wonder my aunt and the other traditionalists are threatened by you," Maia said, then blushed.

Thankfully, Dr. Bingham laughed. "I believe there are some who have the foresight to see that if Saint Dorothea's succeeds, their way of life will vanish forever. Mostly, I fear, they simply don't like anything new or different. Your aunt— Amelia Rawlings, correct?—I would say falls into the former category, though she is at least willing to challenge her own assumptions if given enough impetus, which is more than I can say for some of her colleagues in the Circle."

Len wasn't entirely certain how he felt about it all himself. He was all for challenging hidebound tradition—that was, after all, why he was living as a private detective in London rather than managing his family's estate in Herefordshire. At the same time, he wasn't sure he liked the idea of Magical Intelligence becoming obsolete. After all, he wouldn't be who he was today without that particular institution.

Good heavens? Did that mean he was in agreement with Amelia Rawlings over something? Len shuddered and decided it was time to change the subject.

"Thank you for this splendid tea, Magistra," he said, setting his cup down carefully. "But I think we'd best begin our investigation as soon as possible. If you don't mind, we'll see what sort of hornet's nest we can stir up amongst the secretaries, eh? And then if there's time we really ought to visit Miss Carlyle's landlady and inspect her rooms."

"Of course," the Magistra said. She rose to her feet, and they all naturally followed suit. Dash it, she *did* have an air about her. "Do come to me if you have any difficulties or questions whatsoever. Let us hope you find Charlotte quickly."

It was clearly a dismissal.

* * *

Becket did not rejoin them as they left the Magistra's office, which most likely meant that he had already ingratiated himself with Betsy and was well on his way to blending in with the serving staff. Sometimes Len had to chuckle at his own folly—Becket had been his invaluable ally for years as a valet, a magician, and as a partner in investigation, and yet it wasn't until four years ago (when he had met Maia, in fact) that Len had finally been able to wholly trust that Becket could do his work superlatively without Len there guiding him at every moment. Lord, what an insufferably pompous fool he had been before that! He was lucky Becket hadn't given up on him and gone to work for someone else with more sense. He'd had his reasons for being overly protective, but that didn't change the fact that he must have been dashed irritating to work with.

He shook himself out of his memories as Gwen led the way to the antechamber of the secretaries' office. She nodded at the young woman sitting at the giant mahogany desk, painting her nails a scarlet color to match her lips.

"Hallo, Lil," Gwen said. "Jenny in?"

The young woman—Len couldn't bring himself to call her a lady—glanced up disinterestedly, and then blinked as she took them in.

"Cor, Gwen, is that really you?" she asked, her accent pure East End, startling on the ear after all the well-bred university tones they'd been hearing. "We heard rumors that you were bringing some friends around to inspect the place. So you really came? What do you want to see Miss High-and-Mighty Pelham for? *She's* no attraction to Saint Dot's. Likely to turn people off more than anything, if you ask me."

Len kept an amiable but absent smile on his face and did not allow his eyes to meet those of the young woman, though he could feel her looking at him with appreciation.

"Oh, we have our reasons," Gwen said vaguely. "What's Jenny done now that has you so ruffled?"

The young woman—Lil—rolled her big, brown eyes. "What hasn't she done? Swans around like she owns the place, that's what she does. One of these days she'll try to lord it over the Magistra, and then we'll all have a laugh." She jumped and tried to snatch a handkerchief to her mouth as the door behind the desk opened and a red-haired woman in her early thirties exited with an irritated expression on her face.

"Miss Jamison, what have I told you about gossiping on the college's time? And for goodness' sake, wipe that muck off your lips and clean your nails! If you want to look like a common tramp, do it outside the college, not in." Only then did she look across the desk to the other three. Her flaming red hair, a shade that made Maia's look wholly brown in comparison, was cut in a severe bob, emphasizing her sharp jaw and large honey-brown eyes. Her clothing matched her physical looks, being a navy blue suit with the simplest of lines in skirt and coat, and a crisp white blouse with no ruffles or bows to soften it underneath. It was a striking look, one that helped to emphasize the notion that she was all edges and corners.

"Is there something you need?" she asked in her quick way, biting off each word before hurrying to the next. "Oh—Gwen!" She frowned, emphasizing the angles of her face. "Are you looking for a job …?"

"Oh no, I have one," Gwen said quickly, with a little toss of her head. "I'm looking for Lottie."

"Why?" asked Miss Jamison blankly. She had sullenly scrubbed the lipstick off with her handkerchief, but her nails were still determinedly red. Miss Pelham—at least Len assumed this was the infamous Jenny Pelham—sent her a severe glare, and Miss Jamison ducked her head and shuffled papers together on her desk.

Len would have eased into the conversation and danced around the reason for them being there, but they hadn't had a chance to discuss their approach before encountering Miss Pelham, and truth be told, he was curious to see how Gwen would handle it.

"Let's discuss this elsewhere," Miss Pelham said, glaring again at Miss Jamison and then leading the way out of doors without even a glance at Maia or Len. Once in the open air, she turned on Gwen.

"I don't want my workers to be distracted by gossip at their jobs. I haven't seen Lottie since teatime yesterday, and if you see her before I do, you may tell her for me that she is sacked! I've people enough applying for positions here that I needn't waste my time with a worker who can't be bothered to show up." Her piece spoken, she turned as if to return inside, the matter clearly closed in her mind.

Gwen drew her eyebrows together. "And does the Magistra agree with you?"

Miss Pelham halted mid-turn. "What are you talking about?"

"The Magistra was concerned enough about Lottie's disappearance to ask us to come find her. I would have thought you'd make finding Lottie a priority after that. Or didn't she share that concern with you?"

Len passed his hand over his face to smooth away his smile. Gwen had played that rather nicely. Miss Pelham was clearly a woman who rated herself highly in the ranks at Saint Dorothea's; implying that she wasn't important enough for the Magistra to share information with—when Gwen *was*—would put her on her mettle, and hopefully get more information out of her than when she was armored behind her self-importance.

"I did hear about the Magistra," Miss Pelham snapped. "And I could have told her then it was nothing to fret over! Naturally she has to protect the school by making a show of investigating—it would reflect badly on us if she seemed unconcerned—but it's all too ridiculous. How could Lottie have disappeared? She's merely hiding somewhere, trying to make herself look important, as usual."

Gwen's eyes flashed, and it looked as though she was on the verge of losing her temper. Since that would not help them learn anything, Len decided it was time to intervene.

"You aren't at all concerned for Miss Carlyle's well-being, Miss Pelham? After all, this disappearance does seem rather like the latest in a long line of troubling occurrences."

Miss Pelham finally slowed down. She folded her arms across her middle, eyebrows raised superciliously, seemingly unbothered by the fact that they hadn't been properly introduced. "What occurrences?"

Maia's voice held a sharp edge. "Theft, anonymous letters, an attack, and now a disappearance. This doesn't trouble you?"

Miss Pelham rolled her eyes. "Oh, that nonsense. Lottie is always fussing about something. Thefts! A few missing trinkets, nothing to fret over. Those anonymous letters were too ridiculous for anyone to take seriously. I read one of them, and it was absurd. I even wondered if she'd become mentally unbalanced and written them herself. Why would anyone want to threaten her?"

"That is the question, isn't it," said Len in a dangerously gentle voice.

"I have no time to coddle my workers," Miss Pelham snapped. "Is this really why you're here, Gwen? Ridiculous. If you like to waste your time chasing ghosts, be my guest. I have work to do."

She stalked back inside, ignoring Len as he courteously opened the door for her.

"Well, well," he said in a speculative voice after gently closing the door behind the irate Miss Pelham.

"That is completely unfair," Gwen said. "Lottie never puffs herself up. Jenny's the one who's always trying to come off as more important than she is. It's even worse now than it was when we were all here as students! Back then she was insufferable enough, always going on about how competent all the faculty found her, and how her organizational skills were so much better than all ours, and how her magic was so unique, and how she was going to change the college entirely once she was graduated, and would probably end up as Magistra herself one day … and now she's bullying all the other secretaries and sneering at Dr. Bingham and being rude to guests, and—" She had to pause for breath.

"The question is, why is she so insistent that Miss Carlyle's disappearance is so unimportant?" Maia said, frowning into the distance as she thought.

"Because she can't bear to have people pay attention to anyone but her," Gwen said bitterly.

"Or is it because she doesn't want people to look too closely at the situation?" Len said. "Gwen, your letter from Miss Carlyle—she said that she was encouraging people to report the thefts to the Magistra, but they didn't think it was worth her time. It would be interesting to find out *who* exactly it was who said that."

Gwen blinked. "You mean—you think *Jenny*—hm." She thought for a moment. "I would have thought Jenny would consider it beneath her dignity to stoop to petty theft, or even to take the effort to remove someone from her path who was annoying her, but then, she has changed in the last few years."

"Perhaps Gwen should ask a few questions of the other secretaries, if you can do so without Miss Pelham noticing, Gwen," Len said. He checked his wristwatch. "And I think there's just enough time for you and me, Maia, to pay a visit to Miss Carlyle's boarding house before we need to return in time for dinner. Shall we go?" He crooked his arm at her for all the world like a gentleman at a formal ball offering his lady a turn about the room.

Maia smiled, dropped as elaborate a curtsey as one could manage in the short, slim skirts of the current style, and lightly rested the tips of her fingers atop his arm. "Why thank you, kind sir. Gwen, we'll see you when we return, and you and I can compare notes while we prepare for dinner, shall we?"

Gwen agreed, and they went their separate paths.

Chapter 4

I t didn't take long to get directions to Miss Carlyle's boarding house from Mr. Appleby—who seemed a veritable general information bureau, and would undoubtedly be a valuable ally in their search for Miss Carlyle—and armed with these, Maia and Len set off in the opposite direction of the city center, heading even further into the outskirts of the city from the college's location. Maia was surprised to find herself wishing they could be heading in the opposite direction. Great as her concern over the missing Miss Carlyle was, she couldn't help but think how splendid it would be to be able to enjoy Cambridge without any outside concerns. She had heard such marvelous things about King's College chapel and choir, and she rather fancied herself at attempting to punt down the river Cam.

Alas, duty called. "What are your initial impressions of the case?" she asked her friend and partner.

Len sighed, leaving her to suspect his thoughts had been far from duty as well. "I can't say I cared much for Miss Pelham," he said. "If we were basing our suspicions on attitude rather than hard evidence, I'd put her at the top of our list."

"Not that we've met anyone else to place on that list," Maia pointed out. "Unless you suspect young Mr. Wright or Mr.

Appleby of petty theft, threatening letters, and kidnapping." *Or worse,* her mind added, but she held her tongue. No doubt but that Len was also thinking of the likelihood of Miss Carlyle having been murdered. It seemed an extreme reaction to the situation, but kidnapping wasn't much more reasonable.

Len smiled ruefully. "No, I must say I can't see that."

"The problem is that we don't have enough information," Maia said. "*Why* would a rash of minor crime lead to such a drastic action against Miss Carlyle? Until we know that, we will have a dreadful time finding her and finding the culprit."

"Aye, there's the rub," Len said. "Although I can't help but feel … I don't know." He rubbed his chin. "I feel there's something going on here beneath the surface. Miss Pelham: was her irritation genuine, or was it masking something else? Was the Magistra entirely straightforward with us? Has even Miss Carlyle told Gwen all she knows?" He shook his head. "I can't put my finger on it, but there is something ugly lurking behind all this, I'd stake my life on that."

Maia did not operate by intuition. She considered it mostly rubbish, in fact, especially the idea of Women's Intuition. Her association with Len, however, had led her to reluctantly accept that there were times when his intuition, or instinct, or gut feeling, whatever one wished to call it, was right in the face of all logical reason to believe otherwise.

She wasn't about to start relying on her own intuition, especially as she was still quite certain she had none, but she trusted his.

They had come to another loop of the river by now, and Maia paused before stepping onto the low wooden bridge. "Speaking of the case, don't you think this must be the bridge from which Miss Carlyle was pushed?"

The water the bridge crossed must have been an offshoot of the Cam rather than the main stretch of the river—it was hardly more than a trickle at this time of year. No one was going to come punting down this way, that was certain.

Len glanced around. "I suppose it might be. Difficult to tell, though."

Maia pointed to the railing on one side. "No, look. It's all broken here. Don't you see, this must be where she was pushed in."

"Dash it, I believe you are right," Len said. He crossed over to examine them more closely. "Not that there's much point in looking at it now," he said. "Even if the criminal was obliging enough to leave behind a scrap of cloth or a bit of hair, rain and wind would have blown them free by now. Hmm."

"What's 'hmm?'" Maia asked, joining him in looking over the railing.

"Well, it's just that it occurs to me that this part of the country is in a drought, so rain wouldn't have washed anything away. And it hasn't been all that windy."

"So you think the person might have left something behind?"

"Not the pusher, necessarily—but here. Look how rough and jagged the ends of the wood pieces are where they were broken. Now, imagine yourself crashing through the railing with it being all rough like that. Do you think you'd escape with your clothing intact?"

"I see what you mean," Maia said, touching one of the boards and wincing as her finger immediately picked up a splinter. "There ought to be bits of Miss Carlyle's clothing caught here." She raised her finger to her mouth and nipped out the splinter.

Len wordlessly offered her his handkerchief, but she shook her head and showed him the red mark on the pad of her forefinger. "No blood."

"Another good point," he said, tucking the handkerchief back into his breast pocket. "No blood. You picked up a splinter just from touching the wood. Poor Miss Carlyle ought to have left behind traces of blood as well as scraps of clothing on these broken boards. Yet they are clean as can be."

"What do you suppose it means?" Maia said. "Did the murderer—that is, the pusher—did he come back afterward and remove all evidence of her fall? But why? There wouldn't have been anything to incriminate him—or her—if it was all Miss Carlyle's clothing and blood left behind."

Len shook his head. "I must frankly say that I haven't a clue. Unless—"

"Well, go on, you can't leave it there."

"It's just a thought," he said, leaving the broken rail behind as they walked on. "But you recall how eager Miss Pelham was to dismiss any possibility of the seriousness of these events. What if the pusher came back here to make it look as though Miss Carlyle was making it all up, in case anyone cared enough to check up on the scene of the incident?"

"Trying to make her look like a hysterical woman," Maia said sourly.

"Exactly."

"Only no one cared enough to come and look in the first place," Maia said.

"Except for us," Len reminded her.

"And we are suspicious of everything, so his or her efforts were in vain," she said with a triumphant smile.

"That's right," Len said. "In fact, we're even more suspicious now than we were before. Bit of a blow for the chap, eh?"

Maia laughed, as the twinkle in Len's eye indicated he'd

intended her to, and then felt guilty. How could she be so light-hearted about the matter when a woman's life was at stake?

Possibly at stake, she reminded herself. There was still a chance—a slim one, true—that Miss Carlyle had hidden herself, rather than been stolen away or murdered. Not that that was much better, as surely the only reason she would have done such a thing would be that she was in fear for her life and could think of no other way to protect herself.

Nor did that theory answer the question of how she could have vanished so thoroughly from within the college walls.

"Len," she said abruptly, "How would *you* vanish in plain sight, if you needed to? Or make someone else not noticeable?"

He didn't need any other explanation; they knew well how each other's minds worked by now. "My chameleon spell has gotten me out of more than one slippery spot," he said. "But of course that only helps one blend in to the background, it doesn't actually make one vanish. If a person were looking at me when I cast it, they'd still be able to follow my movement, because they'd know I was there."

"So if Miss Carlyle did want to slip away from the college without anyone seeing her, she might have used a chameleon spell, but if someone was watching her, probably not."

"Right, and don't forget Appleby—she couldn't have gotten past the gate without him noticing. Same with anyone trying to sneak her out. If she were unconscious or otherwise immobilized, the spell would work to cover them both, but it would still require getting through the gate."

"And Appleby is the difficulty with a glamour spell, as well," Maia said, sharing her thoughts from earlier. "He still would have noticed her, even if she'd looked like someone else."

"He would have been more likely to notice her if she looked like someone else, if you ask me," Len said. "Anything out of the ordinary would have drawn his attention. No, as convenient as a glamour spell can be, it isn't likely to be the answer here."

Maia blew out her breath in frustration. "So what we need is someone who can turn truly invisible and incorporeal, or was able to fly over the tops of the walls."

Len shook his head. "No spells I know of that will do any of those things." His expression turned wistful. "Mind you, I've always wanted to fly. I used to hope I could come up with a spell to make myself grow wings, but never quite managed it."

Maia was instantly enraptured by the thought. "Oh, wouldn't that be lovely! A bit of a nuisance, though, having to hide one's wings in everyday life."

"Yes, I assume that's why there is no magic that will permit such a spell," Len said. "It isn't just we magicians who prefer to hide magic from the ordinary world; it tends to protect itself, you know. Even if we didn't attempt to keep it concealed, it would practically do the job for us."

"Ah," Maia said. That explained something that had been niggling in the back of her mind for a while now. When Maia had first discovered magic, Aunt Amelia had impressed upon her the dire importance of keeping it a secret from all magic-users. At that same time, almost in the same breath, Aunt Amelia had informed her that magicians rarely ever used their magic directly on another human, as it was generally considered a gross violation of one's autonomy. The general exception to this was healers, though Maia had also learned that they relied heavily on potions for their healing in order to avoid the temptations that came with repeated use of magic on another person.

Those two facts—magic being secret from all outsiders, and magicians almost never casting a spell on another person—seemed to rather contradict each other. If a non-magician accidentally stumbled upon magic, how could a magician keep him or her from remembering it and proclaiming it without a memory-altering spell? And surely, in all the centuries past, something of that sort must have happened, and must still be happening on occasion. Why, even Maia's first introduction to magic had come as part of an attempt to keep a non-magician who knew about magic from revealing the truth to the world.

But if magic, not only magicians, kept itself hidden, that would help reconcile the two. "Then we needn't have fretted so over Sir Bertram?" she asked, mind ranging back again to that first adventure she had shared with Len.

"What?—Oh, that. No, it was good that we stopped him, as he had physical evidence of the Circle, which could have revealed the truth beyond any ability to hide it—written words are difficult to forget or gloss over. You will be interested to know that Sir Bertram himself has practically forgotten about the magical aspect of that little escapade, though, and is more than halfway convinced he had set out to expose a governmental conspiracy, not a magical one."

"Fascinating," Maia breathed.

There was no time for further discussion of the matter, as they stepped off the footpath at their destination just then.

From the outside, at least, the house—the middle of a row of terraced housing—looked respectable and pleasant. Tall and narrow, made of light golden-grey stone with white trim surrounding the prominent bow windows bulging out the front, and front door painted a cheerful blue. It wasn't Maia's cup of tea, but it certainly wasn't the dingy, depressing place

Miss Carlyle had insinuated from her letter.

Nor was the woman who opened the door to them the slatternly, shrewish landlady of popular literature. She was an Indian woman of small stature, plump and bright-eyed, her hair stylishly bobbed and curled, her pink housedress clean and trim, her smile warm and welcoming. She was wiping her hands on a tea towel, and the scent of something delicious wafted out the open door from behind her.

"Yes?" she said, her accent pure Birmingham, a quizzical smile on her face. "If you're looking for a room I'm afraid I'm full up, but I might have one available at the end of the month."

"Actually, we're looking for one of your lodgers," Maia said. "Miss Charlotte Carlyle. Is she in?"

"Well, that's a funny thing, that is." The woman looked sharply at them before continuing. "Are you friends of hers?"

"Acquaintances," Len said simply, rather than getting into the tedious explanation of their exact relationship. "We understood she was expecting to see us today, but we rather embarrassingly can't seem to find her."

"Have you asked at the college she works at?"

"They've not seen her either," Len said.

The landlady frowned. "Well now, that is troubling. You'd best come in so's we can discuss it in comfort, Mr …?"

"Lennox Davies, at your service," Len said with a slight bow. "And this is Miss Maia Whitney."

"Pleasure to meet you both, I'm sure," the landlady said. "Layla Hawkins. Come in, do."

Even after removing his hat, Len had to duck his head to go through the door. He wiped his feet carefully on the mat— Maia wondered if that was his mother's training or Becket's— to Mrs. Hawkins' visible approval.

"Have a seat," Mrs. Hawkins said, motioning them through a door on the left. "I'll just fetch some scones and tea. How lucky that I had the kettle on!"

Still full from crumpets and tea with the Magistra, Maia would have preferred to forego any more refreshment, but she recognized that they had a far better chance of getting on with Mrs. Hawkins over a nice cuppa than they would any other way.

Then she stepped into the parlor and all other thoughts fled.

Bright pink cabbage roses with vivid green leaves on a pale blue background papered the walls, broken only by the countless photographs hanging all around—almost all of them of the same individual at various stages of his life, from a solemn baby in a white christening gown, to a young boy riding a pony, to a young man wearing a naval uniform. There were none of him any older than the Navy snapshots.

The floor was highly polished wood, with an Oriental rug providing softness underfoot, though the bright greens and blues clashed rather with the shades on the wallpaper. Knick-knacks in the shapes of flowers and birds that were made of painted porcelain and glass covered every flat surface. Lace curtains at the windows and lace doilies on the backs of the overstuffed chairs and sofa completed the room.

"Well," Maia managed. "It's very cheerful."

"Do you like my front room, dear?" Mrs. Hawkins asked, bustling back in with a tray holding a steaming teapot, three cups, and a plate piled high with scones. "I like colorful things around me. Miss Carlyle, she complains about the colors giving her headaches, but there, I tell her, it's better than some boarding houses, all dull brown wallpaper and hard furniture. Oh, thank you, sir," as Len courteously took the tray from her hands and waited for her to seat herself before carefully setting it down in the only clear space he could find on the side table.

"I couldn't agree more," he said. "So Miss Carlyle is not happy here?"

"Her? Now, I don't mean to speak ill of an acquaintance of yours, but it's my opinion that one wouldn't be happy in Buckingham Palace! Nothing is ever right for her—the bed too soft, the parlor too colorful, the windows too tall, the food too strongly seasoned ..."

Len's mouth was already full of scone, but he managed an outraged expression at that. "Rubbish," he said after swallowing quickly. "This is one of the finest scones I've ever had."

"Go on with you, then," she said with a happy little toss of her head. "Take another, dearie."

"I wonder you let her stay at all," Maia said, sipping at her tea—not too strong, and not too weak. Len was right; whatever her taste in home decor, Mrs. Hawkins was an artist in the kitchen.

"I wonder the same, sometimes," the small woman confessed frankly. "It isn't as though I need to take in boarders—my husband left me plenty well off when he died, and since our boy Robbie—" Her voice faltered.

"Naval man, was he?" Len said, his voice full of warm sympathy.

"Always wanted to be a sailor like his old dad," Mrs. Hawkins sniffed. Maia was not as good at sympathy as Len, but she wordlessly handed Mrs. Hawkins a handkerchief. "His ship was torpedoed, you see, during the War, and here I was, with the house on my hands and nothing to distract myself. I moved here when Robbie was accepted to Cambridge, you see, since him and me only had each other—it was his idea, if you can believe it, I didn't think he'd want to be bothered by his old mum while he was at uni, but he said he wouldn't be happy knowing I was all the way back in Birmingham without him to look after me, so I up and moved, and then he was gone but I couldn't face moving again, so I started to take in boarders just to give myself something to do and keep me company. There's a Miss Jones on the first floor, and Miss Carlyle on the second. Another thing she complains about, that she has to climb two flights of stairs to get to her room instead of only one. Lucky, I call her—Miss Jones has to share a bathroom with me, and Miss Carlyle has the entire second floor to herself!"

"And when did you see her last—Miss Carlyle, I mean?" Maia asked.

"She didn't come to the table for supper last night, but that's no real surprise, sometimes they don't. The agreement is that I fix them a tray of cold foods and take it up to their rooms if they miss supper, so that they can have a bite to eat whenever they get in. But this morning, when I went up to change the linens and fetch back down Miss Carlyle's tray, her bed hadn't been slept in and the food was left untouched, just as if she never came home! And whatever else I may think of her, I will say she isn't that sort of person at all."

"So then the last time you saw her was yesterday morning?"

"Yes, when she left for work."

Len swallowed the last bite of his scone and leaned forward. "Mrs. Hawkins, I should tell you that Miss Whitney and I are private inquiry agents, and we are here at Miss Carlyle's request on account of some threatening letters she had received. Do you know anything about them?"

The landlady's eyes widened at this revelation, but she shook her head. "Threatening letters? Who would want to threaten her? What would be the point?"

"So we keep hearing," Len said. "Answer me this, then: Is Miss Carlyle the type of person to ferret out secrets about another person and then use them against that person?"

Maia opened her mouth to protest, then closed it again wordlessly. This was an angle they had not thought of before, but it did make sense, and it could explain why someone might want to cause Miss Carlyle harm—the petty thefts did not seem to justify this on their own, not unless she had discovered the thief's identity and held it over his or her head. Blackmail—whether it be emotional or physical—could be awfully tempting to those whom society overlooked or despised.

However, Mrs. Hawkins shook her head again. "Never. To be honest, I don't think she'd have the gumption."

"Do you mind if we look at her room? We might be able to find a clue to her whereabouts," Maia said now. "And at some point we'd like to talk to Miss Jones, see if she knows anything helpful."

"Miss Jones has been out of town for the last two weeks, visiting a 'friend' in Hertfordshire," Mrs. Hawkins said, quashing that hope. "It's my belief she's going to be marrying that friend soon enough, that's why I said I might have a room available at the end of the month when you first rang. I suppose I can let you look at Miss Carlyle's room, though I don't like the idea of invading her privacy like that."

"If her life is in danger, though, it might be the only way to save her," Len said."

Mrs. Hawkins rose to her feet. "If you say so. I must say, though, I have a hard time believing anyone as wet as that girl could have any enemies at all, much less ones who would want to harm her! Come along, then."

They followed her up the two flights of stairs—neither particularly steep, not much call for complaint there—to the second floor.

"Her bedroom is on the right here," Mrs. Hawkins said, unlocking the door. "And this is her bathroom on the left. Since she's the only person up here, I let her use this as her private bath. Which is more than most landladies would do, let me tell you!"

With this parting shot, she went back down the stairs, likely to return to the kitchen, and left the two sleuths to examine the room in hopes of finding a clue to Miss Carlyle's whereabouts.

There was always something melancholy about seeing a person's home—be it manor house or single room in a boarding house—without that individual present, and this visit, with the shadow of menace hanging over its absent host, seemed even more haunting.

Wooden floors with a gaily colored rag rug covering the boards. Wallpaper, more subdued here than downstairs, this being a slightly faded cream with small multi-colored flowers. On one wall, a cheap reproduction of Blake's *Oberon, Titania, and Puck*. A needlepoint sampler hung on the wall above the bed. Blue curtains at the window, and a gas light fixture on the wall, which Len lit with a casual wave of his hand and a murmured spell.

"Show-off," Maia said, but she said it with a smile.

"Happy to be able to do it, that's all," he replied. "It's not a bad room, but it feels dreary, doesn't it? I wonder why."

"No personal touches, aside from the books and things on the nightstand and her clothes," Maia said promptly. She looked around again. "Though something is off, but I can't put my finger on it." She shrugged, trusting it would eventually come to her, and moved to the door, where a hook held a knitted shawl and an orange and brown patterned scarf. For form's sake, Maia took each down and shook it out in case it was hiding any secrets.

The shawl held none, and the scarf only revealed that it was torn, leaving a hole right at the end.

"Silk," Maia commented idly. "What a pity. Still, I supposed it could be mended. That's probably why she kept it rather than tossing it in the bin."

Len turned his attention to the nightstand. He picked up a small green bottle and sniffed the opening. "Sleep potion. That's a dangerous road to go down, spelling yourself to sleep. She must have been in a right state to risk it, her having had healer training and all. If anyone knows how risky those are, it's a healer."

Maia paused. "Why, what could go wrong?"

"If you mix the potion incorrectly, you could find you never wake up at all," Len said. "I've always had a hunch the tale of Sleeping Beauty had its roots in a poorly mixed sleeping potion, to be honest. Or if you increase one ingredient and decrease the other—I think it's more ivory and less talcum powder, but it could be the other way around—you get a memory potion instead of a sleeping potion, which is illegal and also highly dangerous."

"What's wrong with a potion for one's memory?"

"This is a potion to wipe a person's short-term memory, not enhance it. You can imagine the temptation for an unscrupulous magician. And there again, if something goes wrong, a person could end up losing their entire memory, not just the immediate past. They are so dangerous the recipes for them have been removed from almost all potion books these days. I only learned about them as a side note to the training that all agents get in recognizing the smell of a sleep potion, among others, to be cautious when accepting drinks while on the job."

Maia shuddered. "Ghastly." She moved toward the wardrobe. "Nothing useful in her bag or coat, only the usual items. Compact, lipstick, handkerchief, a few coins. Dear me, I do hate pawing through her things like this. Mrs. Hawkins is right, it is a violation of her privacy."

"Better than respecting her privacy and having her get murdered," Len said. He picked up the top book on the stack, a nondescript brown thing with no title visible. Maia was distracted from her task by a letter fluttering to the floor from between its pages.

"Hullo, what's this?" Len said, picking it up. "It must be the most recent threatening letter. I suppose she stopped bringing them into the office when it seemed nobody cared, poor devil."

Maia was by his side in a flash, standing on her tiptoes to lean over his shoulder to read it. "It's typewritten."

"That could be a clue, if we can match it to the machine. We should look at the college."

The letter read, quite simply, *You were warned. You did not listen. Now you will see.*

"Rather tame, for a threat," Len commented.

"For you, perhaps," Maia said. "Imagine being a young woman of twenty-two and receiving that, having previously lived a blameless life and never experiencing anything more exciting than going off to university."

Len considered. "You have a point." He folded the letter and looked around.

"What?" Maia asked.

"Where's the envelope?"

Maia looked around as well, even going so far as to pick up the wastebasket and look through it. Plenty of crumpled paper and sweet wrappers, but no envelope. "She must have taken it with her," she said.

"Strange. Why would you take the envelope and not the letter?"

"Maybe she meant to take both, and accidentally left the letter behind," Maia offered. "Or—" Her eyes suddenly sparkled as the thought came to her. "Perhaps there was something on the envelope that gave her a clue as to the letter-writer, and so she took it—"

"And confronted the letter-writer, who then kidnapped her to keep her quiet," Len finished. "Brilliant."

"But who was it? And where is Miss Carlyle now?"

That was the question indeed.

Chapter 5

Len and Maia returned to Saint Dorothea's to find Becket waiting for them in the Porter's Lodge, whither Appleby escorted them and bustled off to find two more thick cups for the inky fluid he called tea before Len could protest they were full up, and which Becket seemed to be drinking with great enjoyment.

"Dash it all," Len whispered with dismay, "don't tell me you're actually swallowing that?"

"Of course not, sir," Becket said back from the corner of his mouth, and indicated the potted plant near his comfortable seat.

The Porter's Lodge—or "plodge" as it was colloquially known—was a cozy little room just off the side of the gate. There was barely room for two in there; with Maia and Len crowded in as well it was an almost impossible squeeze.

"Now that's an odd thing," Appleby said, shaking his head and coming out of the tiny side room where he kept his kettle and sorted the students' mail into their pigeonholes. "I always keep some extra cups on hand in case I have friends stop by, and I can't for the life of me find the other two. The cleaning staff must have taken them away. I do apologize."

"Not at all," Len assured him, feeling some relief that Becket had so adroitly arranged things so he and Maia wouldn't have to endure the tea without hurting the old man's feelings.

"We do appreciate the offer," Maia chimed in.

Becket appeared to drain his cup, and stood, moving his body in such a way that Appleby couldn't see him empty the dregs into the plant, though Len could, and was hard put to keep a straight face. "Thank you kindly, Mr. Appleby. Mr. Davies, Miss Whitney, I believe Miss Zhang is hoping to see us now that you've returned. I've also taken the liberty of removing our luggage to the rooms Dr. Bingham has kindly allotted to us."

"Lead on," Len said briefly.

"Pleasure sharing a cuppa with you, Mr. Becket," Appleby said, coming to the doorway of the plodge to see them off.

"Likewise, Mr. Appleby," Becket responded.

As he led them down the short path back joining the Porter's Lodge to the administration building, he explained how he had spent his time since the other two left. "I was able to establish cordial relations with Miss Elizabeth through sharing her washing-up duties after tea, and from there she introduced me to the rest of the kitchen staff and cleaners. In the course of our conversation about the difficulties of waiting on the thoughtless privileged classes—apologies, sir, but I thought you would not mind my maligning your character in the cause of justice—"

Len turned a chortle into a cough. "Not at all," he managed. Really, Becket *was* coming along. Five years ago he wouldn't have felt comfortable speaking poorly of Len even if Len had ordered him to do so in the course of a case.

Becket continued. "Quite so. In the course of said conversation, I managed to introduce Miss Carlyle, by mentioning her thoughtlessness in inviting Miss Gwen for a visit and then not being here upon our arrival. As most of the staff is familiar with Miss Gwen and knows the two of them were friendly, I thought that a more natural way of bringing in Miss Carlyle's disappearance and a reason for Miss Gwen being here."

"Well done," Maia said warmly.

"I learned from the staff that Miss Carlyle is universally disliked among them, I am sorry to say. The cooks and wait staff say she regularly complains about the food and service, and the cleaners say she frequently lurks in the halls to point out dusty corners or high cobwebs they've missed in their cleaning, though rightly speaking that is none of her affair. None of them were surprised she had invited Miss Gwen and then failed to make an appearance, save for one perceptive lass who did say it seemed odd that she would miss an opportunity to try to make herself look more important to Miss Gwen than she really was. The girl went on to speculate that perhaps she realized that with Miss Pelham 'bossing all the secretaries to death' Miss Carlyle wouldn't in fact be able to persuade Miss Gwen of her importance, and that was why she hid. None of them seemed in the least bit concerned about her disappearance, though Miss Elizabeth did admit that it was odd how she had managed to either get past Mr. Appleby without him noticing or remain hidden on the grounds without any of them noticing—but then she considered that even a 'damp rag' like Miss Carlyle probably knew some spell to help her hide, and that was how she was doing it."

"Not overwhelmingly helpful, but it is good to get a clearer picture of Miss Carlyle's character and lack of popularity," Len said.

"No wonder she wrote to Gwen when she became alarmed over the threatening letters and attack on her," Maia said. "She must have known no one here would take her seriously."

Maia's voice was cold and hard, Len noted, and her eyes had an angry sparkle that alarmed him. She was prone to take up the cudgels on behalf of those society overlooked, but this seemed different, somehow—as though something about this case affected her personally. He would have expected anger from Gwen over the lack of concern from everyone here toward her friend, but why should Maia seem so offended?

There was no time to ponder the matter, as Becket continued his account.

"I also introduced the topic of petty theft to the staff, inquiring as to if that's ever been a problem here, with so many different classes and standards mingling—" Here Becket actually looked sheepish, though Len knew for a fact that the man was a traditionalist at heart, no matter how much he repressed his natural belief in the class system in order to align with Len's more egalitarian viewpoint.

"Appealing to reverse snobbery is an old and respected method of establishing rapport," Len assured him.

"Thank you, sir. At any rate, none of them seemed aware of a rash of petty thievery lately, though the same bright lass who spoke up before about Miss Carlyle's likely reason for vanishing did mention that one of the secretaries had been complaining about losing a lipstick from her handbag recently. She doubted anyone had stolen it, though—she thought it far more likely it had gotten lost."

Len shook his head. If no one was likely to take Miss Carlyle seriously with her concerns about the thefts, why should the thief feel the need to threaten and remove her? Why not let her protests continue to fall on deaf ears? Unless the thefts were a precursor to something else, and the thief was afraid of a connection being made after that something else happened … but that was speculating wildly.

It seemed, however, that wild speculation was all they had at this point. They kept running into dead ends at every turn in this puzzle.

He was more than half inclined to write it all off as a wild goose chase and take everyone at their word concerning Miss Carlyle, save for the undeniable fact that she had vanished and no one could explain how. And there were those threatening letters, and the broken railing at the bridge …

No, clearly there was something boiling beneath the surface here at Saint Dorothea's, even if he couldn't make sense of it yet. Even aside from all the physical evidence, his instincts told him that something was amiss here. He only hoped he could uncover what it was in time, before something worse than a missing woman happened.

In his heart, he was beginning to be all too afraid that it already had. It was undeniable that it was easier to hide a dead body than a live woman.

"Ah," said Maia looking across the gardens to the back gate. "There's Gwen."

As they strolled along the path to join the fourth member of their team, Maia said, "Len, couldn't we use a shadow spell by Miss Carlyle's desk, see if it could show us her final movements from there?"

Len considered the idea and reluctantly discarded it. "If her desk and the room itself had been kept empty ever since she vanished, it would work, but given that it's been a few days, with the other secretaries continuing to work and walk around the room, I doubt we'd be able to pick Miss Carlyle's shadow up from all the others."

"Yes, I suppose it would be rather muddled," Maia said sadly.

"One of these days you'll have to come up with a shadow spell that allows the caster to distinguish between individuals, rather than seeing them all as—well, shadows," Len said.

Maia shook her head. "I fear that is beyond my skills! I'm still struggling to master that shield spell I told you about last month."

"The archaic spell you found in the magicians' section of the British Library, the one that no one in two centuries has attempted because of its complexity?" Len affixed a mock frown to his face. "For shame!"

Maia tried to maintain her straight face, but couldn't help but laugh. "Very well, perhaps I am over-reaching. If I could only figure out how the original creator managed to continue to breathe within the shield, I think I would have it. Right now it blocks air as well as anything solid, which is less than useful."

"Indeed." Len rubbed his chin, thinking it over. "I wonder … it's a spell from the 12th century originally, yes?"

Maia nodded, and he continued.

"Then I wonder if it was designed to act more as chain mail, rather than a solid shield, or plate armor. If you think of it as a curtain or veil made up of hundreds of closely-interlocked rings, rather than one solid piece, would that help? It still should block anything solid, but then it would still allow for air to move freely."

"Good heavens, Len," Maia said, her eyes wide. She stopped walking to turn and face him. "That's brilliant! That must be the answer."

He grinned. "Don't thank me until you've tried it. I could be entirely wrong."

"That's not likely, the way the spell is set up," she retorted, beginning to walk again. "You know, it's absurd that we restrict training to master magicians. With your way of looking around the edges of spells and always considering alternative ways to use magic, you would be a far better tutor for apprentice magicians than half the masters out there. It isn't enough to be able to perform great acts of magic oneself; one must be able to show others how to use their wits along with the spells."

Len didn't quite know what to say in response to this. Luckily, they had reached Gwen by now, and he didn't have to say anything.

Still, it was jolly nice to know Maia held him in such high regard, even if he wasn't sure he deserved it.

* * *

Gwen's information didn't amount to much more than Becket's, as Len had feared. This case wasn't giving them anything to grab hold of—dashed irritating.

"None of the secretaries had noticed anything unusual with Lottie," Gwen said, leaning up against the sun-warmed brick wall by the back gate. "Only a couple of them even remembered her mentioning about getting threatening letters, and they didn't take it seriously—just thought it was a crank, or something of that sort."

"In my experience, cranks might write anonymous letters making far-fetched accusations, but threatening letters ought to be taken seriously," Len said dryly.

"Quite," Gwen agreed, as though she had years of personal acquaintance with such matters. "But I suppose, in fairness, one can't expect college secretaries to have the same knowledge as a former MI agent."

Len conceded the point with a wave of his hand.

"I have a list of the items that were stolen from various secretaries," Gwen continued, flourishing a sheet of paper covered with her cramped handwriting. "None of them except one took *that* seriously, either—most assumed they had simply misplaced the items. Leah Fischer was genuinely upset about her loss. She had a bracelet that was gold and garnet, handed down from her great-great-grandmother to the eldest daughter of each generation. She said it had to have been stolen, because she's always extremely careful with it, and she was going to report it to the Magistra even before Lottie talked to her about it, but first she reported it to Jenny, and Jenny told her not to bother Dr. Bingham with such a trivial matter, she—Jenny—would take care of it. Leah didn't want to let it go, but she decided to wait for a week or so to see if it was returned before going against Jenny's command and talking to the Magistra about it." Gwen tossed her head. "She knows Jenny would likely sack her if she found out Leah went to the Magistra when Jenny had specifically told her not to."

"Bit of a tyrant, our Miss Pelham, eh?" Len said.

"Intolerable," Gwen said angrily. "She tries to control every aspect of the secretaries' lives, even outside working hours. Leah says, after she made a fuss about her bracelet, Jenny started not only criticizing all her work, but also scolded her one Monday morning for not attending church on Sunday, said it gave a bad impression of the college! When Leah faithfully keeps the Sabbath every week far more diligently than ever

Jenny bothers to live up to Christian principles."

Gwen took a breath and continued. "Some of the other girls told me Jenny polices their wardrobes, sends them home to change if she deems their skirts too short or their outfits otherwise inappropriate—*and* she docks them their pay for the time they are gone. Lipstick, hair, even perfume … I don't know why the Magistra doesn't do something about it!"

It might not have anything to do with Miss Carlyle, as it seemed unlikely that someone as obsessed with image and control as Jenny Pelham appeared to be would also be a petty thief, or would resort to threatening letters, but it was something to keep in mind all the same. If she felt Miss Carlyle were slipping out of her control, to what lengths would she go to tighten the noose back around the other woman's neck?

"All this is very interesting, Gwen, but why are we discussing it back here?" Maia asked now. She checked her watch. "Surely we ought to be getting ready for dinner."

"I wanted to show you for yourselves how impossible it is for someone to get out this way," Gwen said. "It's all right, I cleared it with Tom first."

She placed one hand on the gate and rattled it lightly. "Locked, as you see. It's always kept locked unless Tom is on duty back here, which he rarely is because of all his other duties."

"Such as chauffeuring," Maia suggested.

"And gardening—the head gardener retired this winter, and Tom has taken over for his duties until they find another. Running errands for the Magistra and other staff as well as numerous other chores."

"A veritable jack-of-all-trades," Len said lightly. Somewhat akin to himself, though Len's particular trades were less practical and involved a good bit more skullduggery.

"So then," Gwen said, stepping away from the gate. "Would one of you care to try to open the lock with a spell?"

Len and Maia glanced warily at each other. Clearly this was a trap, and just as clearly one of them had to spring it.

"Ladies first," Len said, bowing in Maia's direction.

"Oh no," Maia said, smiling with saccharine sweetness. "I wouldn't dream of depriving you of a chance to use your magic."

Len ground his teeth together. She had him there, blast it. Sighing, he squared his shoulders and stepped up to the gate, not sure whether this time he was hoping or fearing his magic would fail him.

"*Recludare.*"

A sharp *zip* of energy jolted through him as his spell entered the locking mechanism, causing him to jump despite being half-braced for such a thing. At the same time, a bell rang out somewhere outside the gate, and a moment later Tom Wright's face was grinning at them through the bars.

"It don't half make you leap, do it, sir?"

"Any spell directed at blocking or undoing the lock protection has the same result," Gwen said. "Even if you can steel yourself to push through the shock, the bell still rings and Tom knows you tried to bypass the spell."

"What about picking the lock without magic?" Maia asked.

Gwen waved at the gate. "I was hoping you'd ask that. Go ahead, try it."

Maia glanced at Len. He shook his head. "Weren't you saying just the other day that you needed more practice at picking locks? I wouldn't dream of depriving you of a chance—"

She wrinkled her nose at him, cutting him off mid-speech,

and withdrew a slim wallet from her skirt pocket. Unfolding it displayed the set of lockpicks Len had given her this previous Christmas. Clearly braced for an unpleasant reaction, Maia knelt down and inserted the first pick into the large square lock.

The bell rang again, even as Maia wrenched her hand away and dropped the pick on the ground. "Drat," she said mildly, shaking her arm out. "And I thought I was prepared for that."

Len retrieved the pick and handed it back to her with a bow. He supposed he ought to feel badly over letting her fall prey to the trap as well, but he was equally certain she would not have appreciated him trying to protect her.

"Thank you," she said, cautiously taking the pick back and slotting it into its accustomed spot in the wallet, then slipping the wallet back into her skirt pocket.

"How *do* you do that?" Gwen asked, momentarily distracted. "I'd swear you didn't even have pockets in that skirt, and it doesn't hang any differently once it's carrying something heavy, and even though I know you have something in there I still can't see a pocket at all!"

"Helen," Maia said briefly, which was all the explanation any of them needed. Helen Radcliffe was Maia's friend and flatmate, and a brilliant clothing designer. Thus far most of what Len had seen from her were spectacular designs and magical effects, but it seemed she was branching into practical outworkings of using magic in clothing as well.

"Golly," Gwen sighed in envy.

"She also gave me a spell for collapsing my clothing when folded so that it takes up less room in a valise," Maia said. "And she's worked something into my evening frock so that it won't wrinkle even when it's been packed. Elsie wasn't happy, as it meant she didn't have an excuse to come with me this time, but it's absolutely marvelous. No more pressing!"

Len cleared his throat. Fascinating as this glimpse into the world of women's fashion was, they were drifting from the matter at hand.

"Sorry," Maia said, flashing him a quick smile. "Tom, does it do the same thing if someone tries to come in from the outside?"

The youth now unlocked the gate and came through into the garden, carefully locking it behind him. "Yes, miss. Non-magical folk just think we've got it wired. Not that we've ever had much of a problem with anyone from the outside trying to come in. Mostly it's students wanting to sneak out after curfew." He grinned at Gwen, who laughed.

"I never did quite manage it!"

"And—forgive me, I know this is impertinent—you never forget to lock it?" Maia clearly didn't care for having to ask such a thing. "I do apologize, but it is rather important that we know."

Tom flushed. "Only once, in all the time I've been working here. It was my mum, see. She was ill, and the doctor, he didn't know what to do, and I was awful worried and distracted, and so when I went off at the end of the day I forgot to lock the gate behind me. That Miss Carlyle, she somehow found out—she must have come along and tested it on purpose to see if I had remembered, because she had no call to be going out the back gate anyway, she always leaves by the front—and took it straight to the Magistra!" An angry spark flashed in his eyes. "Didn't even talk to me about it first, or give me a chance to confess myself. And I was going to, believe me. I could've kicked myself the next morning when I came along and found it already unlocked. I was going straight to Dr. Bingham to tell her, except she came to me first and asked me about it, and I told her right out what I'd done, and she said well, don't let it happen again and then she sent a healer to my house to help my mum, and she never said another word about it. I tell you, Dr. Bingham's a real lady."

"You must have been angry with Miss Carlyle," Len observed.

"Sure I was, even tried to have it out with her, but all she would say was, 'I had to do my duty, even if the Magistra thought I was out of line,'" Tom's tone took on a mincing, overly genteel twist as he quoted her words. He laughed a little. "Can't stay angry with someone like that, especially when she admits the Magistra took her down a peg or two. I heard her mutter something about that as I left, something about how Dr. Bingham would have listened if Miss Pelham had reported it. She might have, too—somehow Miss Pelham always makes people listen, whether they want to or not, and Miss Carlyle, well, she's one of those as can't get any attention. She could stand up and shriek 'fire!' but nobody would notice the building burning until someone else called out about it."

Len noticed Maia wince, and wondered why. It was a ruthless assessment of Miss Carlyle, but not any different from anything they'd heard about her thus far.

It did, however, establish more of the antagonism between her and Miss Pelham. It also explained why Miss Carlyle was encouraging the theft victims to report their losses to the Magistra: after being reprimanded for overstepping once, she wouldn't want to run the risk of the Magistra's disapproval by reporting it herself, while still wanting to ensure the right thing was done.

Only it seemed that somehow she had garnered attention,

and someone had felt the need to remove her.

But why—why—why? And even more so, how?

For all the information they were collecting, they weren't any closer to discovering the truth, and every moment they spent running in circles was another moment Miss Carlyle—if she still lived—was in danger. They had to do something soon, or it would be too late.

Chapter 6

The room shared by Gwen and Maia was small but charming, with white-framed sash windows, an oak floor, high ceilings, a fireplace, and walls painted a soft white. It was far nicer than what Maia had expected for undergraduate quarters, but perhaps a magical college treated its students a bit differently from an ordinary college. Someone—perhaps the excellent Betsy befriended by Becket—had already unpacked their bags and hung their clothes in the tiny wardrobe. Maia was pleased to see the spell Helen had worked into her dinner frock was holding steady: there was not a wrinkle to be seen on the lovely dress.

Before getting acquainted with Helen, Maia had paid little attention to her clothing choices, wearing whatever was most comfortable and practical without thought for how it appeared. This was mostly due to the fact that no matter what she wore, one of her sisters, or her mother, or even her friends, were bound to criticize it in one way or another. Maia had eventually come to accept that she was one of those people who had a knack for always choosing the exact wrong thing to wear, no matter how hard she tried, and so she stopped trying.

With the advent of Helen, all that had changed. Maia had gladly handed over control of her wardrobe to her talented and creative friend. Helen used Maia's clothing as a way to test her newest designs and spells, and in return Maia received a wardrobe that was always just right for her stature and coloring, no matter what the situation. At first Maia had demurred at some of Helen's more daring pieces, but after her friend's taste was proven perfect time and again, she had stopped arguing and instead trusted her friend's judgment in these matters, just as Helen trusted her when it came to solving puzzles or organizing their small household.

Tonight's frock was a rich, vibrant green silk covered with swirls of gold embroidery. The scalloped skirt hit just below her knees, and golden gauze fluttered loose behind her from her shoulders. If she wanted, with one word Maia could release the magic in the gold threads and cause the embroidery to sparkle and flash, much the same way as the golden light of the fountain outside. She decided to forgo that for this meal; no sense in showing off this early.

Still, even without magical enhancement, the gown was stunning and made her eyes look even greener than usual. Long gold earrings and matching necklace completed the look. A touch of powder on her nose and the lightest bit of color on her lips, and Maia was ready to face the hordes.

A light tap at the door heralded Gwen's return from the shared bathroom on their floor, looking quite smart herself in a powder blue frock with striking black accents, her black scholar's gown over one arm, ready to be put on over her dress for the dinner. "Ooh, lovely," she said, her eyes lighting up at Maia's ensemble. "Miss Radcliffe's design?"

"Naturally," Maia said.

Gwen sighed enviously, and Maia was struck with a sudden thought. "You know, Gwen, Helen must sometimes get tired of using me as a prototype for all her dresses—she never gets to create anything for someone petite. If you like, I could suggest to her that you'd be interested in trying one of her new designs sometime."

"Oh, that would be lovely," Gwen said. "So long as you don't mind."

"Not at all." There was no need to be greedy, after all. With what Helen had already created for her, Maia already had a closet full of more frocks than she would ever need.

"Shall we descend?" she asked now, changing the subject.

"Yes, let's," Gwen said. "And I should warn you, the Magistra had held good on her promise of inviting us to join her and the teaching staff for after-dinner drinks. I'm sure it will be a good chance to question them more about Lottie, but I'm sure they'll have plenty of questions for you, as well."

"I won't forget my role," Maia promised wryly. How could she, when it wasn't even that much of a role? The more time she spent here in Cambridge, in particular at Saint Dorothea's, the more drawn she found herself to the place and the lifestyle.

She had no intention of giving up her current path—she was no will-o'-the-wisp, to be drawn hither and yon by a mere fancy, to abandon one career in favor of another simply because the second offered attractions that had paled in the first. It was true that detective work was proving less stimulating and fulfilling than she had originally anticipated. It was equally true that this sort of academic setting, for furthering the development of new ways of exploring magic, seemed like a small portrait of Heaven to Maia. That didn't mean she was going to drop everything, abandon Len, Becket, and Gwen, not to mention Helen, turn her back on the commitment she had made to help those overlooked by official organizations and bring justice to those in need.

It was true that since starting up the detective firm of Whitney & Davies, they had had a mere handful of cases, some of which they had gone out after themselves, rather than waiting for people to come to them. Most of the time the people who came to them were either husbands seeking information on straying wives, or wives seeking information on straying husbands. Even for magicians, divorce seemed the curse of the modern world.

Perhaps she had been foolishly naive and optimistic to think that they would at once be plunged into a whirl of cases as exciting and challenging as the Parasite case. (Dangerous, too, but Maia preferred not to think about that part. After all, they had survived, hadn't they? And Len even had his magic back. No permanent harm done, not really.)

Still, it was disheartening to set out to save the world, only to find the world mildly disinterested in being saved.

All the same, this was her chosen work. Maia helped people: it was a dull life, perhaps, but it was what she did best. She had hopefully moved from helping those who neither wanted nor needed her help, but that didn't mean she couldn't still be a helper. She had thought this detective business was the best way to combine her love of puzzles and stretching her wits with her need to help people. She hoped she wouldn't be proven wrong.

It was early days to assume she had failed, and right now there was more important work at hand than pondering her life choices. She must find Charlotte Carlyle before it was too late. And if it was already too late, God forbid, then she would simply have to switch her focus to bringing her murderer to justice.

This was no time to dither about *what might have been* and *if only I had known more* or even *perhaps I should have listened to Aunt Amelia.*

Maia and Gwen left their room and went down the light-filled hallway to the wide wooden staircase that dominated the center of the building. They walked side-by-side down the stairs and out the front door, across the cobbled garden path past the fountain, ever glimmering and splashing, and into the glass rotunda that was the entry to the dining hall. Maia felt plenty of curious eyes on her back as they went, but no one approached them. Awaiting them just inside the large double doors was Len, resplendent in his dinner jacket and tie. Becket was by his side, dressed more modestly in anticipation of eating with the kitchen staff.

The Magistra was there as well, her academic robe somehow looking even more impressive here than in her study. "Welcome to Merriman Hall," she said.

Len raised an eyebrow. "*The* Merriman?"

Maia wasn't sure who "the" Merriman was, but the Magistra nodded proudly. "He left his entire library to our college in his will, and endowed a scholarship for two deserving magicians, one male and one female, each year. His support alone went a great way toward reconciling many of the traditionalists to our existence."

Becket crossed the light-filled rotunda to stand at Maia's elbow and speak in a low voice meant for her ears alone. "Leon Merriman was the leader of the High Council before he retired, and was and still is a legend among magicians not only in England but all throughout Europe. He never married or had children, and the fortune he amassed in his long life was immense."

Maia was grateful for his subtle way of giving her information that anyone raised in the magical world would have known without needing to be told. She did so hate feeling like an outsider.

Len was shaking his head. "Half the magicians in the world would give their eyeteeth for a tenth of his library. He left it all to you?"

"Indeed. Gwen, you will have to show our guests the library when it is convenient. For now, I must leave you and join my staff. Protocol must be observed, you know, and the students would be most perturbed if I entered from the foyer rather than the side room. Gwen, will you accompany me? Mr. Davies, Miss Whitney, a server will show you to your seats."

She sailed away, followed dutifully by Gwen. Becket bowed and left them as well. Len smiled at Maia.

"You look dashed nice, old thing."

"Thank you," Maia answered. "Fine feathers, you know. You look rather splendid yourself."

He shook his head, whether at Maia's disclaimer of her own appearance or his own sartorial splendor, but before he could answer, a server entered the foyer and coughed discreetly.

"Mr. Davies? Miss Whitney? If you would care to follow me," he said. Len crooked his arm and Maia accepted it, and the server led them out of the foyer into the hall itself, where a couple dozen students sat twelve to each long table. Maia barely noticed them, her attention taken up with the high barrel vault ceiling and the windows whose arches mimicked those above. Painted in colors that shifted smoothly as one watched, the plasterwork far above their heads was carved with all sorts of magical beasts and creatures out of legends—dragons, of course, and unicorns, phoenixes, griffins, and more.

There were more details, but Maia did not want to gawk—so uncouth!—so she brought her gaze back to earth and let Len pull out a seat for her at the left-hand table. There was plenty of room, as the tables were optimistically designed to hold far more people than they currently did. Perhaps one day they would.

A ringing tone filled the air, though there was no gong to be struck that Maia could see, and the students all pushed back their chairs and rose respectfully, the visitors following suit. All wearing academic black, the faculty members filed in through a side door, the Magistra bringing up the rear with appropriate gravity, Gwen just before her. They all ranged themselves on the far side of the high table, placed on a dais crosswise to the other two tables in the hall, and waited.

"*Benedic nos Domine et haec tua dona, quae de tua largitate sumus sumptori. Per Christum Dominum nostrum. Amen,*" intoned the Magistra.

"Amen," everyone echoed.

The Magistra seated herself, followed by the faculty, and lastly the students as well, and the servers began bringing in the food.

The first course consisted of clear soup, a light white wine, and equally light conversation with one's dining companions. As speaking with Len, seated on her left, would have been enjoyable but done nothing to further their purpose in being here, Maia turned to the young man at her right hand.

"Good evening," she began conventionally enough. "Lovely weather for this time of year, isn't it?"

The young chap raised his eyebrows, thick and heavy over clear brook-brown eyes. "Is it?"

Only two words, but in them, as well as in his gleaming white teeth, careless but confident manner of dress, and overall air of independence and confidence, Maia distinguished him as an American. "Are you here on a visit, or do you attend Saint Dorothea's?" she asked now.

He laughed. "Guess you've got me pegged! Nathan Quirke, at your service, visiting from Boston. That's in Massachusetts," he added.

It was Maia's turn to laugh. "Believe it or not, I know where Boston is. I've never visited, mind, but I met a soldier once from Boston who told me all about it. Quincy Market, the Boston Tea Party, Paul Revere's grave."

Mr. Quirke did not laugh again, but the dimple in his left cheek deepened. "That about covers it."

"So what brings you to Saint Dorothea's, Mr. Quirke?"

"Nathan, please. And you are …?"

Maia wasn't sure she was comfortable with moving so quickly to first names—but he was an American, after all. "Maia Whitney, also a guest. Actually, I'm considering changing over from a conventional journeyman's path to attending here instead, and I thought it worth visiting to see if it is right for me."

"I am sure they'd be lucky to have you," Mr. Quirke—Nathan—said politely. "Tell me, Miss Maia Whitney, is this your first visit to Cambridge? I've never been here before, and I've been hoping to find somebody who can explain the university to me and show me all the sights of the town."

Maia had to disclaim all knowledge of the city, and then the American asked about London, and by the time Maia had finished telling him about England's capital city the servers had whisked away the soup and replaced it with exquisitely prepared trout, Parisienne potatoes, and glazed carrots.

"I see Saint Dorothea's has a food magician for a chef," Maia said after her first bite. "Absolutely marvelous."

"Not too bad," Mr. Quirke agreed, though somewhat doubtfully. "Have you ever tried French food, Miss Maia?"

It wasn't until the end of dessert that Maia realized he had never actually explained why he was visiting Saint Dorothea's, but had rather neatly evaded all of her queries on the matter. Curious behavior, especially considering how open and forthright Americans usually were.

Perhaps she should keep a closer eye on young Mr. Quirke than she had originally thought.

* * *

Thanks to one of the servers showing them the way, at the close of the meal Maia and Len were able to find their way to the Maximillian Room, where they would be joining the Magistra, Gwen, and Becket for coffee with the staff.

The Maximillian Room proved to be a small room off the dining hall, lit only by candles and the light from the fireplace, as heavy drapes embroidered with the crest of Saint Dorothea's covered the window at the other end of the room. To the left of the door as one entered was a table bearing a silver coffee pot and several china cups, where a few people were serving themselves. The rest of the room's current inhabitants stood in little clusters here and there, most eying the newcomers with distrust and distaste. A white-coated server circulated with a cut-glass decanter of port for anyone who wished. The Magistra stood close to the fireplace, her strong features cast into shadow by the flickering flames.

"Excellent, thank you for joining us. That will do, Williams," to the server. "Leave the decanter, we shall serve ourselves." When the server had exited with a highly injured air, the Magistra continued speaking. "Mr. Davies, Miss Whitney, I wanted to take this opportunity to introduce you to my staff and vice versa. Everyone, Mr. Davies, Miss Whitney, Mr. Becket, and our own Gwen Zhang are detectives from London come to look into the disappearance of Charlotte Carlyle."

It seemed discretion was no longer required of them, at least not among the staff. That would make life simpler, but Maia wished the Magistra had told them ahead of time she intended to reveal their real purpose here; it made their deception at dinner feel absurd and unnecessary.

"Who?" asked one or two people.

"*Has* she disappeared?" was the slightly better question from a pleasant-faced woman with keen blue eyes twinkling from behind her round spectacles.

"It seems so, Dolly," the Magistra said, answering that question directly. "No one seems to have seen her since yesterday morning. She wrote to Gwen two days ago about that rash of petty thefts we've been having, and some threatening letters she had apparently received, and then vanished. You can understand our concern. It doesn't seem a matter for police or Deep, yet we can't leave it as is, either. If something has happened to her, it is our responsibility to find her and make things right." She cleared her throat. "I trust all of my staff to do whatever is necessary to assist in this."

"Well," said the pleasant-faced woman, "I certainly hope you can find poor Lottie, and if in the process you are able to recover my missing silk scarf I shall be even more delighted.

It was such a stupid theft, but that scarf does have sentimental value for me, and I do miss it."

"I still think you misplaced it, Dolly," said another woman. "You know you're scatter-brained when it comes to personal possessions."

"Nonsense," she answered spiritedly. "That is, yes, I can be scatter-brained about things, but not the scarf. Alan sent it to me from France, you know, the first week of the war, back when we all thought it would be over quickly." She sniffed and dabbed her eyes with a spotless white linen handkerchief. "He was killed the very next week. I would *never* lose his final gift to me."

Maia decided she liked this woman. "I'm sorry, your name and position here are …?" she asked, moving closer.

"Oh, sorry. Dolly Archer, chemistry. Yes, I know, why chemistry at a magicians' college?"

"Actually—" Maia began.

"But, you see, a thorough understanding of the composition and structure of matter and energy is crucial to the formation of new spells. If we know how everything in the physical world is built and how it all relates to each other, we can learn how to better shape it and alter it—but there, I mustn't talk shop. My apologies, Miss Whitney. I had both Lottie and Gwen in my supervisory," she added, smiling fondly at Gwen. "It's good to see you again, dear."

"You as well, Miss Archer," Gwen said.

"And you've had a scarf stolen?" Briefly, Maia recalled the torn scarf hanging in Miss Carlyle's room at the boarding house—but it was unlikely to be the same scarf. Surely Miss Carlyle would have returned it to Miss Archer had she found it, and most women did, in fact, own one or more scarves these day. Maia herself had a half dozen, and her sister Ellie had three times that. No, it was much more likely that the scarf in Miss Carlyle's room was exactly what it appeared to be: a favorite scarf that was awaiting mending rather than having been thrown out after getting torn. In fact, it was most likely the scarf Miss Carlyle had been wearing when she was pushed through the railing on the bridge, and had been torn then. A clue to Miss Carlyle's careful personality, to not throw something away simply because it was damaged, but not a clue to her disappearance, alas.

Maia wished she had paper and pencil with her so she could start jotting down notes on why had lost what, starting with Miss Archer and her scarf, but this frock had been made before Helen had perfected her magical pockets, and so it had none.

Dr. Bingham had anticipated her need. "Here, I've made a list for you of everything I know of that's gone missing. Be aware, some of the items may not have been stolen, only misplaced. As you will see when you look at it, there is no rhyme or reason to any of it." She handed the piece of paper to Len, who folded it and placed it in *his* pocket.

"I think it's all nonsense," said a short, slim man with a scowl on his face. "A few items go missing here or there, a hysterical woman gets a few letters as a prank, and suddenly we have detectives from London down? What's next, Scotland Yard and bloodhounds? Miss Carlyle was clearly embarrassed to face her friend and admit she overreacted to the situation, so she faded away for a few days to avoid facing the consequences of her actions. What could be simpler?"

"That is an interesting theory," Maia said. "And you are …?"

"Gerald Foster, mathematics," he snapped. "Magistra, I am shocked you would permit this sort of vulgar questioning in our sacred precincts."

"Don't be so pompous, Foster," said a burly fellow who looked like he would be more at home in a rugby jersey than a dinner jacket. "Our precincts are barely six years old, how can they be sacred yet?" He grinned at Maia. "Steven Gardiner, librarian."

"Ah, so you're the chap in charge of the Merriman Collection," Len said. "Lucky fellow." The two immediately gravitated toward each other and began chatting.

Once again, Maia found Becket at her elbow right when she wished for him. "I didn't realize Len was such a reader," she said to him in a quiet voice. Gwen was happily talking with her former supervisor, and nobody else had come forward yet to speak to the detectives, most appearing to share Mr. Foster's viewpoint rather than Miss Archer's or Steven Gardiner's.

"Under normal circumstances, he isn't, though he does enjoy the occasional novel when he has leisure enforced upon him by injury or his mother," Becket responded in a voice equally low. "However, the late Mr. Merriman had dabbled with ways of strengthening latent magical abilities, with the notion that anyone could become a magician if they only worked hard enough at it, in much the same way that many people believe anyone can become an athlete with the proper training and diet. I believe Mr. Davies is intrigued by the idea of being able to strengthen his own abilities, as they are still weaker than they had been before the Parasite attack."

"I see." Maia felt an ache of dull rage against the unfairness of it all. Though they had stopped the Parasite, it hadn't made things wholly right. Yet what could one do? She had already stretched the acceptable boundaries of propriety by lending him some of her magic in order to rekindle the spark that had gone out of his.

If there was a book in this Merriman Collection that could help Len, she hoped Mr. Gardiner would allow him access to it. She couldn't think of anyone who deserved it more.

"I for one agree with Foster," broke in a loud, strident voice. Maia looked across the room and found its owner: a tall, thin woman with a narrow face and a battle-axe nose. "'Vulgar' is the only term for this. A few trinkets have gone missing here and there from careless individuals, one of our secretaries has proven unreliable, and suddenly we have detectives in the college, treating us as criminals? I object very strongly."

"I am aware this is unpleasant, Marcia," the Magistra said with an air of weariness, as one repeating an old argument, or perhaps a new argument with an old opponent. "But as I have already said, it wouldn't do for the college to gain a reputation of being unconcerned with possible thefts or a missing person, however much we may think it an overreaction. Just imagine if the conservatives in the Circle got a hold of this! They could use it as an excuse to stop our support and force us to close down. Much better to show that we are treating it with all seriousness."

The woman—Marcia—narrowed her eyes. "And how do we know these so-called detectives aren't really secretly working with the Circle, trying to concoct some sort of story about us to justify closing our doors? You—Miss Whitney—you were Amelia Rawlings' apprentice, weren't you? How do we know she hasn't sent you here to try to blacken our reputation?"

Maia felt more than saw Becket stiffen beside her, and Len broke off his conversation with Mr. Gardiner in the middle of a sentence, outrage plain on his face. She wasn't entirely sure why they were so offended; it was not an unreasonable guess, given Aunt Amelia's character, and this woman had no way of knowing that Maia would scorn to stoop to such levels even if she was in agreement with her aunt's principles.

"Really, Miss Linton!" Miss Archer said. "There's no need to be insulting."

"Yes," Mr. Gardiner added, a hint of malice spicing his words. "Someone might begin to think you had something to hide."

Miss Linton drew herself up even straighter, though Maia wouldn't have thought it possible. "How dare you make such an insinuation, Gardiner?"

"Merely an observation," the burly librarian said.

"Please, everyone," Dr. Bingham broke in. "There is no need to take any of this personally. I believe we all have the good of Saint Dorothea's at heart, and I can assure you that Gwen, as well as Mr. Davies, Miss Whitney, and Mr. Becket, have been nothing but respectful and concerned for the wellbeing not only of Miss Carlyle, but of the school."

The tension in the atmosphere eased slightly at that, but Miss Linton was still combative.

"That's as may be, but I still have my opinion about Miss Carlyle and her so-called disappearance. Miss Whitney, I had the misfortune of trying to teach potion-making to Charlotte Carlyle, and let me tell you, she was hopeless, utterly hopeless. Couldn't memorize a single formula. Perhaps you are not aware of how important potions are for healers. Rather than having to expand all their energy on spell after spell, they rely on previously prepared potions to take care of the more common healing, and save their strength for more detailed spells. Without the ability to make potions easily, Carlyle couldn't hope to achieve her goal of joining the ranks of England's healers. Nor did she have the moral character for it. Again, Miss Whitney, you might not be aware of this, but healers must be above reproach in every aspect of their lives, as so much of their work lends itself to abuse of power. It's generally frowned upon for magicians to cast spells directly on other people—another reason potions are valuable—and so a healer is constantly subject to the temptation of improperly using their magic due to the necessity of performing spellwork that directly affects their patients."

Becket spoke before Maia could answer. His voice was as mild as ever, but there was steel underneath that took Maia by surprise. "I do not believe Miss Whitney requires you to instruct her in the restrictions and cautions magicians place on ourselves to prevent abuse of our powers, Miss Linton."

Maia did not consider herself particularly dense, though she lacked Len's ability to leap to correct conclusions based on merely a few words or gestures, but she knew she was missing something here. Clearly Miss Linton was attempting to put Maia in her place, but why? And in what way? Why did Becket feel such a strong need to defend her?

Missing context, Maia decided to ignore whatever implied insult Miss Linton was giving and answer her objection straightforwardly. "I am afraid I do not see what a difficulty in mastering healing has to do with Miss Carlyle's disappearance now."

"Do you not? The woman has the backbone of a dishrag. She has a job here only because Dr. Bingham is too kind to let any graduate of Saint Dorothea's go jobless. She whines and plods and wishes her life would be better without ever doing anything to make it so."

"Those all may be reasons for you to dislike her, Miss Linton, but I must agree with Miss Whitney: I do not see why any of that should matter in our task of finding her now that she is missing," Becket said.

Miss Linton cast her hands into the air with a theatrical gesture. "Because Foster is right! She doesn't have any enemies, and nobody could care enough about such a pathetic thing to want to do her harm. If she is missing, it's because she wants to be."

"Thank you for your opinion," Maia said, tamping down her fury with an effort. It wasn't that long since experiencing anger of this sort would have caused her magic to burst free in all sorts of destructive and embarrassing ways. Len had taught her some methods of control that had worked far better than Aunt Amelia's advice to simply be less emotional, and Maia was pleased that not even a hint of silver had begun to glow around her hands. "We will be certain to bear that in mind as we pursue our investigations."

Was everyone going to attempt to discourage them from bringing about justice for Charlotte Carlyle simply because they found her dull and unimportant? Was there no room in the magical community for plodders and workers-behind-the-scenes, only for those who sparkled and shone?

Maia's head began to ache, and she suddenly devoutly wished the night was over.

Chapter 7

"The brown suit today, sir?" Becket asked, laying out Len's clothing while the morning sun peeped through the clouds to foretell another fine day.

"Indeed," Len said. "The green tie, I think."

"Excellent choice, sir."

Green, like Maia's smashing frock the previous evening. She had looked like a meadow in spring, or a forest in midsummer. He'd never seen her look anything less than beautiful, even when dressed for sneaking around a crime scene after dark, but last night she'd put every other female in the college to shame. Probably every other female in the entire city.

That cat Miss Linton had been green-eyed herself with envy. No doubt she was intimidated by Maia's tremendous potential—Miss Rawlings might not have approved of Maia's career choice, but that didn't stop her from boasting of her former apprentice's magical prowess. The way that she'd attempted to shame Maia for not having been brought up in the magical tradition, as if that mattered one jot, had made Len see red.

Luckily Becket had been there to show her Maia was no one to trifle with, else Len might have lost his head and challenged the fool woman to a wizard's duel, which was not only illegal but also would not have been appreciated by Maia. She was more than capable of defending herself—and him, for that matter—but it went against the grain to stand by silently when someone was insulting the woman he cared for so deeply.

Len paused with one arm inside his coat, frozen in place until Becket discreetly assisted him the rest of the way. Was it time to tell Maia of his deeper feelings for her? Was it fair to keep working alongside her while keeping her in the dark of the truth buried in his heart? Fear of losing her friendship if she couldn't reciprocate had kept him silent thus far, but he couldn't live in fear forever. Surely there had to be a way of phrasing it that would allow her to graciously turn him down if she wasn't interested. Becket might know, but dash it all, there were limits. He'd be hanged if he asked his valet how he ought to confess his feelings to a woman. Sure he ought to be able to think of something himself. What else were novels for, but to give a chap a few clues?

He had brought *Pride and Prejudice* to read on the train, though the conversation had made staving off boredom unnecessary. How was it Mr. Darcy had put it to Elizabeth in his second proposal? "… One word from you will silence me on this matter forever."

There you were, the perfect way to give her a back door to say, "I'm sorry to disappoint you but I wish to remain friends," if that was indeed what she wanted. Miss Austen had known a thing or two about how a chap ought to address the lady he admired most in the world.

Now how to *begin* the confession? "By the way, I love you," seemed a trifle casual. Mr. Darcy's original proposal, along the lines of, "You must allow to tell you how ardently I admire and love you," on the other hand, was more dramatic than Len could see himself saying. "My feelings for you are far deeper and stronger than friendship," was safe, but then it seemed like he was diminishing their friendship, and that wasn't at all right, either.

Perhaps there was something there, though … Something along the lines of, "Much as I value our friendship, I find that I care for you in a different way as well." It was a little rough, but surely in the moment he could make himself clear, along with finishing up with the guarantee that if she could not reciprocate he would never speak on the matter again, and their friendship would continue as it always had.

With one final decisive knot to the tie around his neck, Len made up his mind. He would speak to Maia as soon as this case was wrapped up. Here in Cambridge, if possible, or back in London if that did not work out. One way or another, he would confess the truth, and damn the consequences.

He went downstairs to the dining hall for breakfast in a remarkably elevated frame of mind.

There were fewer students here this morning than there had been last night—Len remembered well from his own student days the tendency to skip breakfast in favor of sleeping later. That American chappie who had apparently been so entertaining—he and Maia had laughed together more frequently than was comfortable for Len, even as he acknowledged the absurdity of his jealousy—was not there, nor were any of the teaching staff.

Len dished himself up a plate of eggs, kippers, and toast from the dishes set on a sideboard that had made its appearance in the dining hall for the morning meal, and found a seat near one of the windows facing the courtyard so he could see Maia and Gwen when they came across.

It didn't take long. A foolish smile spread itself over Len's face as he watched them on the path, Gwen so petite and trim, Maia so tall and commanding. Truly, he was dashed lucky to be working with both of them, and with Becket.

An unpleasant feeling wiggled into the back of his mind, temporarily wiping the smile from his face. What was it? Why did he suddenly feel so uneasy?

An image of his mother's letter floated before his eyes at the same time he heard his grandmother's voice in his memory. "Tempting the gods," she used to say whenever anyone seemed too content with his or her lot.

Nonsense. Granny was a wise woman, but he refused to believe that being too pleased with his life circumstances meant he was asking fate to reverse his situation post-haste.

He also refused to believe that his mother's concerns about the estate would require anything more than a stern letter to resolve.

"Morning," he greeted the ladies cheerily, rising and pulling out chairs for them as they approached the table with laden plates. "Sleep well?"

They indicated that they had, and then Maia, as was her wont, leaped in feet first to the fray. "We must organize a plan of action for today—who to question, where to search, that sort of thing. I don't suppose either of you has any suspects in mind? I must say I didn't care for—"

She was interrupted by the door crashing back on its hinges. Mr. Foster, the mathematics lecturer, burst into the dining hall hatless and with wild eyes.

"Fetch the Magistra!" he yelled, his voice high-pitched and shrill. "Someone find a healer! Hurry!"

A babble of voices rose into the air, and one female began

screaming from sheer panic, so Len imagined, as students rose from their seats and milled around Foster asking what had happened, what was wrong, what was going on. Len's good mood dissipated at once.

"Come on," he told the other two, tossing down his napkin.

"What is it?" Gwen asked, eyes worried. "What do you know?"

"I don't know anything—yet," Len answered, leading them away from the crowd and out toward the main door. "But I have a feeling."

Becket materialized as if by his own particular brand of magic at Len's elbow as they exited Merriman Hall and made their way to the plodge.

"Len," Maia said in a hushed voice, matching him stride for stride. "Do you think—Miss Carlyle?"

"I don't know who, but I know it's murder," he answered.

"How?"

"I don't know, I just know," he answered, somewhat confusedly. After all these years, his instinct for violent death and trouble was well-honed. Maia preferred facts and a steady unraveling to get to the bottom of the problem, but for Len, acting on his gut feelings rarely failed him.

He wrenched open the door of the plodge, and felt no shock, merely a deep sorrow and a stirring of anger at the sight that met their eyes. Gwen's gasp was more of a short scream, quickly cut off when she clapped her hand over her mouth. Maia made no sound, but Len could feel the tension begin to coil in her body. Becket released a long, slow breath and removed his hat.

Appleby the porter did not care for any of these reactions. He was beyond caring for anything. His body lay sprawled on the once-clean floor of the plodge, one side of his head caved in from a heavy blow, his bowler hat cast off to the side.

* * *

The wheels of officialdom did not take long to begin turning. The Magistra, pale but composed, put in a telephone call to the Cambridge City Police, and was much relieved when the spell adapted from Saint Dorothea's for the police worked exactly as it ought, and she was automatically transferred to the very small Sorcerous Crimes Unit within the CID, who sent out their entire force: one inspector, one sergeant, and one constable.

It did not seem like enough for a crime of this magnitude, and Len harbored a slight hope that the inspector would welcome any aid Whitney and Davies could give him since his own forces were spread so thin. He well knew from his time in MI that jealousy and tension were common when one force felt their rights were being encroached upon, whether it was Deep resenting MI, or police resenting private investigators. He had no wish to step on any toes, but neither did he care to see this murder handled in a haphazard manner simply because the inspector was too proud to accept outside help when it was needed.

When he came, Inspector Ashley Dale of the SCU proved something of an enigma, even to Len, who prided himself on being able to read a person's character in their face within a few moments of meeting them. Inspector Dale was small and slender, with a thin dark face and a sardonic expression which seemed habitual, as it did not change even when he examined the crime scene.

"Hm," was all he said, his quick eyes darting every which way.

"And how many people have been in here since it happened?" he asked abruptly, wheeling around to the group at the door.

This consisted of Len, Maia, Becket, and Gwen, as well as the Magistra, Miss Archer, and young Tom. The other residents of the college lurked nearby on the grounds, unwilling to get too close but not wanting to move away entirely, either.

"Only Mr. Davies, to be certain Mr. Appleby was dead," the Magistra said. "He told us to let no-one in after him, and so we did not."

"Hm," Inspector Dale said once again. "Very well, you are all excused. Dr. Bingham, if you would please gather everyone together in one place, and set aside a small room we may use for questioning, I would appreciate it. As soon as my team and I have finished examining the crime scene, we will begin with questions."

"I will have everyone wait in the dining hall," the Magistra said. "And you may use the Maximillian Room for questioning." She hesitated. "You wish to question everyone within the college walls? Including the cooks and cleaners and gardeners …?"

Dale nodded, pulling a pair of gloves on. "Only way to make sure we haven't missed anything. Thank you, ma'am."

He entered the plodge, his silent sergeant and constable at his side, and closed the door to the rest of them, effectively ending any further conversation.

"Well," the Magistra said, her voice mildly uncertain for the first time. "He seems extremely … efficient."

Gwen's eyes flashed. "He didn't even give us a chance to tell him about Charlotte!"

"Oh!" said Miss Archer. "You don't think—oh dear, you don't think these things are connected?"

"It seems highly unlikely they would not be," Len said.

"And now we must find Lottie, before what happened to poor Appleby happens to …" Gwen's voice faltered. "That is, before it's too late."

Len said nothing, but he greatly feared it was already too late. If one murder had been committed, it was all the more likely two had been. A man who killed once was always more prepared to kill again. The question now was, had Appleby been the first victim or the second? And why?

"I wonder if that ledger is still there," Maia mused. When Len looked at her, she clarified. "The one Dr. Bingham told us about, the one where he recorded all the comings and goings of everyone through the gate."

Ah, that ledger. Maia's mind was working along the same lines as his—why would anyone need to kill the porter?

"I will leave you all here to discuss matters with Inspector Dale when he emerges," the Magistra said. "Dolly, help me gather everyone else together in the dining hall, would you? Tom, please make sure the back gate is locked. We don't want anyone slipping out that way while we are distracted at the front."

The members of the college departed, leaving the four Londoners alone outside the plodge.

"Well," said Maia.

That seemed to sum things up quite neatly. Len could think of nothing to add.

Gwen pulled out a handkerchief and dabbed at her eyes. "I'm not crying," she said furiously. "I won't cry. We have to *do* something! Dear Appleby … he was always so kind to everyone. And then there's Lottie, and no one else seems to care that she's missing … we *must* find her, and stop whoever kidnapped her and killed Appleby. We must!"

"I applaud your decision," said a mild voice behind them. "Might one ask why you believe it your responsibility to solve this case, and who Lottie is, and who, for that matter, you are and why you have not followed my instructions to gather in the dining hall?"

Inspector Dale had exited the plodge so quietly not even Len had heard him—that was impressive enough Len wondered if that man had used a spell to make his movements silent. Though his tone was calm his words were sharp, and his pointed eyebrows had risen, increasing his likeness to a sarcastic faun.

Maia smiled at him in a friendly fashion. "Dear me, Inspector Dale, we do seem to have blundered, haven't we? The Magistra thought it best if we wait for you here, but I don't blame you for being irritated that we disregarded your instructions. Maia Whitney, and these are my colleagues: Len Davies, Gwen Zhang, and Mr. Becket."

She paused for a brief moment, looking mildly flustered over not being able to give a first name for Becket. Len sympathized; he had been working with Becket for years, and the only thing he had ever learned about his man's given name was that it began with "G" and Becket loathed it.

"The infamous Whitney and Davies from the Parasite case?" Inspector Dale inquired. Len's neck and cheeks went hot with embarrassment. Curse it, would they never live that case down? True, they had concluded it in a rather spectacular and public fashion, but still. Old habits of secrecy died hard, and while he enjoyed no longer having to live his life as a lie, he wouldn't have objected to a bit more privacy.

Maia patted her hair, one of the few times Len had ever seen her move aimlessly. "Oh … well, yes, I suppose so," she said, stammering a little. "That is …"

Becket cleared his throat. "If I may, sir. We are here on behalf of a Miss Charlotte Carlyle, who has gone missing after expressing concern to Miss Zhang about a recent bout of petty thievery. It seems not only possible but probable that the two matters—Mr. Appleby's murder and Miss Carlyle's disappearance—are connected. Dr. Bingham thought it might save time and assist you in your questioning if we informed you of our purpose here before you began questioning the others. We intended no disrespect, and only wish to help in any way possible."

Well now, good for Becket! Len had never heard him speak so eloquently and clearly. He had an expression on his face, though, that Len had only ever seen him wear when looking at a pair of shoes Len had managed to irreparably damage mere hours after Becket had cleaned them to perfection. For whatever reason, it seemed Becket had taken a dislike to the police inspector.

"I see," said Dale after a pause. "I suppose you'd better tell me about it, then."

Len expected Maia to speak, as she was usually the best as summing things up incisively, but as she still stood there silent, he took up the tale from his manservant and managed to bring Dale up to date on their investigation.

"Curious," Dale said when he finished. "Could be a coincidence. It's a long step from pilfering a few trinkets here and there and mailing childish threats to kidnapping and murder.

You say everyone here is convinced Miss Carlyle has vanished of her own accord?"

"Yes, but how?" Gwen broke in. "She's not that talented of a magician, and there are all kinds of safeguards in place to prevent people using magic to sneak in and out anyway, so how could she have been here and then disappeared willingly? And why? She knew we were coming to help."

"True, but by the same token, how could someone kidnap or murder her here without running afoul of those same safeguards? It is easier for a person to willingly sneak past such precautions than for a villain to take him or herself past them along with his victim."

Len had to admit the man made a reasonable point.

"But someone with more magical talent, and especially someone with more knowledge of how the safeguards here work, could manage it better than Miss Carlyle could herself," Maia countered, seeming more like her usual self.

Inspector Dale conceded the point with a nod. "Then you suspect one of the staff," he said.

"Oh," Gwen said suddenly. "And that would explain Appleby." She glanced at them all, not seeming to realize she had cut off the inspector. "Don't you see? Someone circumnavigated the spells at the front gate, but even if they managed to hide themselves, they couldn't fool Appleby completely. You remember, he told us there was something odd about the day Lottie disappeared, even if he couldn't remember it. What if he did remember, and was going to tell us?"

It made sense, but Len felt instinctively that somehow it didn't quite hang together. He looked over across the grounds, to where Tom was still hanging by the back gate.

What if … what if it wasn't that someone got around the

front gate? What if that was what Appleby remembered, or rather knew without understanding? What if the old man had realized that if Charlotte hadn't left by the front, she had to have left by the back, which meant that either Tom had forgotten to lock it again, or that Tom himself was the one who had taken her? What if Appleby had spoken to his junior about it, and desperate to protect himself, Tom had lashed out at the old man?

Who better to be their petty thief? Stealing trinkets and little things for his mother, other items to sell to give himself more pocket change? He already had a grudge against Miss Carlyle because of how she reported his carelessness to the Magistra when his mother was ill. It wouldn't take much for that grudge to fester, and, when he learned that Miss Carlyle was encouraging the victims of his thievery to report their losses to the Magistra, for it to spill over into threats. Then, when she found out—somehow—from the envelope of the latest threatening letter that he was the one behind them, and when he learned that there were proper investigators coming from London to look into the matter, he panicked, managed to overcome her, and took her out of the college through the back gate.

It all fit together. He wished it didn't.

"Len?" Maia said, and he realized the conversation had continued around him while he had thought this all out. He ruffled a hand through his hair and pasted a smile on his face.

He would discuss this with Maia when they had a moment of privacy; he didn't want to accuse Tom of anything in front of the inspector. That wouldn't be fair to the lad, and there was still a chance Len was wrong.

"Sorry," he said. "Lost in thought. What did I miss?"

"Inspector Dale suggested that we continue our search for Miss Carlyle, while he pursues the investigation into Mr. Appleby's murder," Maia said.

"Since you are already here for that purpose," Dale added. "And I haven't enough men to search for a missing woman and catch a murderer."

Not to mention that solving a murder would be far more likely to gain him accolades and a promotion from mere inspector to chief inspector, Len thought cynically, while the search for the missing woman was most likely to result in finding her dead body dumped in the river somewhere, and lead to nothing but grief and more puzzles.

Still, it was better than being ordered to return to London or to sit on their hands and keep their noses out of the affair entirely, so he acquiesced with as much grace as possible, and went back to worrying about Tom.

If he was the killer and kidnapper, how to prove it? And if he wasn't, who was?

Chapter 8

"I think Jenny did it," Gwen said.

They had adjourned for lunch at a nearby pub, sitting at a table which gave them a clear view of this quiet stretch of the river, today with few punts traversing it, though Maia had seen a family of swans serenely drifting by. The meal finished, Len had gotten them all a refill of cider, and they settled back to discuss the case.

"Miss Pelham?" She was unpleasant, to be sure, but Maia wasn't sure that she was a thief, kidnapper, and murderer.

"Out of everyone at the college, she's the one who was in the most regular contact with Lottie, seeing her on a daily basis," Gwen said. "She would have the best opportunity to do—something to her. She's also the one who was loudest in calling Lottie's ideas about the thefts rot, and she actively discouraged anyone from reporting the thefts to the Magistra. Not to mention she is, for all her faults, terrifyingly efficient; if she set out to do something wicked, she would do it well."

"Fair enough," said Len. "But what's her motive?"

Gwen raised her hands, palms up. "What is anyone's motive? Hasn't that been the difficulty all along, trying to determine why anyone would engage in petty theft to begin with, and then why they would feel the need to threaten and kidnap

Lottie to prevent her from drawing attention to the theft? I would think that once we know who did it and how, the *why* will make itself clear."

Maia frowned—not in disagreement, but in contemplation. "Lennox, may I see the list the Magistra gave you, of the items stolen?" He handed her the piece of paper from his pocket. "Isn't it curious," Maia continued as she smoothed the paper free of its fold lines, "that the thief went to all this trouble to prevent anyone from reporting their loss to the Magistra, only to have her put together a list of all the missing items within hours of learning about the matter? So much bother, and all for nothing."

"Speaking of terrifyingly efficient," Len murmured.

Gwen blinked, startled. "Len, you can't mean—you don't— you can't possibly suspect Dr. Bingham!"

It was his turn to look startled. "What? No, not at all! Although … hm. No, no, that's rubbish. No, I was thinking that if there is one person at the college more efficient than Miss Pelham, it's Dr. Bingham, and seeing how little time it took her to learn the details of all the missing items and organize them into a list gives us at least some insight as to why the thief wanted it kept from her: once she takes a matter seriously, she bends all her formidable will toward it, and succeeds more often than not. If she weren't distracted right now by Miss Carlyle's disappearance and Mr. Appleby's murder, I'm sure she'd have already determined who the thief was and apprehended him or her."

Maia thought he looked unhappy, but she wasn't sure why. Come to think of it, he had seemed distracted ever since their chat with the inspector. Perhaps he was as flustered as she had been at the fact that the inspector knew their names and their reputation from the Parasite case? But if that was so, surely he wouldn't be bothered by it *still*.

She looked down at the list. "If the Magistra could make sense of this lot, she has my deepest admiration, and I would like to recruit her for our detective agency."

"Read it aloud, would you? Let us all share in your bafflement," Len said.

Maia did so.

"Red lipstick (Lily Jamison, secretary)

Linen handkerchief (Marjorie Cooper, secretary)

Fountain pen (Gerald Foster, mathematics)

Powder compact (Sally Linton, student)

Silk scarf (Dolly Archer, chemistry)

Carved wooden bear (Robert Robertson, student)

Umbrella (Elaine Green, secretary)

Garnet and gold bracelet (Leah Fischer, secretary)

Ink bottle (Stephen Gardiner, librarian)."

There was a pause, and then Len borrowed the list back.

"Let's see," he said. "Six females, three males. Four secretaries, three staff, two students."

"No servants," Becket commented.

"Indeed. I wonder why?"

"They didn't have anything the thief considered worth stealing?" Gwen suggested.

"But most of what was stolen was nonsensical," Maia said. "None of it was worth stealing, save the bracelet and perhaps the fountain pen."

"More ladies, and more secretaries, than anything else," Gwen said. "It must be Jenny. Oh! Of course!" Her eyes were very bright as an idea occurred to her. "Don't you see? As you said, the thefts themselves are irrelevant. I bet she's been stealing from people who irritate her, as a sort of twisted punishment. So what she takes doesn't matter so much as who she takes it from—that's why there are more secretaries than any other role on there, and more women, because that's who she is most apt to be annoyed with. And no servants, because she would consider it beneath her to be irritated with them. You remember her scolding Lily Jamison about wearing lipstick and nail varnish at work? Well?" She tapped one finger on the first name on the list. "What was stolen from Lil? *Lipstick.*"

"That does make a certain amount of sense," Maia said. "Well reasoned, Gwen."

Gwen beamed, while Len looked thoughtful. "That is a different direction than I was thinking, but it's worth pursuing. We should follow up on these people, find out their interactions with Miss Pelham and if they've annoyed her at any point. If that is the common thread, well …" He spread his hands.

Only Becket seemed unconvinced. "I think there's another common thread in those items, sir, if you'll excuse me saying so."

"Of course!" Len answered. "What is it?"

Becket's face wrinkled in a frown. "I'm afraid I can't put my finger on it. It's something … not obvious. Something related to magic." He shook his head. "I'm sorry, sir, I can't remember. I'll have to do some research, with your permission."

"You know you don't even have to ask," Len said. "But until you can determine what the connection is, I think the Miss Pelham angle is one to follow. It would be worth seeing if the theft victims have anything else in common, as well, though without knowing what questions to ask it's going to be more a matter of hoping they reveal something in conversation that gives us a clue."

Maia lacked a pencil to tap on the table—for once she wasn't taking notes—so she drummed her fingers on the wooden surface instead, halting only when she saw Len's involuntary wince.

"Right. Gwen, you've already spoken to the secretaries once. Will it be better, do you think, if you question them again, or would it be best to come from one of us?"

"If I'm asking them to complain about Jenny, they won't care who's asking," Gwen said wryly. "I'll do it."

"Then, if Becket is doing research, Len, shall you and I split up the students and staff?"

Len hesitated before answering, to Maia's surprise. Truly, he was not himself.

"There's something else I need to look into first. Why don't you get started with the list, and I'll come along and take whatever you haven't gotten to yet after I've finished with my little matter?"

She was instantly suspicious, but decided she could challenge him later, when they had some privacy.

"Very well," she said. "And in the meantime, we all need to turn our minds to thinking where Miss Carlyle could be, and how Miss Pelham, or anyone, could have spirited her out of the college. We are four bright detectives and magicians; surely we can think of some way to find her, either through deduction or magic or some combination thereof!"

* * *

Upon Maia's return to the college (the gate now guarded by the stolid Constable Wilson, who let her enter without comment, clearly on orders from the rather dashing Inspector Dale), the first person she spotted was the American Nathan Quirke, accompanied by a young woman with a daringly short blonde bob and a vividly pink frock, cut in such a way as to disguise her unfashionably curvy figure, much as Maia suspected the hairstyle was meant to disguise an adorably cute button nose and ingenuous face.

"Miss Maia Whitney!" the American hailed her. "Wretched business, this, isn't it?"

"Dreadful," Maia agreed.

"Perfectly ghastly," the blonde girl said with a shudder. "We had to sit in the dining hall for simply ages waiting for the police, and then they were so unsympathetic when they finally did talk to us—or to me, at least, I don't know about Nathan—and they strongly hinted that we should stay indoors afterward but I knew, I absolutely knew, that I was going to scream if I had to sit with everyone else speculating and worrying and all that one moment more, so Nathan kindly offered to accompany me on a stroll around the grounds." She drew a fresh breath and smiled up at Maia. "So you're the Miss Whitney everyone is talking about! I overheard my aunt and Miss Archer talking about the possibility of you completing your journeyman work here, and Miss Archer said we'd be lucky to have you, as you have already started introducing new ways of perceiving and using magic, and that's just what Saint Dorothea's needs, and my aunt *sniffed,* and so I knew I should like you very much."

Maia blinked, taken aback by this flood of confidence, as well as flustered at this naive recounting of her supposed abilities. Just what had she done to introduce "new ways of perceiving and using magic?" She'd helped Len regain the use of his magic after the Parasite had drained most of it away, but surely that wasn't anything worth noting, not that she'd told anyone besides Aunt Amelia about that anyway. She wouldn't have even told her aunt save that she had needed an expert's opinion as to whether she could do it without causing him further harm. Her aunt had thought her mad, but made no other objection, and to Maia's delight the dangerous experiment had worked. Yet truly, she didn't think it was that remarkable, nor any of her other small steps forward in her journey with magic.

"This charming child is Sally Linton, and the sniffing aunt is the infamous Miss Linton, feared and loathed by all at Saint Dot's," Mr. Quirke explained.

"Oh," Maia said. "*Oh.*"

"Gosh, yes. If my aunt doesn't like the idea of you coming here, everyone else will," Sally Linton said, widening her blue eyes. "I think it's smashing. Only you have to promise not to despise me, like everyone else, just because of my aunt. *I* didn't choose her. I'd much rather have gone somewhere she isn't, except there isn't any other college like this one, and Father said we had to support her because she's family, but you'll notice *he's* not here."

Mr. Quirke patted her hand. "Not everyone despises you, Miss Sally."

She beamed up at him. "No, that's true, and since you've been so nice to me the other students aren't quite so snooty, because they are all wondering about you and hoping that I'll be able to tell them all about you, and even though I don't know anything because you are wretchedly close-mouthed for an American, and here I always thought you lot were willing to talk about *everything, especially* yourselves, they still hope

I will learn *something* and so they're accepting me into their ranks at last. And hopefully by the time you've left they'll have gotten used to talking to me and including me in their midnight bashes and what-nots, and seen that I won't turn them in to my aunt for breaking the rules, and I'll finally be one of the crowd. But it will all be even better when you come, Miss Whitney, as long as you don't give me the cold shoulder."

Maia could hardly tell her now that the possibility of attending Saint Dorothea's was a fiction designed to cover her presence here, even if the fiction was unnecessary now that poor Mr. Appleby was murdered and the police were here. She was recalled to her purpose, though, in thinking about Appleby and the police. "Miss Linton … am I correct in thinking you recently had a compact stolen?"

"Goodness!" Miss Linton said. "However did you hear about that? I say it was stolen, even though my aunt insists I misplaced it. I know I *look* and *talk* like a featherbrain, but honestly, I am awfully careful with my things, and I *know* I had the compact in my bag at the start of the day, and it was gone at the end, and I looked all the places where it could have fallen out and it wasn't in any of them, so it *had* to have been taken by someone."

Mr. Quirke was looking at Maia with some curiosity. "What makes you ask about that, Miss Maia?"

Maia smiled at him but directed her response to Sally Linton. If he intended to be cagey about his reasons for being here, she would do the same. "Do you have any suspicions as to who could have taken it?"

"One of the servants, I would have said, but Miss Carlyle, she said that the servants would never risk being sacked for stealing, so it must have been someone else."

"Oh? When did she say that?"

"As soon as I noticed it was missing—I had come into the secretaries' room to ask about something, can't remember what now, some letter or something I was hoping one of them could type for me, but Miss Pelham said no, that wasn't their job and I shouldn't even have asked, and then Miss Carlyle caught me up in the corridor outside and said she was so sorry for Miss Pelham's rudeness, and perhaps she, Miss Carlyle, could do it for me after hours, but I said no, I couldn't dream of asking her to do that, never mind the fact that Miss Pelham would no doubt be very cross at Miss Carlyle using one of the school's typewriters for such a thing." Young Miss Linton paused here for a breath before continuing. "Miss Carlyle agreed, though she was awfully sorry to not be able to help me out, and then she tapped my arm and leaned in close to let me know I had a smudge on my nose—in a friendly way, you know, so I wouldn't be embarrassed to discover later that I'd been going about with a smudged nose, unlike my aunt, who would have told me in a 'how could you be so careless, you disgraceful girl?' sort of way—and so I opened my bag to get out my compact so I could powder my nose, and it wasn't there, and Miss Carlyle was awfully sympathetic and said it wasn't the first theft around the school, and I ought to tell the Magistra about it, and I said, oh, probably one of the servants took it, and she said—well, what I told you before."

"And did you tell the Magistra?" Maia asked, though she knew what the answer would be.

"No, because my aunt came along then and scolded me for keeping Miss Carlyle from her work, and when I explained about the compact told me not to be ridiculous, I had probably just misplaced it, and even though I knew I hadn't, I thought the Magistra might agree with Auntie, so I didn't bother. It wasn't a terribly valuable compact, after all."

So it was the elder Miss Linton, not Miss Pelham, who had prevented Sally from reporting the theft. Maia recalled hearing her scorning Miss Archer's loss as well. Yet the compact had gone missing after a visit to the secretaries' room and a conversation with Miss Pelham, who was curt in her dismissal of Sally's request. Not a very strong reason for stealing something, but they had agreed, hadn't they, that her sense of proportion was all out of place?

The American was still eyeing her with speculation, though Sally didn't seem to think anything odd of Maia's questions, so she hastened to allay any suspicions and end the conversation, especially as she could see Len approaching from the back garden.

"Well, I do hope you find it eventually, and I commend you on your fortitude. I'm glad you don't think Saint Dorothea's is a likely den of thieves overall—I wouldn't care to attend a place where one had to constantly fret over having one's things stolen."

With a courteous nod, she hurried away from the pair before Sally could burst into another long speech or Mr. Quirke could say something cynical. She still didn't know what to make of the man, but he was far too close-mouthed and perceptive for her liking.

"Len!"

He saw her and stopped, courteously waiting for her to reach him before he continued walking.

"How go the interviews?" he asked.

Maia wasn't having any of it. "Just what is troubling you, Lennox? And don't try to charm me or slither out of answering—I've had enough of that from the enigmatic Mr. Quirke."

His eyes began to twinkle, and he laughed. "Thank goodness! I should know better by now than to try to put one over on you. You're the perfect antidote to my ingrained habit of keeping everything to myself."

Unexpectedly, Maia felt a twinge at that. She didn't have time to analyze why it bothered her—so many things had been giving her unpleasant twinges since the start of this case, she'd almost stopped wondering why—as he continued.

"If you don't mind casting the spell to ensure we aren't overheard, I'll tell you all about it."

She briefly focused her mind and rattled off the incantation which would transform their words into a meaningless buzz to anyone within earshot, and followed him to sit on a bench facing the golden fountain.

"The plain fact of the matter is, I think I've solved the case, and I'm dashed unhappy about it," Len said.

Well! He went from secretive to blunt in a matter of moments. No dodging here.

"Do explain," Maia said.

"It's like this," Len began, then stopped.

"Yes?" Maia said encouragingly.

"It's like this," Len said again, then made a heroic effort. "I think it was young Tom."

"What, Tom the chauffeur and odd-job man?"

He nodded, his face set in unhappy lines. "I rather suspect he started pilfering little things here and there for his mother— you remember, he told us about her, how she had been ill— meaning no harm, but wanting to bring some pleasure into her life that he couldn't afford otherwise on his salary. Then he became nervous when Miss Carlyle started making noise about telling the Magistra, so he sent her letters, even pushed her off the bridge, in an attempt to frighten her into silence, not meaning any real harm. Then when he somehow gave himself away with that final letter, the one in her room with the missing envelope, and she confronted him, he lost his head and abducted her, taking her out via the back gate, where no one would see. Then, when he realized that Appleby had confirmed that she didn't come out through the front gate, he realized suspicion would naturally turn to him—probably our questions made him nervous—and so he tried to redirect attention to the front. My hunch is that he didn't intend to kill Appleby, only injure him, but got carried away, probably due to nerves, and hit him harder than intended."

"I see," mused Maia, turning the theory over in her mind. "It's certainly plausible. But why all the secrecy?"

"Because—because dash it, Maia, I hate to see a chap incarcerated for life for something he didn't intend to do!"

"Len, if you are correct, he stole, threatened, kidnapped, and murdered. Why this sudden pity for him? Shouldn't you save your pity for his victims?"

Len ran his hands through his hair, a sure sign of agitation. "Things aren't that simple. I can see how easily a chap like that could slide into all of that, never intending evil. If I'm right and he did kill Appleby, I'd swear he didn't mean to. He's not that sort of person. And as for Miss Carlyle—if it hadn't been for her nosing into business that didn't concern her, none of this would have happened. Oh, I'm not saying she deserved to be kidnapped, but you've heard what everyone has to say of her. A person who always wants to be more important than she is, someone who always felt put-upon and under-appreciated even when she wasn't, someone never happy with her lot. You can see how a boy like Tom could feel panicked when she starts pushing, and to try to harmlessly stop her. Is it his fault things got out of hand?"

Maia tried to calm her racing heart. "I can't be understanding you correctly," she said. "It almost sounds as though you are advocating letting Tom escape justice for his crime because Charlotte Carlyle is unlikeable?"

"Of course not!" Len leapt to his feet and began to pace in short, jerky motions. "Of course there has to be justice. But … isn't there room for some mercy as well? Even the Magistra, when she found out he'd left the back gate unlocked, reprimanded him but also sent help to his mother."

"Murder is hardly the same thing as forgetting to lock a gate," Maia said shortly.

"I know that," Len said, sounding exasperated. "It's the principle of the matter."

"Yes!" Maia flared, losing her calm. "That's exactly it! We cannot change our principles simply because we like one person and dislike another! They aren't principles then, they are—preferences! If murder is wrong when one person does it, it's also wrong when another does it."

"Yes!" Len said, agitated in his turn. "And also no! People do matter, circumstances do affect our principles. We acknowledge that killing is wrong when it is done by one individual to another for personal gain, but not when it is sanctioned by the government in a time of war. But the act is the same— one person taking another's life. Our principles are shaped by circumstance, even when we think they aren't. And this has nothing to do with liking or disliking Miss Carlyle, only that Tom, left to himself, would not be the sort to resort to violence, only lashing out to protect himself, and surely we ought to take that into consideration."

"Every murderer has an excuse that seems reasonable to their own mind, or they wouldn't murder," Maia flashed back. "If we start making excuses for one, we can make them for another. Perhaps Tom wouldn't have resorted to violence if he hadn't felt trapped—but that doesn't change the fact that it was his wrong act to begin with that put him in that position. Nor does it change the fact that someone of better character could feel trapped and *not* resort to violence."

"Is it really our place to judge and condemn, though? Are we—any of us—so much better? When our backs are to the wall, will we respond in a manner we can be proud of afterward?" Len closed his mouth abruptly, his eyes staring into the distance, as he seemed to recall something from his past.

"If I don't, I hope there is someone there to stop me from carrying it so far as murder," Maia said tartly. "We are not judging him, Len. We are uncovering the truth. I thought we agreed that was our role, our calling. To serve the truth at all costs."

"I didn't say I wanted to let him off the hook," Len said, coming back to the present. "Only that I wish there were a better way to handle this."

Maia didn't know what to say in response. She had never imagined she and Len could disagree about something so fundamental. It was almost as revelatory a moment as when she'd learned of the existence of magic: everything she thought she could rely on was shaken.

Except discovering magic had transformed Maia's world for the better. This? This was *devastating*.

Chapter 9

Len, frankly, was appalled at himself. Whatever had possessed him to rattle off all that rubbish to Maia? Doing it badly as usual, no less. He hadn't half expressed what he wanted to say—no wonder she was horrified.

"Look here—" he began, without exactly knowing what he was going to say next. He couldn't retract his view—he'd presented it poorly and in a muddled fashion, but it was true that he felt some responsibility toward mercy as well as justice, to the wrongdoer as well as to the victim, without in the least wishing to let the wrongdoer go scot-free—but neither could he stand here letting the distance grow between them by the second.

Maia jumped to her feet. "I think I need to take a walk," she said in a strangled voice. "Perhaps we can finish this conversation another time."

Len held out a hand toward her, aghast. "Oh, I say," he tried again.

Maia cut him off with an abrupt gesture, then turned and walked away, burying her hands deep in her invisible pockets and hunching her shoulders as against a blow.

He had made a mess of that, right enough. His instinct told

him to go after her and apologize, try to straighten things out, make things right. His better sense told him to respect her desire for privacy and talk to her again when they were both calmer. For once, he rather thought his instinct was wrong.

He ought not to have mentioned Charlotte Carlyle at all. He hadn't meant what Maia seemed to think he did, that he didn't care about finding justice for her because nobody liked her. He'd only meant to use her as an example: every person's character and actions were in part shaped by those around them, and no one could stand apart and claim that he and he alone was responsible for the person he was and the deeds he did, and surely, *surely* they ought to take that into account in how they dealt with someone who had gone so far astray. Only he'd not managed to put it that way at all, and instead given Maia the wrong notion about him entirely.

Dash it all. Even Mr. Darcy wouldn't have blundered *that* badly.

He dragged his mind back to the case when he saw Tom emerge from the tree-shaded path and approach the back gate, keys in hand. If he couldn't explain his attitude to Maia, perhaps she'd understand better by him showing what he meant.

As an agent for Magical Intelligence, Len had frequently made use of what he called his "chameleon spell," a spell that allowed him to blend into the background and go unnoticed. Invisibility spells were dashed hard, nearly impossible in fact, but the chameleon spell required much less energy and concentration. It wasn't perfect, and one could train oneself to notice the small details in shadow and light that gave away the person trying to blend in, but for the average chap it sufficed. He hadn't cast it since regaining his magic, and he felt some trepidation now as he prepared himself for it. What if his magic wasn't enough for even this, his favorite and most-used spell? What if he was stuck doing small spells and nothing more for the rest of his life?

He reminded himself that a few months ago he thought he would never recover any of his ability to use magic, and that he had been trained in ordinary forms of sneaking as well as magical—Harrison, his superior, had warned all of them of the dangers on relying too much on magic and not enough on one's own wits.

"On day you'll be in a situation where you can't use magic or you're too distracted to cast a spell, or you don't have the energy for it, and then where will you be? An agent who depends solely on his magical ability has no place here."

If Len couldn't cast the chameleon spell, he would follow Tom on his own. The chameleon spell would simply make things easier, that was all.

He steadied his mind and his breathing, put his distress over hurting Maia out of his mind until he could do something about it, and spoke the Latin words to begin the spell.

"*Abscondo meum in manifestis conspectu.*"

There was a slight pull on his energy as the spell took effect— more than there used to be, but not so great as he had feared. Len looked down at his hands, spreading his fingers wide. The sunlight dappled them, and they shifted in and out of view as the shadows from the trees branches overhead moved in the light breeze.

It wasn't the best chameleon spell he'd ever cast—if someone looked directly at him they would surely notice something odd in the landscape—but so long as he was sneaky enough, it would do.

Len hurried along the path, thankful most of the college inhabitants were indoors either still being questioned or recovering from being questioned so that there were fewer people out here to avoid, and managed to slip out the back gate right behind Tom, flattening himself along the outside wall and breathing lightly when that young man turned to lock the gate behind him.

If he hadn't already been suspicious of Tom, Len would be now. Why would he exit the college when everyone was supposed to stay in place until Inspector Dale gave them permission to leave?

Keeping his distance and choosing his steps with case, Len followed Tom along the narrow footpath that led to the larger road. Was it possible Charlotte Carlyle was still alive, and Tom was going to wherever he had stashed her? It didn't seem likely, but if Len was right and the lad wasn't a killer at heart, it could be so. Len could hope, in any case.

It was a beautiful little pathway through here, and if Len hadn't had to concentrate so hard to keep up the chameleon spell he would have been able to appreciate it more. Bordered on one side by a brick wall covered in ivy just starting to turn red, on the other by blackthorn bushes with the sloes hanging ripe off the branches, the path echoed with the cheerful song of robins and the harsher cry of magpies seeking something shiny. The weather was still unusually sunny for early autumn, though there was a nip in the air, and Len once again wished this dratted case was over and done with and he and Maia could be strolling gently along arm-in-arm, enjoying being together and in Cambridge.

Provided Maia still felt she could be friends with him after the end of this case.

Once Tom stepped onto the road, Len had to move more carefully—there were more people out walking and cycling here, and his disguise didn't serve him quite so well. He noticed more than one person blinking and looking twice when he sidled past. The spell was getting more difficult to maintain, as well—he was sweating by now with effort.

That Gardiner fellow had encouraged him to come take a peep at the Merriman Collection and see if there was anything in the books that might help Len to strengthen his magical muscles, so to speak. If he had a chance to breathe at all during this trip, he would do just that. Brilliant fellow, Merriman. Absolute genius when it came to boosting one's own magic through outside means. Most of them had been deemed unsafe or unethical by the Circle now, which was one reason why his research wasn't more widespread, but was instead confined to his own published work and contained in one collection, but even so, the chap had been the most daring and forward-thinking magician of his time or most time since.

Rather like Maia, in fact. The spell she had come up with to bring back his magic—unsafe and doubtless horrifying to most members of the Circle, but brilliant. Even before she had begun her proper training, she had come up with new and inventive ways to use her magic. It was as though she had grasped the principles behind magic so thoroughly that she could build on them in entirely new ways, ways that magicians who had been trained in English magic since their youth were simply incapable of conceiving.

Len himself had learned a few different ways of doing magic through his time spent working with magicians of other countries, but Maia, now, Maia understood magic on a deeper level that he could never dream of attaining.

In many ways, he realized, she really was wasted on detective work. He would never dream of discouraging her from this career, as it was so important to her, but she was capable of so much more.

Len was disgusted at his new sense of sympathy with Amelia Rawlings, who had been furious when her niece gave up a more brilliant, specialized career in magic for something as mundane as detective work. It was not Len's place to dictate to Maia what she ought to do, though, and if working together as detectives was what she wanted, he certainly wasn't going to complain. He only hoped she wouldn't lament missed opportunities when she was old, and wish that someone— namely Len—had encouraged her to spread her wings and dare more.

Len was so consumed in his own thoughts that he nearly missed it when Tom stopped at a small house tucked in the middle of a row of terraced housing, opened the door without knocking, and went inside.

Safe now from his suspect's view, Len glanced around to make sure no one was looking at him to be surprised as he gradually appeared from the background, and dropped the chameleon spell, using his handkerchief to dab away the perspiration from his temples and upper lip as he did.

Now, what were they doing here? This was far too public a spot for Miss Carlyle to be hidden. So why was Tom here?

Only one way to find out. Hiding himself hadn't gotten Len very far; it was time to try boldness.

Stepping through the front gate, Len pressed his finger to the bell and waited for someone to open the door.

* * *

Tom himself answered the door. Surprise followed by dismay flashed across his face at the sight of his visitor.

"Mr. Davies!" he said, making no move to step back or otherwise invite Len to come inside. "What are you—that is, how did you—I mean, is there something you need, sir?"

Before Len could answer, a woman's voice, sweet and a bit shaky, called out from further in the house. "Who is it, dear?"

"Someone from the college, Mother," Tom said over his shoulder.

Mother? Len felt like an idiot. Of course Tom had come home. If his mother was frail, he would want to check in on her to ensure she was not worried or in need while he was stuck at the college.

"Oh how nice," said the woman's voice, gaining in strength and volume as its owner presumably moved closer. Then Len could see her over Tom's shoulder, a small, dainty woman with silvery-white hair and a face that, despite the lines etched into it by pain and age, still retained something of a flower-like sweetness and purity. "Welcome to our house, Mr...?"

Tom glanced over his shoulder, saw his mother, and with a slump of his shoulders moved aside so Len could enter if he chose. Len contented himself with an abbreviated bow from where he stood. "Davies, Mrs. Wright, Len Davies. I won't intrude, but I wondered if I might have a brief word with you, Tom?"

"Oh, but you must come in and have a glass of lemonade," Mrs. Wright said. "We so rarely get anyone from the college visiting us, though that nice Dr. Bingham did stop by briefly when I was unwell—such a kind woman, though a trifle brusque in manner, I found. Still, I was most grateful for her concern. Now Tommy, invite your friend in!"

Tom muttered something about "not really my friend," but did manage to ungraciously motion for Len to enter.

Len felt like a heel. He could not—he absolutely *could not* impose upon this sweet lady as a friend when he was here to accuse her son of kidnap and murder.

"You are too kind, but I really can't stay," he said again. "Tom, would you mind stepping out for just a moment? I won't keep him long, madam."

Mrs. Wright looked as though she was going to continue to protest, but a flash of relief crossed Tom's face and he slipped out through the open door and pulled it closed behind him, cutting off whatever his mother had been going to say.

"Thank you, sir," he said before Len could speak. "I know I oughtn't to have left the college grounds, especially when that inspector told us all to stay put, but mother, she worries if I'm not home when I should be, and I was afraid she might hear some rumor of what had happened and worry even more, and I just couldn't leave her without giving her a story about why I wasn't going to be home for supper like I normally am. I didn't think anyone would mind so much that they'd send you after me."

"I'm not here for that," Len said, just biting off the "son" that wanted to come out of his mouth. No doubt Tom would find that patronizing from a man only ten years or so older than himself, and rightly so. "I am here for Miss Carlyle."

The puzzlement that stamped itself across Tom's open features seemed genuine. "Miss Carlyle? I don't—"

"I am sure you never meant any harm," Len said. "And I'll help you in any way I can. But she must be freed, you understand? I can't help you if you refuse to confess to what you've done."

"I don't understand," Tom said steadily. "You seem to think

I've done something with Miss Carlyle. But I haven't seen her for days. I couldn't have done anything to her, nor would I have a reason to. What's it all about?"

"The thefts?" Len pressed, watching him closely. Was it possible the lad was telling the truth? Len had been wrong before, but this had made such perfect sense. Nothing else fit all the facts so neatly. "Miss Carlyle pressing to investigate them, so she had to be silenced, one way or another?"

Red slowly suffused Tom's cheeks, and his eyes flashed. "You think I'm a thief? What, just because I'm not posh, like you, naturally I must be a thief? I've never stolen anything, nor told lies, nor nothing like that. My mother raised me proper, she did, and I'll thank you to keep your filthy insinuations to yourself, sir!" He stopped and gaped. "Wait a moment … if you think I did those things, you must also think I did for Mr. Appleby. How *dare* you?"

Len held up his hands. "No, no! I never thought for a moment you intended any harm to anyone, only that, perhaps, things went a little awry for you. It has nothing to do with your class, I assure you, or the way you were raised. I only—"

"You get off our property," Tom cut him off. "And don't you dare come back here pestering my mother, you hear? I'll talk to Dr. Bingham about this, see if I don't!"

There was nothing for it. Len dropped his hands and moved back, acutely aware of curtains pulled back in the front windows of all the neighboring houses, and what a sight he and Tom must be presenting. He had meant to spare the lad shame by not talking about this in front of his mother; instead he had made both the Wrights a source of gossip for their neighbors.

"Wait," Tom said suddenly, coming down the step and stopping him by the gate. "When did Miss Carlyle go missing, and what time was Mr. Appleby killed?"

"Miss Carlyle was not seen since right before teatime two days ago," Len said, seeing no reason to hide this information. "I'm not entirely certain when Mr. Appleby was killed, but judging by how warm his body was when I saw it, he must have died shortly before Mr. Foster discovered him."

Tom folded his arms across his chest. "Well, then. Two days ago at teatime I was here, on account of Dr. Bingham allowing me to cut my day short so's I could have tea with mother. Her cough had come back, see, and I was that worried about her. You may ask the Magistra yourself if you don't believe me! This morning, Miss Archer came in by way of the back entrance, so's I unlocked the gate for her and she chatted with me—asking about mother's cough, in fact—for a good quarter hour. No sooner had she left than I heard the commotion and come running to see what it was all about. So you see, I couldn't have done nothing, neither of those times."

As alibis went, those were both exceptional. They shattered Len's theory all to bits. He ought to have asked the Magistra about Tom before coming out here to confront him, but he'd been so concerned about damaging the lad's reputation that he thought it would be best to deal with him privately first, and then control how the information was released to others.

"I am deeply sorry to have made such an error in judgment," Len said. "I'll leave now."

He went through the gate and made his way off the road to the nearest footpath as soon as he saw one, following it as it meandered alongside a tributary of the Cam until he came to a willow overhanging the water, with a space between two of its roots that seemed made for sitting and brooding.

What a fool he'd been! Maia was right—of course she was.

He let his concern for Tom overshadow his commitment to finding out the truth, and the result was a right mess. He'd insulted the lad badly, blundering in like the fool of a condescending, overbearing bully of the upper class Tom now considered him to be—everything Len hated in his own class, everything he'd tried to escape by leaving the estate. He'd never wanted to play God with other men's lives, but that's exactly what he'd done here.

"Tell the truth and shame the devil," his nanny used to say whenever he'd tried to prevaricate with her, usually to protect Pippa from taking full responsibility for her misdeeds. That was Maia's mindset as well, and he ought to have stuck with it.

Although … Len frowned. Even in the midst of his self-flagellation, a glimmer of another viewpoint tickled his ear.

Dash it, even though he'd been wrong about Tom, and wrong in how he handled the matter, he still believed he was right in considering mercy alongside justice. Not in place of it! But if it was wrong to play God in men's lives by determining one knew better than they how they ought to live, it must also be wrong to play God by standing apart from humanity and saying, "I have the right to dispense justice, and the ability to know the truth perfectly."

Humility, the word came to him. That was what he was looking for. The recognition that even old Sherlock Holmes had come to: "There but for the grace of God go I."

If Len had lacked humility in how he handled everything with Tom—and he was willing enough to admit that he had—then he still believed there was a lack of humility in trying to cling too closely to an ideal without acknowledging one's own faults and failings.

Did that mean he thought Maia was arrogant? Surely not!

Len raised his head and stared unseeing across the smooth surface of the river. He wasn't thinking of Maia; he was thinking of himself.

He'd gone from Magical Intelligence to private detective with the highest of motives: to work openly for justice, rather than the shadowy deeds he'd done in the name of the greater good before. To serve truth rather than living a lie. It had all seemed quite noble, really. Was it arrogant? Not intentionally, no, but perhaps there was some latent arrogance beneath it.

And, if he were perfectly honest with himself (and what was the point in claiming to serve truth and be done with lies if one couldn't even be honest with oneself?), he had done it in large part so that he could be with Maia. She had been the driving force behind Whitney & Davies; she was the one who had felt the deepest burning passion for justice. If she had suggested opening a draper's shop, Len would most likely have cheerily gone along with that as well. It had been … convenient, that was all, that what she had wanted them to do fit so nicely with his ideas of a gentleman magician's duty to society.

Hang it all, he *was* a snob, after all.

"Damn and blast!" Len said aloud, shoving his hands through his hair and knocking his hat off in the process. This was where too much thinking got one. Twisted around in circles, trying to see through the back of one's head, proving irrefutably that two plus two equaled five, not four.

He picked his hat up before it could be blown into the water by the breeze that had picked up. There was something in that. Two plus two equaling five … why did that stick in his mind?

He gave his head a short, sharp shake, and stuffed his hat back on. It would come to him. Likely at three in the morning, or some other equally inconvenient time.

In any case, whatever sort of existential crisis he was having or about to have, one thing was clear: he still had a job to do, and he couldn't fall apart until after it was complete. If there was one thing he had learned in MI, it was this:

Finish the task at hand. No matter what else, complete the mission.

Chapter 10

Maia had made three circuits of the college grounds and her stomach was still churning, her thoughts still whirling. She kept her hands buried in her pockets so that she wouldn't see the glimmer of silver outlining them—she had almost entirely overcome her tendency to leak magic when she was upset, but this was distress on a deeper level than mere anger.

On her fourth circuit, she was hailed by Inspector Dale.

"Miss Whitney!" the slim, short man called, walking toward her from the direction of Merriman Hall. "A word, if I may?"

Maia forced her feet to a stop and took in several deep breaths to calm herself. When she was reasonably sure she could speak coherently, she faced the inspector. "Of course. What can I do for you?"

"I was wondering if you'd made any progress in finding the missing secretary, of course," he said, raising his eyebrows as though surprised.

A spurt of annoyance jolted through Maia, but she kept her expression calm and forced her voice to sound wry rather than angry. "It's only been a few hours since we left you, Inspector. Even we are hardly that talented."

"One never knows," he answered obliquely. "To be perfectly

honest with you, Miss Whitney, I am somewhat surprised you haven't found her already. It hardly seems that much of a puzzle. You merely trace her footsteps, find where she was last and who was with her, and there you go. Not much of a challenge for the great Whitney and Davies."

"You do make it sound simple, but—" Maia stopped. She pulled her hands from her pockets and looked at them. The silver traces of her magic had faded, but all she had to do was cast the simplest spell and it would return.

"Miss Whitney?"

"One moment," she said.

What was it Len had said about the shadow spell? That one day Maia would have to come up with a way to determine an individual through the spell, rather than a vague shadow.

Generally, magicians could not see each other's magical auras. There were a few exceptions to that rule—she and Len, for example, had mingled their magic more than once, though the first time had been accidental, and as a result could now see the other's magic. What if there was a way to duplicate that serendipitous effect deliberately, even if only for a short time? What if they could create a spell to trace Miss Carlyle's magic?

There was no guarantee that she had used magic to defend herself against an attack—but it was likely. In fact, she might even have had a defensive shield spell in place beforehand as a precaution, if she was intending to confront the individual who had written her those threatening letters. Following her physical trail had proven to be a dead end, as she was unmemorable enough that no one seemed to have noticed when she was no longer around. Following her magical trail might assist them in any number of ways. If she had released a burst of magic in the library, for example, that would tell them that it was most likely there that she met her opponent, and that would allow them to narrow down the suspects to who had been in the building at the time.

Or if they were very, *very* lucky, she would not have had time to end her spell before being overcome and kidnapped, and would have left a trail of magic all the way to wherever she was being held.

If only they were in time! Magic traces faded over time, and Miss Carlyle's might be gone by now.

And if only they could put together the spell—Maia was by no means sure it was possible. It ought to be, but she couldn't say for certain.

"Excuse me," she said. "I need to find—"

"Yes?"

Oh, bother it all! She needed *Len*, but she had all but ordered him to leave her be, and she had no idea where to find him now. Curse her childish behavior! He had wanted to sort the disagreement right then, but no, she had to go off and sulk about it, and now look at the result!

There was no time to fret about it now. She could scold herself later. Now she needed someone who could help her determine if this spell was even possible.

"I need to find Miss Archer," she said decisively. "So long as you have cleared her from any possible guilt in murdering Mr. Appleby."

"Miss Archer and the junior porter were together at the back gate when Appleby was killed," Inspector Dale said. "She is clear."

"Thank you, I—did you say the junior porter?" Maia stared at him.

Inspector Dale nodded. "Yes, Tom Wright. Why, is he on your suspect list?"

"Not anymore," Maia said.

After all that fuss, Tom wasn't guilty in the slightest. Not that it mattered that much—the disagreement had been more about principles than about the specific individual—but Maia still felt sick to her stomach as she walked toward Merriman Hall in search of Miss Archer.

To her surprise, Inspector Dale accompanied her. She wasn't sure why—he didn't seem to approve of her, taking every opportunity to needle her about Whitney and Davies' so-called fame. She wanted to disapprove of him in return, yet she had to admit there was something fascinating about him. She just didn't quite know what.

Perhaps it was that, despite his utterly professional behavior, he made her very aware that she was a woman, and he was a man. She wasn't smitten or any such silly nonsense like that— she had been attracted to the trim, compact type when she was younger, but in recent years had found her taste shifting to men who were taller than her, with broad shoulders and deep voices (theoretically, she added hastily in her own mind). All the same, something about Inspector Dale made her want to check her hair and powder her nose. It was most irritating when she had a job to do.

Yet for all that, she couldn't deny that it was pleasant to have him walking beside her now, even while she wished she *didn't* find it pleasant.

Honestly, who would have ever thought she could be so schoolgirlish?

"Might one ask why you need to see Miss Archer, or is it a trade secret?" he asked now.

With almost anyone else, Maia would have stopped and demanded to know why everything he said had an edge to it, why he seemed so sour against their team. Without in the slightest understanding why she wasn't responding in that now, however, she merely replied, "Certainly one might ask. Another one might even answer."

She thought she saw the slightest trace of a smile flicker across his olive face, but it was gone too quickly for her to be certain.

"Very well, then. Why do you need to see Miss Archer?"

"I've thought of a spell that might help us find Miss Carlyle, or at least her magic, but I need to consult with a more experienced magician to know if it's possible," she answered. "As Mr. Davies is out pursuing other clues, I must rely on other sources."

"I'm surprised you feel the need to check," Inspector Dale said. "From what I have heard, you specialize in spells that no one else can dream of."

"I am not sure where you heard that, but it isn't remotely true," Maia said, impatience with that rumor overtaking her. "I wish I knew who began it; it's frightfully annoying."

"Really?"

"Yes, really. I am not some prodigy at magic, Inspector. I only wish I were. I came late to my apprenticeship and have been trying to make up for lost time ever since. If I have done anything unusual with spells, it is only through my ignorance of what is and is not acceptable, ethical, or safe. I hardly think that is praiseworthy."

After a short pause, he said, "I apologize. I believe I was operating under an incorrect understanding. As for who began that rumor, though, I can tell you that. Your aunt, Amelia

Rawlings."

"What?" Maia stopped in her tracks at that. She laughed aloud. "No, I can hardly believe that. Aunt Amelia never once praised my magical ability, she only told me how slipshod my methods were. And she was furious with me when I did not pursue a more specialized career for magic. On top of all that, she has been in France more often than England these last six months."

"Whatever she might say to your face, behind your back she boasts endlessly of her niece's remarkable talent. The stories, perhaps, have grown a little in the sharing, but they do originate with her."

"Well!" Words failed Maia. After all her aunt's reprimands, not to mention her declaring she washed her hands of Maia when Maia decided to take up detective work! "Of all the nerve!"

To her surprise, it was Inspector Dale's turn to laugh.

"She might not approve of you, but she is more than willing to capitalize on your fame—and even nudge it to grow."

"I shall have to change my name if I ever want to accomplish anything more," Maia mourned. "How *could* she do this to me?"

"Relatives," Inspector Dale said, as though that explained everything.

Thinking of her family, Maia conceded that perhaps it did.

"At any rate, Miss Whitney, if you can forgive my former rudeness, would you consider sharing your idea with me? I am by no means the expert on spells Miss Archer is, but I admit you have piqued my curiosity, and I would be pleased if you would confide in me."

"Oh!" Maia said. "Well ..."

She was not accustomed to sharing her ideas about magic with anyone except Len, and perhaps sometimes Helen. Inspector Dale was supercilious enough as it was, though he had apologized nicely. What if he thought her an awful fool, or downright dangerous in her ideas?

For heaven's sake, did it matter? Miss Carlyle's life was at stake, and here was Maia wringing her hands over whether or not her idea was silly. If she was willing to risk Miss Archer's scorn, why not Inspector Dale?

She told him.

To her utter relief, he didn't laugh or gasp in horror. Instead, his brows drew together in thought. "A bloodhound spell," he said.

"Yes, that's a very good name for it," Maia said. Then she had a thought. "Oh, or did you mean that such a spell already exists, and it's called a bloodhound spell?"

"What? Oh, no, no, I've never heard of anyone attempting such a spell. It's a good idea, though. I can see it having many applications beyond this one. Finding a rogue magician comes to mind. It might even be a good way of discovering new magicians, ones who aren't aware yet of their own abilities. In fact, now that I think of it, I'm not sure why no one has ever tried it before."

"It obviously would take quite a bit of work to establish the parameters," Maia said. "You'd have to have an example of the person's aura for it to begin."

"Exactly like a bloodhound, then—give it a scent to follow. Hm, yes, I do see the difficulty. How do we let it 'sniff' the aura without knowing the person's aura?" He frowned.

"Unless we were to set it up in a place where we knew that person had cast a spell, knowing there would be lingering traces behind."

"Oh, well done, Miss Whitney! That's it exactly." For the first time, Maia saw Inspector Dale's genuine smile directed at her. Her stomach leapt up and did a small flip.

"We would need to put firm boundaries around it," she said hurriedly, to keep herself from blushing. Goodness, what *was* it about this man that had the ability to fluster her so?

"Yes, we wouldn't want it leaking out to get confused with other auras," Dale agreed. "I think we ought to take this to Miss Archer after all—she may be a chemist first and foremost, but even if she herself is not able to help us, I think she'd be able to direct us to those who can. I think we need more minds on this." He hesitated, then looked directly at her. "You may not agree with your aunt's assessment of your abilities, Miss Whitney, but even from this conversation, I can tell you that I don't think she exaggerated as much as you believe she did. I am impressed."

This time nothing Maia did could prevent her blush from warming her face and neck. "Thank you," she managed to say through an unexpectedly tight throat.

Of all the silly things—now why should that make her feel as though she needed to cry?

* * *

Miss Archer was tentatively excited but immediately concerned about the ethics of Maia's proposed spell.

"Oh dear," she said. "It's very ingenious, yes, and I do see its benefits—but a person's aura is a very personal thing, you know. People might feel exceedingly uncomfortable knowing that it could be seen by others. Then there are the other difficulties. Is it quite the thing to track down every place a person has done magic recently, or is it a violation of their privacy?"

Maia fell back on Dale's bloodhound analogy. "Is it any different than tracking a person using dogs to follow their scent?"

"Oh well, when you put it that way, yes, but I can only imagine the outcry from ordinary magicians, most of whom don't even like putting up with Deep investigating magical infractions. Well then, I think the best thing is to put this to Dr. Bingham. If she approves, we can put our best spell-crafters on it. I assume you want to be part of the design process, Miss Whitney?"

Maia opened her mouth to agree—of course she wanted to be part of it, this was her idea, after all! Nor had she ever been part of a group effort at creating a brand-new spell from scratch, and that sort of collaborative effort intrigued her.

But then—was it right, to take time away from the active investigation in order to dabble with spell-making? With Len on an entirely wrong trail after Tom Wright, and Becket doing research for something that might or might not prove relevant, that would leave only Gwen to continue with questioning and following up on leads. Was this mere indulgence? Wouldn't it be better to let the experts follow through with the spell while she, Maia, continued the less exciting but still necessary detective work?

Inspector Dale touched her elbow lightly. When she looked at him, he held her gaze steadily with his eyes and said,

"If I may be so bold, Miss Whitney, I think you ought to work with them. Only you know exactly how you want the spell to be formed, and if you are not there to guide its formation, some crucial part might be left out. And," he lowered his voice, while Miss Archer looked up at the ceiling and did a good impression of a person who was not there, "if you are not there, those who are overly concerned with limiting the spell might well make it unusable. I have seen that you are truly concerned to find justice for Miss Carlyle and Mr. Appleby. This seems to me the best use of your skills in bringing that about. Anyone can do the type of questioning Miss Zhang and Mr. Davies have been doing. Only you can create this spell."

Maia's cheeks burned. "Thank you for your insight," she managed. She turned back to Miss Archer. "Under the circumstances, yes, I would be delighted to join you. So long as we can begin work on it as soon as possible. Every passing moment means it gets harder and harder to find Miss Carlyle."

"Certainly," Miss Archer said, brisk now that she had a plan in place and did not have to fret over the ethical implications of the spell herself. "If you'll excuse us, Inspector, Miss Whitney and I will go find the Magistra at once."

"Of course," Inspector Dale replied. "Do keep me informed. I shall be most eager to learn how the spell works."

The next hour was tedious in the extreme. The Magistra hesitated initially over concerns regarding the spell, but finally reluctantly agreed that it seemed their best chance at learning more about what had happened to Miss Carlyle, and perhaps even where she was now. She put Foster on it to assist with setting the limitations, as well as two magicians Maia had not yet met, a Miss Woodward and Mr. Henderson. Maia was not entirely certain of their specialties, as by that point the Magistra's study had turned mildly chaotic as everyone talked over each other and pencils flew wildly over paper and everyone, it seemed, had a question for her as to what they ought to do for the spell and how she thought it ought to be done.

It was exhilarating in a way Maia hadn't experienced since she was first learning about magic and Len introduced her to her first spells.

She had been home from the War for three years at that point, feeling trapped in the role of "responsible eldest sister and daughter" and seeing no way of ever escaping her self-imposed duties. Discovering magic—and her ability to wield it—had not only given her a new purpose and goal, it had opened her eyes in other ways as well. Maia still winced as she remembered the argument with her sisters which had culminated in her realization that her martyrdom to her family was neither wanted nor needed, that she had in fact been holding her sisters back from discovering their full potential by her insistence of taking on full responsibility for everyone in the family, and that her "help" often placed a burden on those she was helping as well as herself.

It had been horribly painful to realize, but it had also brought her freedom. At the end of that particular adventure, she had broken the chains of her own forging and gone to apprentice under Aunt Amelia. When her aunt's expectations had started to weigh her down in a similar fashion, she had broken free once again, moving to a flat shared with Helen and beginning work as a general magician and detective.

So when had that work started to feel like a burden as well, that doing something of this sort should feel so energizing and exciting? When had that freedom—for it *had* been freedom, and joy—turned to drudgery?

Maia frowned, distracted even in the midst of all the bustle around her.

What if the problem was her, not her circumstances? Was she the sort of person who was doomed to always feel bored and burdened after a stretch, always seeking something new and never finding contentment?

Gracious, what a dreadful thought. She'd never thought of herself as the restless, perennially discontented type. In fact, she'd always despised people like that.

There was no more time to dwell on personal matters; the work picked back up and Maia was swept back into the middle of it, and she could do nothing more than focus all her energy on the spell.

The Magistra insisted they take a break for refreshment around nine o'clock that evening. Maia, standing away from the table that held the diagrams and preparations and stretching with one hand on her back, was amazed at how long they'd been at it. Only now that they had paused did she realize how ravenously hungry she was. She took a sandwich from a tray being held out to her, took an enormous, unladylike bite, and then saw that the individual holding the tray was Becket.

"Oh!" she said, quickly chewing and swallowing. "Forgive me, Becket, I did not mean to be so rude."

Becket gave her a half-bow, the tray held steady in his hands even as he bent forward. "Not at all, Miss Whitney. I have assisted at spell creations more than once, and am well aware of how much focus they take."

"Thank you," she said.

Becket handed off the tray to another server, exchanging it for a tumbler and glass bottle. "It is only ginger beer, I am afraid—no alcohol while preparing a spell, nothing to cloud the mind or judgment—but it is cold."

"That sounds marvelous," Maia said, absently finishing her sandwich in two large bites while watching the stream of golden bubbles flow from the bottle into the glass. It was almost as mesmerizing as the fountain outside. Becket handed her the full glass, and the soft drink tasted like ambrosial nectar in her parched mouth.

"Might I inquire how things are progressing?" Becket asked, producing another sandwich from somewhere, as well as a plate for at least the appearance of civility. Perhaps that was his magical talent, Maia thought fuzzily, conjuring items out of nowhere to make people's lives a little more comfortable.

"I believe they are coming along nicely," she said, this second sandwich helping restore some clarity to her thinking. "I had no idea this would be such a massive undertaking, though. I know Helen's dress design spell to qualify her for mastery required an enormous amount of work ahead of time, but I suppose I thought that was only because of its many layers and complexity. I would have thought for something like this, all one would have to do would be to decide on a precise enough Latin phrase and concentrate one's focus on the desired result. Setting some parameters, of course, but still ...!"

She had learned early on the danger of attempting an unproven spell without setting parameters, and nearly killed herself in the process. Ever since, she'd been cautious when trying new ideas, but even when working with Len to restore his magic she'd worked mostly from logic and precision, nothing of this sort of scale.

"Any magic that has to do with other magic-users must be formed very carefully," Becket explained. "No one wants to run the risk of a spell warping or damaging another person's magic."

Maia shuddered, memories of the past spring's Parasite all too vivid still in her mind. "No indeed," she said.

The precautions and warnings from Miss Archer and the Magistra suddenly seemed a little less nonsensical. She changed the subject.

"Has Len returned?"

"Yes, Miss Whitney. Mr. Davies returned to the college several hours ago. He wished me to tell you that he has learned of Mr. Wright's innocence, and that he has every confidence in the efficacy of your spell when it is completed. In the meantime, he ..." Becket hesitated for a moment before continuing. "He has questioned the staff not occupied here while Miss Gwen interviewed the students once she finished with the secretaries. I am not yet sure if they have ascertained anything useful."

Maia felt a brief pang of guilt for leaving the others with the more dull, thankless task while she got to work on something exciting and enjoyable. She quashed it down firmly. As Inspector Dale had pointed out, this was valuable work, not mere self-indulgence, and besides, Len *liked* talking to people. And he was—generally—good at seeing beneath their words to what was really going on beneath. Though clearly he had missed something vital with Tom Wright. Still, one couldn't hold one mistake against him.

Maia sighed quietly, knowing that at some point, she and Len were going to have to address their disagreement earlier. She was just as glad to be able to put it off. Not that she would ever stoop so low as avoiding him, but ... well, the timing of this bloodhound spell was convenient, that was all.

"And how has your research progressed?" she asked.

"Slowly, I fear," Becket answered, his brow wrinkled. "I

believe I might need to abandon this line of investigation and focus on another. Even if I uncover whatever it is that eludes me now, it will likely be too late to do any good."

"I sympathize," Maia said. "My greatest fear is that even if this spell works, by the time we are able to test it, there won't be any traces left of Miss Carlyle's spell-casting for it to follow, and it will all have been so much wasted time and effort."

"Never fear, Miss Whitney," Becket said encouragingly. "This will be a spell with many fine applications, whatever happens here and now."

"Perhaps," Maia said. "But if it doesn't help Miss Carlyle in the here and now, I'm not sure any future success will make up for it."

Chapter 11

When Len had returned to Saint Dorothea's only to be informed that Maia had come up with a brilliant idea for magically tracking Charlotte Carlyle and was ensconced in the Magistra's study along with several of the college's best spell-crafters putting it together, his first reaction was a spurt of hot jealousy.

Maia had thought up another new spell and hadn't come to him first about it?

Because you were off wallowing, said a dry, sharp voice in the back of his mind.

Len winced. True. He had no right to indignation, and this was not a sign of rejection by Maia.

"Well," he said to Gwen, who was the one who brought him the news, "that's good! Means we'll finally get this case cleared up sharpish, eh?"

Perhaps his voice was too hearty. At any rate, Gwen cast him an odd look.

"I finished speaking with the secretaries," she said after a long, drawn-out moment of silence, while Len squirmed internally. "Here are the notes from our interviews." She handed him a sheaf of papers.

Len glanced at the notes, then looked closer. "This is a word-for-word transcript, not shorthand or notes," he announced.

"Yes, I used a spell to copy down what we were saying," Gwen said blithely. "That way I wouldn't miss anything."

Blimey. Even when he'd been at the height of his magical powers, he couldn't have sustained a spell like that for … he flipped through the papers … over a dozen interviews. It seemed their Gwen was going to always be impressing them.

"Splendid," he said, the false heartiness in his voice modulated now to a genuine approval. "Maia probably didn't get to any interviews with staff and students before her spell idea, did she?"

Gwen shook her head.

"Then I'd best read through these quickly and get to it myself," he said, stifling a sigh. All this was time consuming and tedious, and he resented having to do this sort of drudgery instead of getting *out* there and finding Miss Carlyle and taking care of her kidnapper.

But this was the backbone of detective work. Just because he was accustomed more to sneaking around, luring people into confidences by his false persona, digging out buried secrets, using magic to set careful snares for unwary villainous feet, picking apart seemingly innocuous comments to read the truth beneath them … just because that was what he used to do didn't mean it was better than this. In fact, hadn't he decided on detective work because he was tired of all that, tired of living a lie? Hadn't living in the shadowy world of spies and deceptions ended up sickening him to his very soul? Now he was going to start complaining about the very lifeline he had grabbed so desperately last April?

He shook his head. He knew perfectly well what had caused this *ennui*. First his instinct had led him astray about Tom—

something that had only ever happened once or twice in his life—and now he was working apart from Maia, with no way of knowing how badly their friendship had been damaged by his idiocy. He wouldn't mind at all doing endless questioning if she were beside him.

"I can help with that," Gwen said, voice still cheerful. "Although it's probably best if I take the students while you question the staff." At his querying look, she explained. "To most of the staff, I'm still Gwen-the-former-student, which means they don't necessarily take me as seriously. Even the Magistra, to a certain extent."

Thinking back over their interactions with Dr. Bingham as well as many of the other faculty, Len couldn't help but agree. "That doesn't bother you?" It would have driven him mad.

Gwen shook her head. "Oh no. It's only natural, isn't it? Besides, this way they'll be all the more impressed when I do something spectacular, because they weren't expecting it."

Len chuckled. He wished he had half her confidence and wisdom. Even when he was her age, he didn't think he'd been so sanguine about the future, or content with the way things were.

"The staff will be more accepting of you questioning them, and be more likely to give you proper answers," Gwen said. "But the students shouldn't have such preconceived ideas, and might even respond better to someone closer to their age."

"Gwen," Len said. "Are you calling me old?"

Gwen giggled. "Maybe," she said.

Len tried to affix a properly outraged expression on his face, but that only made Gwen laugh harder.

"Children these days," he muttered, just loud enough for her to hear.

Gwen opened her mouth for a rejoinder, but they were interrupted before she could speak. A secretary, hurrying out of the office, spotted them standing by the fountain and rushed up to them.

"Mr. Davies! I'm so glad we found you, I thought we were going to have to hunt all over the college. There's a telephone call for you, Lil says you can take it in her office if you want privacy. Miss Pelham's at tea, so you won't be interrupted."

Len furrowed his brow. "A telephone call?"

Who would be phoning him here? Who even knew "here" existed? The only person he could think of who would keep this close tabs on his whereabouts was Harrison, but Harrison would have no reason to track him down here unless … unless something dreadful had happened in the family, or MI needed him for something urgent.

Without further ado, Len turned his steps to the office, where Miss Jamison held the telephone receiver.

"The call is from Hereford," she said, her eyes wide with curiosity. "He seems to think he has reached your flat in London. I didn't tell him otherwise."

Len thanked her with a nod and took the receiver. Not Harrison, then. Someone from home. Who? And how? He put the receiver to his ear and drew nearer the mouthpiece. "Hullo? Davies here."

The rich, broad accent of his former steward reached his ears. "Mr. Len! Mackenzie here. I received your letter and decided to telephone rather than write—too easy for misunderstanding when one had to wait for letters to cross. Since when have you had a secretary, my lad?"

Len's brain reeled. Mackenzie was the last person he had expected to hear from. Indeed, the matter of his family's estate had slid so far to the back of his mind since coming to Cambridge that it might as well have not existed. And how was Mackenzie speaking to him here when he had clearly telephoned Len's flat …? Ah.

The answer to that question, at least, he could guess. Becket, of course. Becket must have set up some sort of spell to forward important calls here. It was just the sort of spell his man would do—complicated, delicate, and unobtrusive.

Len cleared his throat. "Mac! Never mind about the secretary, it's, er, a temporary situation. Good of you to phone, old man. How's the family?"

He wanted to skip right to asking about the estate so he could get it over with, but it would hurt old Mac's feelings terribly if he didn't start out with the appropriate small talk.

"Not so bad, not so bad. Bessie's like to make me a grandfather again. This will make six little ones!"

"Splendid news," Len said heartily. He had been madly in love with Bessie Mackenzie when he was sixteen and she eighteen, captivated by her curls the color of honey and the laugh that flowed so easily from her red lips. She had been far more sensible than he, well aware that the heir to the Davies estate and the daughter of the steward would never be allowed to form an attachment. Instead, she had married Jonas Wayland, the blacksmith, that same summer and settled down quite happily to raise a family with him. It had taken Len a long time to get over feeling betrayed, but in the end, he realized she had done the right thing, and even came to be grateful for the quiet way she had handled the situation.

Now, with Maia in his life, he could only be all the more grateful that he hadn't already bound himself to someone whose lifestyle and sensibilities were so far removed from his own. Never mind the class difference, how could he live with someone who had no knowledge of magic, or who wouldn't want to share in the thrill of solving an impenetrable mystery, or who wouldn't challenge the way he viewed the world? Bessie had been a fine girl and was still a fine woman, but there was no one in all the world for him but Maia Whitney.

"I'm sure Mrs. Mackenzie must be delighted," he said. "She probably started knitting as soon as she heard the news."

There was a small pause on the other end of the line. Then Mac cleared his throat. "Well now, no doubt she would have, were she her usual self. But she's not been at all well since … since I retired. Most days she can't even get out of bed, sorry I am to say it."

"I say, I am sorry," Len said, genuinely shocked. "I hadn't heard." Why had Mother not told him?

Because she didn't think you would care, a bodiless voice whispered in his ear. Len hunched one shoulder in a fruitless effort to dislodge the voice. "Is there anything I can do?"

"No, no thank you, Mr. Len, though it's kind of you to ask. It's just … she did love our little cottage, you know, and I think it fair broke her heart when we had to leave it. Mrs. Davies was very kind indeed in helping us find a little place in town, but it isn't the same. We don't have roses here." Despite himself, Mac's voice sounded forlorn. A fist grabbed Len's heart and squeezed. Mac's roses had been famous in the county, and Mrs. Mackenzie, a delicate, gentle soul, did so love them.

"I hadn't even heard that you had to leave the cottage," Len said. "That can't be right, Father left it to you in his will."

"So I had thought, sir, but Mr. Norris, he said no, the cottage went with the job, and if I was no longer steward, I would need to find a new place to live. Your mother, she was none too pleased with it, but Mr. Norris said he had your full confidence to make whatever changes he deemed best for the estate, and even got a fancy solicitor from London to back him up, and your mother—well, she didn't back down, but she bided her time."

That determined, conniving old woman, casually mentioning in her letter that she didn't approve of how Norris was handling the estate, and never breathing a hint of the details! It was just like her. Len shook his head. She must have known the news would have far more impact on him coming from Mac rather than her. Mother might exaggerate in order to make her point; Mac never would.

"I shouldn't have to tell you that's rubbish," he said now. "I never would have given my blessing to Norris forcing you out of your home, not to mention letting you go in the first place. Why Mac, you've been our steward since before I was born! You have more right than any of us to keep on there."

"Mr. Norris now, he said that was the very reason I should retire, that I had earned a chance to rest, and that it was time to let younger men step up. It wasn't that I wanted to leave, Mr. Len, but he didn't give me a choice. And I will say it, though some might think it sour grapes, that young jackanapes Ames he got in to replace me is mishandling everything! Young fool wants to grow wheat in that lower field without the proper drainage, and he's even started cutting down some of the trees in the north wood."

Len actually gasped at that. Outrage swamped his vision so that he temporarily saw red. First Mac, and now the trees? "Those trees have been there for generations! It isn't a coppice, dash it, there's no reason to cut them."

"That Ames, he thinks to sell the wood from them," Mac

said.

"But there's no need," Len said, trying to grasp this. "The estate is not suffering for lack of funds, unless things have gotten far worse than anyone has told me. And even so, there is plenty to do to retrench before cutting down the trees."

"I doubt me the money from the sales would be going back into the estate, if you take my meaning, sir," Mac said sourly.

Len took it. His hand tightened around the telephone receiver. For a moment, he wanted nothing more than to fly back to the estate and thrash both Norris and his worthless steward. He forgot that he had moved to London specifically to escape the boredom and drudgery of managing the family estate: generations of Davieses rose up in his blood and demanded an accounting.

"Well," he said at last, his voice sounding peculiar even to his own ears. "It seems matters are more serious than I thought. Thanks very much, Mac, for your honesty. It looks like I'll need to come back and take care of it myself. Keep that under your hat, though, will you? I'd rather Norris not hear anything about my arrival until I'm there. I want to hear what he has to say for himself without giving him an opportunity to think up excuses."

Mac's low chuckle vibrated through the telephone wire. "You can count on me, Mr. Len. Awfully glad to think of you returning home, sir. It isn't the same without you here, and that's a fact."

Len bid him farewell and replaced the receiver back on its hook, breathing as hard as if he had just run ten miles.

What the devil was that fool Norris about? How could he possibly think he could get away with robbing the estate and not having to face up to his actions?

Because for as long as he's known you, you've wanted as little to do with the place as possible, answered the same dry, pitiless voice as before.

"Shut up," Len muttered between clenched teeth.

Yes, he had fled the estate. He wanted excitement, adventure, action. He had wanted to do something more, something greater, contribute something important to the world rather than prop up a stuffy old system that had bound England for generations. As much as he enjoyed reading Miss Austen's books, he didn't want to be a Mr. Darcy. Being a good master to his servants and a good landlord to his tenants, marrying a suitable wife and raising sons to carry on the family traditions was all well and good, but it wasn't enough for Len. He wanted to *matter*.

He'd said nothing about this while his father lived, knowing the old man would never understand. Mother had suspected— as soon as he apprenticed himself to Harrison, she'd started to carry a certain grimness in her eyes and around her mouth. She never said anything, though. That wouldn't be the mater's way.

Len had played the dutiful son as long as he could, but as soon as his father died, he started looking for a tenant for the estate so he could live in London and pursue his Intelligence work without hindrance. Old Mr. Norris—Charles's father— was a long-time friend of Len's father, and had seemed the perfect fit. And indeed, for as long as he lived, the place ran smoothly. Neither Mother nor Mac had ever had reason to complain of his lifestyle or management of the estate.

So like a fool, Len allowed the tenancy to transfer over to Charles when old Mr. Norris passed on, assuming things would continue as they always had. Only they hadn't, and now he had a duty to tend. Charles Norris couldn't be allowed to turf old Mac out, not after all these years. Nor could Len stand by and do nothing while the fields were mishandled and the ancient woods felled and the cottagers turned out and goodness only knew what else.

There was nothing for it. He was going to have to go home just as soon as this case was solved.

* * *

Following the disquieting conversation with Mackenzie, Len found it difficult to concentrate on the reports from Gwen. His feet itched to fly back to the estate *at once*, throw Norris and the new steward out on their ears, and put everything back to rights. His mind buzzed with thoughts of the best way to handle it all. He'd need to talk with Amos next, find out just how badly they'd mangled the stables. His brother-in-law wouldn't be happy if they'd done anything to the horses. The Cameron stables were some of the finest in the land, and Cam had worked hard since marrying Pippa to bring the Davies stables up to a comparable level—or at least, as Cam put it, to a level that wouldn't embarrass him through their connection.

Dash it, he wasn't supposed to have to worry about any of this! He was supposed to be able to lead his own life, while knowing the estate was in good hands.

Supposed to be enjoying yourself while others do your work, you mean.

Len scowled unseeingly at the papers in his hand. That dashed voice was getting dashed irritating.

Meanwhile, he was stuck here until they solved the case,

since he couldn't exactly fob off one responsibility for another. Then there was Mother's visit—though she would be the first to cancel that if it meant him returning to the estate. Perhaps it was a lucky thing that cases had been so few and far between. He didn't have to feel guilty about leaving Maia and Gwen with too much work.

Leaving Maia … the thought twisted in his heart. Would she understand? Would she consider it a betrayal? Her father was an estate owner, surely she would understand Len's responsibilities there. Only then would she despise him for letting things get so out of hand?

And would they ever have a chance to straighten out that disagreement between them, or were they doomed to separate still misunderstanding each other?

One thing was certain. He couldn't unburden his heart to Maia now, not when everything was so muddled. That would have to wait—wait until he had his responsibilities sorted, wait until he was in a place to offer her something other than a blighted mess. Wait until he had regained her respect, most likely.

Len's hands clenched around the papers, crumpling them into a ball. He breathed deeply and smoothed them out with a muttered spell.

"Get a hold of yourself, Davies," Len said under his breath.

First step was to find Miss Carlyle, or her body, and bring the person who had abducted her and murdered Appleby to justice. Everything else could wait until that was accomplished.

Len forced himself to focus, skimming through the reports quickly, grasping the salient points of each before setting it aside and moving on to the next. Lord knew he didn't want to discourage Gwen, but it would have been simpler had she simply jotted down the main facts rather than copying the entire conversation verbatim. That was something she'd have to learn for herself eventually, and heaven forbid he do anything to dampen that shining enthusiasm of hers.

Unfortunately, there wasn't much in the reports that they hadn't already learned. Jenny Pelham ruled all the secretaries with an iron fist—and did not even bother with a velvet glove—and nobody paid enough attention to Charlotte Carlyle to notice anything unusual about her interactions with Miss Pelham.

With that in mind, Len set off to track down those of the staff members who were not currently locked in the Magistra's study with Maia.

After a couple of junior faculty who could give him nothing useful, he was able to track down Gardiner, the librarian. The fellow was, unsurprisingly enough, in the library, sitting behind the enormous wooden desk at the front where he could keep a sharp eye on anyone coming or going. He glanced up at Len's footfall, even softened as he instinctively made it entering into the large, dim room lined with shelves and shelves of books.

"Davies!" Gardiner said in a muted tone. "Glad to see you again. Are you here to peruse the Merriman Collection?"

"I wish I was," Len replied, his voice as heartfelt as it could be when one was speaking barely above a whisper. "Actually, I'm here on a much more boring mission. I need to ask you a few more questions about Miss Carlyle, and about your missing ink bottle."

A startled expression crossed Gardiner's face before it quickly smoothed back to his previous amiable appearance. It was so quick that Len might have thought he'd imagined it, save there was something in the very amiability of face that reminded him—well, it reminded him of *him*. All those years he had worn the mask of courteous, friendly, and mildly dim-witted English gentleman for the sake of MI.

Was Gardiner's face a mask as well, or was Len imagining things?

His instinct told him Gardiner could be trusted—but after what had happened with Tom, Len wasn't entirely certain he could trust his instincts right now. Too much else distracting him, between his family affairs and the odd undercurrents swirling around Maia. It wasn't just their argument from earlier in the day; he had started feeling out-of-tune with her ever since they arrived here, perhaps even before. He couldn't put his finger on what the issue was, worse luck, and there was no time to ponder the matter with everything else happening.

He shook himself out of his introspection as Gardiner responded.

"My ink bottle! I wasn't expecting that." He glanced around, then motioned with his head toward the entryway. "Come, we can talk more easily out there, and I can still see if someone comes to the desk needing me."

They stepped through the open glass-paneled doors, Gardiner closing them most of the way behind him as he went. "There, that's better," he said in a normal tone. "Now, who cares about my old ink bottle going missing? And what do you want to know about Miss Carlyle? She rarely visited the library, you know. Not many of the secretaries do—I think Miss Pelham discourages them from coming in, doesn't want them getting above themselves, or some such nonsense." He rolled his eyes. "Rubbish, of course, but what can one do?"

"Indeed," Len said. "So you haven't seen Miss Carlyle in the last couple of weeks?"

Gardiner rubbed his chin as he thought. "As a matter of fact, she did pop in last week briefly—not for herself, though. She said Miss Pelham needed a book for refreshing the spill-proof spell on the secretaries' ink bottles. Seemed a bit odd to me, as those spells ought not to need refreshing, but she shrugged and said it was what Miss Pelham had told her. I couldn't let her take the book out of the library, of course, but I helped her find it and even let her use my pen and a scrap of paper to copy the spell out." He blinked. "Come to think of it, it was shortly after that my ink went missing. I say! You don't think *Miss Carlyle* could have been the thief, do you?"

That was an idea. Len turned it over in his mind before deciding it didn't make much sense. Why put up a fuss about reporting the thefts if she was the one committing them? And if she was the thief, who had sent her the threatening letters, and why?

"Not likely," he said. "Were there other people in the library at the time?"

"Oh yes, we always have students and staff alike in here for one reason or another. We don't let anyone take books out of the library, so if they want to study something they have to do it in here."

Len had it. The spill-proof spell was a ruse—Gardiner had said it ought not to need refreshing. Miss Pelham had wanted the book it was in for another reason, and in retaliation for not being able to get it had pinched the ink. Petty, but wasn't everything about this case petty? Save Appleby's murder, and even that felt as though it had been done out of panic, or even an accident, rather than something coldly planned and deliberate.

Except … none of that fit with Miss Pelham's character as they'd seen it thus far. She was a small tyrant, but coldly disciplined and in control of everything. Was she really the type to indulge in small retaliations or to lash out at an old, frail man in a panic?

Unless the image she presented to the world was just that: an image. Perhaps that domineering veneer was meant to cover up her insecurities and weaknesses?

Len repressed a sigh. Every time you thought you had an insight into this case it twisted around and led you right back pointing in the opposite direction. They were no closer to finding Miss Carlyle than they had been the day they arrived.

As a detective, he was proving to be a fine spy.

"I don't suppose there was anything special about your ink bottle?" he asked hopelessly.

"Nothing in particular," Gardiner said. "Just your standard Hoffman's glass ink bottle." His face colored ruddily. "I do use green ink—awful affectation, I know, but I like it—but that's the only thing that's different from the dozens of other ink bottles around."

Len considered that. Magicians preferred to use a particular type of ink where the dye came from organic sources rather than artificial—as magic only worked on the natural world, it was far easier to do a spell on one's ink if the compound was made up of mostly natural parts. Hoffman's was the largest manufacturer of magic-friendly ink in this country.

Did any of this matter? Sadly, Len had to discard the possibility. Practically everyone at a college like Saint Dot's would be using Hoffman's ink, so why would someone need to steal Gardiner's? The color? He was vague on what went into green ink, but he thought it had something to do with green plants. Or was it copper? Bother it, he had no idea.

"Might I see the book Miss Carlyle was copying from?" he asked as a last resort. If his half-baked theory about Miss Pelham was correct, there would be another spell in that book that would be the one she had really wanted. If he could figure out which one it was, that might be enough to give him the clue to this whole case.

It didn't seem likely, but one never knew.

Gardiner opened the door again. "After you," he said cheerfully.

Len stepped inside, then followed Gardiner deeper into the mellow room. Despite its youth, the library had already taken on an air of stability and peace, as though it had been there for centuries. Len breathed deeply of the scent of leather, paper, and that indefinable *something* that made up old books, and felt something in his soul start to uncoil and relax.

Gardiner stopped by a case with leaded glass panels in the doors and an iron lock. Squinting to see past the lines of leading, Len saw about two dozen red-covered books in the case.

"Is that the Merriman Collection?" he whispered reverently.

Gardiner nodded. "In its entirety," he said, pride evident even in his muted tones. "Marvelous works. I haven't been able to read them all yet—too much other work that I can't neglect even though I'd rather spend an entire year doing nothing but poring over them—but what I have read is marvelous. Amazing how the old fellow had a grasp of magic none of our modern magicians have been able to match. You'd think we would have been able to build on his work, but instead we're still trying to understand it."

Maia could understand it. Len wasn't sure where the thought had come from—he hadn't even looked in the books yet—but he was absolutely certain it was the truth. He'd have to see about her taking some time away from the agency to come study them once this matter was settled.

Gardiner pulled a slim volume off the shelf nearest the locked case. "Here is the spill-proof spell," he said, rifling through the book until he came to the relevant section. "You can go through the book at one of the tables here, if you like. Don't bother re-shelving the book, just bring it to me when you're finished."

Nodding his understanding, Len sat down at the nearest table with the book and flipped back to the table of contents. From the look of it, this was an ordinary spellbook for basic household spells—nothing interesting or extraordinary in it. Perhaps there would be something within it that would stand out to him once he started skimming, but his hopes, never high to begin with, sank even lower.

If they didn't get a break soon, this case was going to grind to a halt through sheer attrition.

Grimly, he set himself to reading.

Chapter 12

The hands on Maia's wristwatch (a gift from her father for her sixteenth birthday, back when wristwatches were the newest thing) stood at midnight when the assorted magicians finally stood back from the table and Miss Archer said,

"I think that's done it, don't you?"

There were nods of agreement all around, though Foster looked uncertain. "I'm not entirely sure about those calculations for the parameters," he said. "I'd like to go over them again."

Miss Woodward groaned. "Oh honestly, Gerald. You've gone over them four times already. They're solid."

He raised his eyebrows, but subsided.

"Right then," Miss Archer said. "Time to present the finished work to the Magistra, and then we'll test it. Who wants to volunteer?"

There was an uneasy silence.

"To cast it, you mean?" asked Mr. Henderson at last.

"Nonsense," Miss Archer said. "That honor goes to Miss Whitney, you all know that. This is her spell, after all. We merely assisted in its formation. No, who will volunteer to have it cast upon an object of theirs to see if it works to reveal their aura in all the places they have done magic recently?"

Again, silence descended over the room.

Maia shrugged one shoulder. She could not understand why everyone was so fussy about this. They acted as though having others see the traces of their magic were as intimate and embarrassing as—as—showing their knickers in public! She was about to offer to allow someone else to cast it on her— though as she had used hardly any magic since arriving at the college it would be an inconclusive test—when Foster spoke again.

"Since the purpose of this spell is to help find Miss Carlyle, why not use her as the test subject?"

"Oh." Miss Archer considered this. "Yes, I suppose that would work. Very well. Gerald, would you kindly fetch the Magistra? And you, Ethel—see if there's anything in the secretaries' room that belongs to Miss Carlyle. If not, we'll have to visit her boarding house and try to find something there. Goodness, that *does* feel like a violation of her privacy," she added in an undertone.

Fortunately for Miss Archer's tender conscience, by the time Foster had returned with the Magistra, the others had found a scarf belonging to Miss Carlyle, left behind at her desk when she vanished.

"Perfect," Miss Archer said. "I recall her wearing that nearly every day, and it is silk, so it will have absorbed significant traces of her magic."

The Magistra laid down the notes she had been perusing. "Excellent work, everyone. Miss Whitney, will you begin?"

"Certainly," Maia said.

She breathed deeply as she took the scarf from Miss Archer's hands and laid it on the clean work table. Now that it came to it, with all eyes on her, she was nervous. True, this wasn't her own work, it was a team effort, and she was not being judged on anything—but this was still her first time creating a spell in community like this, and it suddenly meant a great deal to her that she not fail.

The notes were on a side table, but she didn't need them; she had pored over them so much over the preceding hours that they were engrained in her memory. She placed her hands on either side of the scarf and closed her eyes, gathering up her magic within her and concentrating it on the scarf. Carefully, she set the boundaries of the spell in place, so that the magic would not spill out and start searching for anyone and everyone's aura. The parameters Foster had been so worried about fit smoothly into the working of the spell—Maia didn't understand the equations perfectly, but they established the limitations of the spell exactly as they were meant to.

Within the boundaries, Maia guided the seeking magic into the scarf, directing it to identify Charlotte Carlyle's magic, take the "scent" of it, so to speak. *Discere exemplum unius cuius gerit hoc."*

There had been considerable debate about the wording of that incantation. Initially Maia had intended to use "aura," since that was what everyone called it. That, apparently, would have been too vague for a spell that relied so heavily on precision. The other magicians had also rejected words such as "aroma," "flavor," and "feel" as being too literal. Finally Maia had hit upon "pattern," and, after a bit more argument, that one stood.

The problem was that magic was by nature difficult to define, and nobody was entirely sure of what made one person's magic unique to them and not another—or even what allowed one person to be able to use magic when so many couldn't. While magic did tend to run in families, that wasn't guaranteed, and it was also quite likely to crop up in someone with no history of magic in their line ever.

This was the main reason why the seeking spell had taken so long to craft. How to create a spell to learn and hunt for a person's magic when the spellcasters knew so little about how that magic came to dwell in a person to begin with? Between that and the need to set so many boundaries to keep the spell from finding other people's magic, Maia had begun to fear she had set herself too hard a task before the team finally agreed it could be done.

So far, it seemed to be working. Maia opened her eyes to see the scarf surrounded by a pale mauve nimbus. It was similar enough to the translucent silver cloud surrounding her own hands as she directed her magic, and to the copper cloud she saw around Len whenever he worked magic, that she knew it was the leftover residue from the spells Miss Carlyle had cast while wearing this scarf.

"It's working," she said in a hushed voice, not wanting to distract herself from the spell but also knowing the importance of sharing the progress with the watching magicians. "I can see the aura."

She heard murmurs in response, but closed her eyes again and sank back into her magic, shutting out the outer world.

Now that the spell knew Miss Carlyle's "scent," it was time for the final step, the incantation to send the magic out of the scarf to find the same scent of magic anywhere else on the college grounds (another mathematical equation in setting up the boundaries—otherwise, Foster had warned, the spell-caster could drain themselves of all magic by casting the net too wide and exhausting their resources).

"*Idem inveniet,*" she said in a clear voice, then opened her eyes once more.

"Oh!" she said, catching her breath.

"What?" chorused a number of voices.

Maia couldn't answer for a moment, caught up in wonder.

For there, floating in the air before her eyes, was a faint mauve haze. The spell had worked! She could see the memory of magic from where Miss Carlyle had cast a spell!

"It works," she said, her voice quiet in direct contrast to the joy and triumph singing through her veins. She was reminded of the first spell she'd ever cast—a spell to bring light—and the awestruck delight she had experienced then. Len had been beside her for that, and she suddenly, searingly, wished he was here for this, as well. It didn't seem right to go through something this momentous with her magic and *not* have him by her side.

"How do you know?" Foster asked, and Maia tore her eyes away from the visible spell residue to look at her audience.

"I can see it," she said, gesturing to the mauve cloud, though she knew no one else could see it—that was the entire point of this, after all, that while the spell was active she could see the magic that no one else could.

Foster frowned, but it was Miss Archer who spoke. "But how can that be? Miss Carlyle has never cast a spell in here, has she, Magistra?"

"Certainly not," Dr. Bingham answered. "I don't permit casual spell-casting in my rooms. In fact, I don't even think she has been in my study for months—not since she came to speak to me about Tom Wright, last spring."

Maia's heart checked in its soaring as a cold tendril of doubt wound around it.

Could she be mistaken? But then how could she see anything at all? Surely if the spell had gone awry she wouldn't be able to see any trace of Miss Carlyle's magic, not a trace where there wasn't one.

"Perhaps it's simply drifted there from the scarf," Miss Archer said. "Let's go around the college a bit, dear, and see if things become clearer."

"I told you the parameters were off," muttered Foster.

Maia ignored this, but the doubt remained as she dutifully followed Miss Archer and Dr. Bingham out of the study, the other half dozen magicians trailing behind, unsure whether to be excited or disappointed.

There was another mauve wisp in the corridor, and once in the grounds, Maia could see them *everywhere*.

Bobbing over the fountain. Hovering near the entrance to Merriman Hall. Scattered around the back gate. Clustered thickly by the gatehouse. Shining through the windows of the secretaries' rooms. In the trees and bushes.

"Oh dear," Maia said, a catch in her throat.

This couldn't be right. There was simply no reason for Miss Carlyle to have cast this many spells in all these places in the last week.

She turned to Miss Archer, who read the disappointment in her face before she even spoke.

"Well, no sense in giving up now," the older woman said briskly. "We'll look in each building for thoroughness' sake, and then we'll go from there."

The interior of the buildings matched the grounds for being host to traces of mauve magic. Maia held out some hope right up until she (blushing furiously) entered the gentlemen's cloakroom and even saw one in *there*. The only rooms they did not enter were bedrooms which currently held sleeping students and staff, but even Miss Archer admitted there was no point in continuing after the cloakroom.

"Better end it now," she said with a sigh.

Maia drew her concentration back together and spoke one word:

"*Finiatur.*"

Abruptly, the mauve traces vanished from her sight, and at the same time, she became aware of a throbbing headache behind her temples.

"I know you all want to put your heads together and discuss what went wrong," Dr. Bingham said, eyeing them all with a mixture of compassion and shrewdness. "But I am going to strongly recommend bed now. After a good night's sleep, breakfast, and a hot drink, you can go back at it."

"If there's any point," muttered one of the other magicians.

Maia wanted to protest that *of course* there was a point, but her disappointment was too severe to respond at all, much less in her own defense. She nodded dispiritedly, and stood back while the rest dispersed, some with a sympathetic smile in her direction, others with irritated looks—likely annoyed that they had spent so much time and effort on a failed effort.

Miss Archer patted her shoulder as she left, and eventually even Dr. Bingham went back to her rooms, leaving Maia standing alone in front of the gentlemen's cloakroom in Merriman Hall, her heart somewhere near her toes.

She knew she ought to take the Magistra's good advice about sleep, but she couldn't seem to summon the will. It wasn't just the disappointment—the spell had taken an enormous amount of energy, and in addition to leaving her with a headache had left her with extreme lethargy in all her limbs, and a numbed mind.

She might have stayed there all night had not the main door opened a crack, and a man's shadowed form slipped through.

It didn't even occur to Maia to be alarmed.

"Hullo, Len," she said.

He dropped the spell that had cloaked him in darkness—not his usual chameleon spell, but one Maia hadn't seen him use before—and spoke in an equally quiet voice.

"I gather it didn't go exactly as planned?"

Maia didn't want to talk about it, but somehow the words came tumbling out without her volition.

"I thought it had worked, at first. I could see her magic! I could see the residue of her spells. Except then I kept seeing it, and saw it in places where she couldn't have even been, much less cast a spell, and I don't understand how it could make me see something that isn't there, rather than not see anything at all." Her shoulders slumped as she finished.

"Rotten luck," Len said, the warmth in his voice coming through even in a near-whisper. He came closer. "I say, you're just about done in, old thing. Have a seat."

His hands were on her shoulders, steering her down to sit on the floor and lean back against the wall. Then a soft weight draped over her as he took off his coat and swooped it expertly over her front to settle like a blanket. For the finishing touch, he dipped one hand into his pocket and brought out a package of digestives.

"Biscuit?" he said.

Despite herself, Maia felt significantly better just for his care. She even laughed a little. "What, no tea?"

It was still too dark to make out his features, but she heard the grin as he answered, "Sorry, I haven't yet managed to fit a kettle and cups into my pockets. Bet Becket could manage it, though. Did I tell you about the spell he worked to have telephone calls automatically transferred from my flat to here? Dashed if I know how he managed it."

Maia managed another laugh. "Perhaps we should have had him working on this spell."

"As much as I admire Becket's skills, I don't believe he could have done anything with this spell that you didn't already do," Len said, his voice serious for once. "You're the finest magic-worker I know."

Warmth stirred in the bottom of Maia's stomach at his words, but even they weren't enough to ease her bitterness. "Not fine enough," she said.

Len stretched his long legs out beside her. "Oh well, hardly anybody gets a major working like this right the first time. Trial and error, my friend, trial and error. That's what it takes. You keep at it, you'll sort it out."

Either the digestives or Len's confidence or both were starting to help. "Do you think so?"

"I'm certain of it," he said. "I can't imagine you failing at anything you set your mind to, even if there are setbacks along the path."

The warmth in Maia's stomach spread at that, but she also felt embarrassed. How was one to respond to such a sweeping statement? A deprecating laugh smacked of false modesty, but a "thank you" seemed to indicate an improper pride and agreement with the sentiment. After an awkward pause, she settled for,

"That's very kind."

"Simple truth," Len insisted.

Was it, though? Maia reflected on her discouragement with the detective agency, and her stomach curdled. How dared she criticize Len for not living up to her standards of right and wrong, when she couldn't live up to his belief in her? He would be as disappointed in her as she had been in him if he knew how the work on this spell had raised such a fierce longing to be done with detective work so she could come here to Saint Dorothea's and do this sort of thing all the time.

Maia's thoughts stuttered to a stop here. Was that really what she wanted?

Yes, she had to admit to herself. It was.

All at once, her unspoken desire kindled to full life. She was *tired* of doing work that nobody cared about, that didn't matter. It had felt fine and grand at first, the thought of bringing justice to the overlooked in society, but it seemed the overlooked weren't all that interested in justice, and the petty crimes and misunderstandings Whitney and Davies had cleared up in the last six months could just as easily have been done by Deep or a police division akin to this one here in Cambridge.

But studying the nature of spells, learning how to use magic in new ways, discovering more about its very nature and how magicians could shape it to better serve their community—ah, what satisfaction there would be in that!

That was why it had been so important to her that this spell work, she realized now. That was why she had been so crushed when it failed. She wanted to know that she had done something important. Something no one else had ever thought of, and she brought to life.

Oh, the hubris of it! It was no wonder she had failed. With an attitude like that, she had deserved to fail. Where was her sense of duty? Where was her compassion for Miss Carlyle?

One taste of glory, and Maia was ready to toss it all aside.

She was no better than Len, letting his sympathy for Tom Wright get the best of his sense of justice. Worse, because at least he had been distracted by care and concern for someone else. Maia had gotten distracted by her own desire for recognition and appreciation.

"I should get some sleep," she said abruptly, struggling to her feet. "So should you. Since this spell didn't work, we'll need to go back to old-fashioned detecting tomorrow to continue our search for Miss Carlyle."

"Oh, I say," Len said, standing as well and helping Maia up. "Surely you're going to keep working on the spell?"

"I would like to come back to it once Miss Carlyle is safe, if I can find anyone to volunteer to be a test subject," Maia said. "But it's too much of an indulgence now. Even if I am able to make it work, I doubt it will come together in time to be of use for finding Miss Carlyle."

"Seems a shame," Len said.

"Perhaps," Maia said, keeping her voice calm with an effort. "But we must put Miss Carlyle first."

"Of course," Len agreed. "That goes without saying. I simply—I suppose I simply wish you didn't have to make such a choice." He sighed. "If I were half the detective I thought I was, I could solve this case for you so you would be free to spend as much time as you needed on this spell."

"And if I were half the magician you think I am, I'd have come up with a spell to solve it for us," Maia rejoined.

Len chuckled under his breath at that, opening the door for her to precede him out. "Now that, I think, might very well be beyond even your capabilities. Even Merriman couldn't do that! No spell will ever truly do away with the need for human creativity and intelligence. Magic is a tool, not a substitute."

It was the last thing either of them said before they parted to retire to their respective rooms.

Maia did not realize until she was changing into her pyjamas that she was still wearing Len's coat. She smiled a little as she smoothed it out and draped it over the back of the chair. Dear Len. Where would she be without him?

It occurred to her only as she was drifting into sleep that she would need to tell Inspector Dale that the spell had failed. She couldn't help but wonder how his reaction would compare to Lennox's, but sleep claimed her before she could speculate any more.

* * *

"Drift," Len said the next morning at breakfast, setting his filled plate down beside Maia's at the long oak table.

"Beg pardon?" Maia said, looking up at him blankly as he seated himself.

Breakfast was far less formal than dinner. Though the high table was still reserved for faculty and their guests, in the mornings anyone was free to come and help themselves from the long sideboard at any time between seven-thirty and ten. Until Len's arrival, Maia had had the table entirely to herself, as the only other students there at the hour of eight in the morning had gathered at the other tables, many of them reading their notes in preparation for their lectures or supervisions to come later.

Maia herself had a notebook by her elbow and a fountain pen in her hand, but the page remained blank for now.

"That's the problem with the bloodhound spell. The magic drifts! The leftover residue from the spells doesn't stay in the same place, it drifts about everywhere."

"Oh." Maia frowned. "You could be right. That would be an insoluble problem, then, wouldn't it?"

"It means the spell worked perfectly," Len pointed out.

"Perhaps, but it also means it's useless for tracking the progression of someone's magic," Maia replied sharply.

"I hadn't thought of that." Len scowled at his eggs and bacon. "Bother. There must be some way to compensate. Or maybe I'm wrong."

"Now that is hardly likely," Maia teased lightly.

Len grinned wryly. "You'd be surprised." He nodded at her notebook. "Jotting down some ideas for the spell?"

"No, as I told you last night, I'm putting that on hold for now." Maia tapped the pen on the table's surface. "We've been dithering around this problem for too long now, speculating *who* could be behind Miss Carlyle's disappearance, *why* it happened, all that. We need to move forward on finding her."

"I applaud the notion, but admit I haven't the faintest idea how to do that. What do you suggest?"

Maia began to write as she spoke, pushing her plate away still half-full. "We've agreed, haven't we, that Miss Pelham is our chief suspect?"

"Er—yes," Len said, his face going red.

Maia had almost forgotten about his conviction of Tom Wright's guilt, and even about their disagreement. They would have to come to terms with that at some point, she supposed, but not today. Today they needed to find Miss Carlyle.

"Then I think we should learn where she lives, and pay a visit to her home when she's not there, see if we can find any clues to Miss Carlyle's location," Maia said. "We also …" She bit her lip, then continued valiantly. "We also should cast a spell at the river, to see if there's a human body hidden anywhere in its depths, particularly downriver from here."

Len shuddered. "I hate to do it, but you're right. As much as we all hope she's still alive, you and I both know there's a good chance she was dead before we even arrived in Cambridge."

"I'd also like to take a look at Mr. Appleby's ledger of who went in and out of the college the day she disappeared, especially around teatime," Maia said. "We'll have to ask Inspector Dale for permission, of course."

"You think there might be a clue there?"

Maia raised one shoulder in a helpless shrug. "I don't know, but we have to try something. A discrepancy would be nice— someone who, like Miss Carlyle, was signed into the ledger in the morning but didn't get signed out. That would tell us that somebody else snuck out, most likely with her in tow. Or perhaps a glamour was used after all, and so there's evidence of someone signing out who didn't sign in that morning. Or—I don't know, anything!"

"Both jolly good notions," Len approved. "We ought to have done that first thing, if we'd been thinking clearly."

"Dithering, as I said," Maia said, directing her ire at herself.

"It can be difficult at the start of a case to know what the first steps should be," Len said peaceably, spreading marmalade on his toast. "There's usually a lot of stumbling around trying to decide what is important and what isn't. Besides, you never know. Some of what we have already done may prove to be crucial to solving the case even yet."

Maia was not convinced, but she held her tongue. "I'd like Gwen to check one more time around the college grounds to see if there's any possible way someone could have gotten in or out, or if a body could be hidden anywhere. I know the Magistra already organized a search before we arrived, but I would feel better if we could confirm that for ourselves. If Becket is free from his research, perhaps he could assist with that? It's a large job for one person."

"You know that the police will also be searching the grounds," Len said, not criticizing, but stating the facts.

"Yes, but they are looking for clues to a murderer," Maia said. "We are looking for Miss Carlyle."

"Right you are." Len reached across Maia to pick up the notebook and close it. She looked over at him, startled, but he merely smiled and drew her plate back toward her. "First, though, you must finish eating. No good chasing down clues on an empty stomach."

"Goodness," Maia said, startled into a laugh. "You sound just like my old nanny!"

He was right, though. She felt considerably better once she finished her breakfast. They met Gwen on their way out, as she was coming in, and Maia stopped to give Gwen her instructions for the day. Gwen grimaced at the thought of having to go over all the buildings and grounds with a fine-tooth comb for any sign of Lottie or of a way she might have been smuggled out anywhere except the gates, but agreed it was the logical next step.

"Now," Maia said afterward, "for Inspector Dale and the ledger."

She tried to ignore the quivering in her stomach at the thought of seeing him again. For heaven's sake, she was not some silly schoolgirl to be getting a pash for the man! Whatever this odd attraction was she felt toward him, she was not going to let it affect her judgment or her actions. One need not, after all, be controlled by one's emotions.

In this militant spirit, she led the way to the gatehouse.

Chapter 13

"The book isn't here," Inspector Dale said.

"Is it at the station, then?" Len asked, a little irritated at the fellow's attitude. If he didn't want to share evidence, why didn't he just say so, instead of dancing around the subject and making them grovel for it?

Dashed if he was going to grovel, even for important evidence.

The inspector's expression didn't change by so much as an eyelash flicker. "No, I mean it was missing when we inventoried the contents of the porter's lodge."

"What?"

That was important information they ought to have been given right away! What was the blasted fellow thinking, keeping it from them?

He was likely thinking that the murder was his problem to solve, not theirs, said a reasonable voice in the back of Len's mind that sounded like Maia—or possibly Harrison, and he didn't even want to think about why he couldn't tell the difference.

Regardless, this still should have been shared.

"Any particular reason you waited until now to tell us?" Len asked, not even trying to hide the edge in his voice.

Inspector Dale sighed. "Because by the time we were certain it was gone and not merely misplaced, Miss Whitney was in the middle of creating an exceedingly complex spell, and you were nowhere to be found. And because you did not ask until now."

It was a fair point, which only irritated Len all the more, especially as Maia was blushing at the compliment. Maia! Blushing! What was the world coming to, dash it?

"Is there anything else missing that we should know about?"

Len couldn't help the sarcasm in his voice, but to his surprise, Dale actually seemed thoughtful. "Not missing, no … something odd, though. I don't see how it can have anything to do with the murder or the kidnapping, but it is odd. We found two mugs hidden in the pot of that Jerusalem Cherry he had in the lodge. They had only a light layer of dirt brushed over them, so they couldn't have been there long, or Appleby would have noticed them when he went to water the plant."

"Unless Appleby hid them there himself," Maia commented, her blushes gone now that she had a point to grapple with.

"But why?"

"Why would anyone hide two mugs?" Maia countered.

Len started. That made him remember. "Sorry, Inspector—I think my man might be responsible for that. You remember, Maia, when we came back from the boarding house, and Appleby was going to make us tea but couldn't find the extra mugs? I recall thinking at the time how adroit Becket must have been to hide the mugs so we could get out of drinking it without hurting the old man's feelings."

"He was sitting near a plant at the time," Maia said slowly. "You think he got hold of the cups and hid them?" Her expression was faintly skeptical. "I know Becket is good, but could even he have anticipated the issue and provided a solution so adeptly?"

"If anyone could, it would be Becket," Len assured her. He looked over at the Inspector. "There you have it, I'm afraid. I can confirm with Becket later, but I'm sure that's the answer."

"At least that's one mystery solved," Dale said sourly.

Len couldn't help but feel cheered at Dale's obvious displeasure. "Sorry that it couldn't turn out to be the key to solving the entire mystery," he said. "Now, do we have any way of figuring out what was written in the book?"

"Unless Miss Whitney can think of another brand-new spell that would reveal the words when we have neither the book nor the writing instrument, no," Dale said.

Len wanted to think of his tone as sarcastic, but he had to admit that it actually sounded ... hopeful. Not to mention respectful.

He was glad more people were appreciating Maia's talents, of course, but did it have to be this fellow? Maia was blushing again, and it was becoming dashed bothersome.

In theory, Len strongly disapproved of jealousy. If this were anyone else, he would have laughed at the situation. What right did he have to be jealous? He'd never even told Maia of his deeper feelings. Even if he had, she was under no obligation to return them, and was perfectly free to blush at whomever she wanted.

Nevertheless, the sight of Dale smiling at her and her smiling back at him with a shyness Len had never seen from her made him wish dueling was still socially acceptable, so he could slap a glove in Dale's face and challenge him to name his choice of weapon and his second.

Between his treacherous tenant, the still-unsettled argument between him and Maia, and now this unexpected jealousy, this case was turning out more full of personal difficulties than any other, and that included that one time in Russia he had to be undercover for months and would have been killed out of hand if his disguise had slipped for a moment.

This was supposed to have been a lovely jaunt to a university town with a pleasingly challenging locked-room puzzle to solve before wandering the golden streets arm-in-arm with Maia, feeding the swans and marveling over the Mathematical Bridge. Why did nothing ever go according to plan?

"I'm afraid I'm right out of clever spell ideas," Maia said, her voice carefully neutral.

"Then we are at an impasse," Dale replied.

There was a pause as they regrouped.

"At least we know the book was important, and might even have been why Appleby was killed," Maia said at last. "Perhaps Miss Carlyle's kidnapper returned to steal the book, and Mr. Appleby caught her or him, causing the kidnapper to lash out in fear, inadvertently killing him."

"You think it was an accident, not deliberate murder?" Dale asked.

Maia motioned to Len. "Len says it doesn't have the feel of deliberate murder, and I trust his judgment."

Len couldn't speak. What a woman! Not one woman—no, not one *person* in a thousand could be so fair-minded after the idiotic way he had behaved over the Tom Wright matter. For Maia to still trust his judgment even after he had muffed that—for her to publicly declare her trust in this way—Len didn't deserve a friend like her. How dare he suffer jealousy for her favor? He ought to be dam' thankful for her friendship, and never mind raising his eyes and his hopes to anything higher.

Dale didn't look any too pleased about Maia's declaration, but he didn't argue with it outright. "Hmm," was the only answer he committed himself to.

"What is your next step, Inspector?" Len asked, trying to keep his voice pleasant. He didn't quite manage it, but at least the edge was gone.

"Continue to sift the evidence and the witness statements," Dale answered. "Routine police work. It's dull, but more often than not it's what gets the job done. Flashes of brilliance and the genius detective building a case out of thin air are all very well in stories, but in real life, it's the slow, plodding work that goes unappreciated that does the trick."

Len felt more than heard Maia's catch of breath at that statement. Now why should that have affected her? It was a simple enough statement. Abrasive and defensive, but nothing out of the ordinary.

"Couldn't agree with you more," Len said, and meant it. He knew he relied too heavily on intuition and those "flashes of brilliance," but in his case, it was the years of experience behind the intuition that guided him, and the flashes of brilliance came about only after his subconscious had been working away on the disparate parts of a case for a long time and finally handed him the answer.

And even then, it wasn't a reliable method. It worked well for MI, when his business was more spying and hunting down international magical crimes, and the only thing that mattered was staying one step ahead of the opposition. Intuition and doing the unexpected had kept him alive then, and allowed him to bring more than one malefactor to justice, but when it came to this sort of detective work, it wasn't anywhere near as useful. Sometimes it worked, but often he felt he was simply stumbling in the dark hoping for a spark of light to show him the path.

This case in particular.

Maia cleared her throat. "Ahem," she said. "Sorry. Yes. That sounds quite reasonable, Inspector. I believe we'll be doing something similar."

"Good old-fashioned legwork," Len confirmed. "Following in the footsteps of our main suspects in hopes that they lead us somewhere useful."

"I see," Dale said. "Do you mind if I ask who your main suspects are?"

Len glanced around out of habit, but as they were talking near the plodge, and nobody wanted to be near there unless they had no choice, they didn't have to worry about being accidentally overheard. "Miss Pelham tops our list right now."

"Curious," Dale said. "She is near the bottom of mine."

"Really. Why is that, if one might ask?"

"Certainly one might ask," Dale replied. "One might even receive an answer." He gave a quick glance at Maia and relented. "She has an alibi for the time of the murder. She was scolding one of her secretaries for wearing lipstick when Foster came screaming out of the porter's lodge."

Len grimaced. How had they missed that in the witness statements?

Because they were investigating the kidnapping, not the murder, said the Maia-Harrison voice again.

This business of splitting the two crimes was hurting their ability to solve either one, and was a blasted nuisance to boot.

"Of course, she could have bullied the secretary into giving her an alibi," Maia said thoughtfully.

"Possible, but I doubt it. The girl—Miss Jamison—spoke freely and bitterly about it. She didn't even seem to realize she was giving Miss Pelham an alibi by her complaint."

"Bother," Maia said under her breath. She looked at Len. "Do we still track down where she lives?"

"Might as well," Len said. "It is just possible that she is still our thief and kidnapper, and is not the murderer. Or that she killed Appleby and then dashed to the secretaries' office to find someone to scold just to give herself an alibi." That last bit had come to him only as he was speaking, and he was rather proud of it once he finished. He was pleased to see Dale looking annoyed over it, too.

"I didn't think of that," the inspector admitted. "I suppose it is possible."

"Who is at the top of your list?" Len challenged him.

"Foster," Dale surprised him by answering readily. "He is deeply uneasy over having investigators here at the college, clearly a man with something to hide, and he was the one to report the death. All too easy to kill the man and then pretend to have found the body. It would make it easier to explain any blood on him or any fingerprints left behind, too—all he would have to do is claim he tried to check for a pulse or picked up the murder weapon without thinking."

"Has he done that?" Maia asked with interest.

"No," Dale said with a wry twist to his mouth. "And we haven't found his fingerprints anywhere they shouldn't be, nor have we found the murder weapon yet, but he's still a good suspect."

"Perhaps we should find where he lives as well and investigate," Maia said to Len.

"Fair enough," Len agreed. "Better add Miss Linton to our

list as well."

They both looked at him.

"Why?" Maia asked. "You haven't said anything about suspecting her."

"I don't," Len answered. "I just don't like her."

"And that's a good enough reason to spy on her?" Dale said, his nostrils pinching together.

"Not under usual circumstances," Len said. "But here and now? I'll take whatever is offered. Goodness knows we're flailing in the dark. Any light is going to be helpful."

* * *

Miss Pelham lived in a flat out toward Grantchester Meadows, and Mr. Foster boarded only a few streets over from her. Miss Linton lived in the opposite direction, north toward Coton. While it might have made more sense for Maia and Len to split up, one to go north and one to go south, Len very carefully made no such suggestion, and he was pleased when even Maia's ruthlessly logical mind didn't come up with the solution, either.

"We'll simply have to tackle Miss Pelham's place and Mr. Foster's house first, and then work our way north," Maia said. "If we're looking for places they might have hidden Miss Carlyle along the route between their homes and the college, it makes sense to cover and re-cover our tracks anyway."

"Absolutely," Len agreed. "If we miss seeing something going south, we'll catch it going north."

They left the college through the back gate, as the porter's lodge was still closed and a policeman was still on duty at the front. Tom Wright let them through the back gate, scowling at Len the entire time, and not vouchsafing either of them a pleasant word or nod.

"Came an absolute cropper with that one," Len admitted once they were clear.

"We all make mistakes," Maia said generously.

It was dashed decent of her to gloss over it so smoothly, but Len couldn't forget the horror with which she had faced him after she thought he had wanted to show mercy to Tom because he thought Charlotte Carlyle was unlikeable, or the way he'd ruined the perfect trust they had shared because of his blundering.

"Got things a bit muddled in my head, I suppose. I know I disappointed you with the way I was flailing about, trying to get it all clear. Frightfully sorry and all that. I'm still trying to sort it all, but I won't inflict my tortuous thoughts on you again. Awfully good of you to still stand by me and my opinion on the murder even after that whole mess."

It wasn't the most polished of apologies, but dash it, a man couldn't throw himself to the ground, beating his breast and wailing his abject remorse these days.

"I believe I over-reacted as well," Maia said after a pause. "It is easier to see flaws in others than recognize them in oneself. I had no right to set myself up as better than you."

That was unexpected. Len wanted to ask what had caused her to come to that conclusion, but it was an awkward sort of question at the best of times, and with this new fragility between them, even more so now.

"I'd have said there was no question but that you're the better person by far," he said, striving for a light tone. "But it's generous of you to say that."

At last, she looked him in the eyes—the first time she had done so since the previous afternoon, Len realized—and smiled fully. "Thank you."

Things may not have been fully back to where they had been prior to arriving in Cambridge, and Len knew they would still have to come to a reckoning eventually over what their role was as detectives, but this was a step toward reconciliation, and he was glad they had been able to take it.

"Rather shattering about Miss Pelham, eh? If her alibi holds true, that's our best suspect gone," he said now.

Maia plunged her hands in her coat pockets and scowled at the cloudy sky. The weather had shifted overnight from golden autumn sunshine to clouds and the promise of rain, and with the wind picking up as well it was a mite chilly. Len was thankful for his good wool scarf Pippa and Cam had sent him from Scotland last Christmas. Aside from their own selves, only a few other hardy souls were out and about on the footpath.

"Every time we think we're moving forward, we find we're no closer to the truth," she said. "And poor Miss Carlyle is as absent as ever. We must be missing something, but what?"

"With any luck, we'll find that out today," Len said. "But I agree, there is something about this entire case that has felt askew from the start. As though we aren't asking the right questions, or looking in the right places ..."

"We wanted more interesting cases," Maia said, her lips curving upward ruefully. "We should be careful what we wish for."

"Indeed."

Aside from the cold wind and the gloom, it was a lovely walk toward Grantchester Meadows. Len wished yet again that they had been able to visit Cambridge on a different matter entirely from this case, so as to enjoy the ancient town more fully. He believed there was a tea house out this way as well as several pubs; a walk on a day like this would be all the more enjoyable if one were expecting a cozy cup of tea and a scone at the end, or a pint of cider and a ploughman's lunch.

The block of flats where Miss Pelham lived was astonishingly modern and expensive looking, all chromium and glass and angles. It looked horribly out of place surrounded as it was by brick and stone terraced housing, and seemed well out of reach for a secretary, even a head secretary such as Miss Pelham.

"By Jove!" Len exclaimed under his breath.

"What?" Maia said. She had been scanning the surrounding lanes and fields, presumably looking for places to hide a body, but her head whipped around at his exclamation.

"Embezzlement!" Len said triumphantly.

"Sorry?"

"What if our Miss Pelham's been embezzling from the college? What if the petty thefts have been to cover up the greater theft—if the embezzlement is discovered she can point to all the little thefts and say, 'there, see, we have had a thief in our midst all along,' and divert suspicion from herself. And then when Miss Carlyle comes along to inadvertently expose the plot, well ... naturally, she must go."

"But then wouldn't she want the thefts reported, if they are to be her alibi?" Maia said slowly.

Len shook his head. "No, because that would cause people to look into the matter too soon, and perhaps uncover the larger theft before she has taken what she wants. This way, they are there if she needs them, but small enough to be dismissed if nobody finds out about the embezzling."

"I must say, that does fit together quite nicely," Maia said. "Well done, Len!"

"We still need to prove it," Len warned. "And I've seen no sign of Miss Carlyle on our way here, have you?"

Maia shook her head. "No, but if we can get into the flat, perhaps that will change. How do you feel about a spot of breaking and entering?"

"My dear lady, I thought you'd never ask."

* * *

It ended up being a fairly tame breaking and entering—no breaking at all, merely entering. They loitered casually near the front door of the flats until a young matron left to go for her morning shopping. Len sprang forward as soon as she began to open the door, holding it open courteously for her so she didn't have to struggle with the heavy door and her cumbersome shopping basket, he explained with a dazzling smile. She was so charmed she didn't even notice that he continued holding the door open even after she left, enabling him and Maia to slip inside easily, where they could check the names on the board next to the stairwell to see which flat belonged to Miss Pelham.

"1B," Maia said, spotting it first.

"After you," Len said with a bow.

Up the stairs to the first floor, the second door down the hall, was 1B. Here, some breaking was required, as Miss Pelham conscientiously locked her door behind her when she left for the day. Len courteously stood back and let Maia go at the lock with her lockpicks.

"I say!" she said after a few moments.

"What's that?"

"Someone else has been having a go here. Look, you can see the scratches on the plate." She moved and let Len take her place.

He vented a low whistle. "So you can. Fairly fresh, too. Now, who do you think would be needing to break into Miss Pelham's flat aside from us?"

"Miss Carlyle?"

"It seems out of character for her, but if she had found that Miss Pelham was behind the threats and the thefts, could even someone as lacking in gumption as Miss Carlyle find the will to break in looking for evidence? I think so."

Maia gripped his arm. "Oh," she breathed. "*Oh.* Len, I've got it. I know what happened."

"What?" he urged. "Go on, what?"

"Miss Carlyle never came to the college at all that morning. Miss Pelham caught her here and imprisoned her. She crafted a magical *doppelgänger* to look like Miss Carlyle—you notice nobody spoke with her that morning—and then simply let it fade away as the day progressed."

"Oh, I say," Len said appreciatively. "That's dashed clever. Well done, old thing. That hits the nail whang on the crumpet, I should think. All that's left now is to go inside and look for the evidence."

He hoped very much that the evidence would not include Charlotte Carlyle's dead body, but at this point, he feared it was most likely. The expression that crossed Maia's face at his words indicated a similar mindset for her.

"Right," was all she said, as she bent back to her work.

A few more moments, and the lock was undone. Visibly

steeling herself, Maia put her hand on the doorknob and turned it, pushing the door inward and stepping through, Len on her heels.

No dead body awaited them. In fact, the flat appeared entirely innocuous at first glance—clean, polished, sparkling brightly, and empty of all personality and life. The modern chrome and leather furniture only enhanced the sterile feel of the place.

"I suppose it was too much to hope she kept Miss Carlyle tied and gagged in the entryway," Len said. "I'll take the kitchen and sitting room, if you want to do the bedroom and bath?" He would rather not have to paw through a woman's underthings unless he had to.

Maia accepted the division of labor with a brisk nod, and they set to work.

Len had only been at it a few minutes when he heard a cry from the bedroom.

"Oh—damn!"

He rushed to the other room, knowing that Maia had to be in dire straits before she would use such strong language. "What is it?" he blurted, before seeing she was unhurt, merely standing with a small notebook in her hand and an expression of thwarted fury on her face.

"We were wrong, wrong, wrong about everything," she spat out, thrusting the small red book at him. "Look at it!"

Len opened it and whistled softly as he read within its pages.

"Not embezzlement after all—blackmail," he said.

Written in small, black, pinched handwriting were the plain details of a marriage recorded at a church in France between one Gerald Foster and Hilde Dreher in 1916. Underneath the information was a list of sums—presumably paid by Mr.

Foster to keep the secret of his marriage to a German woman while the two nations were at war. They started out small and grew over time.

"No wonder Foster is so nervous," Len said. "He must be barely scraping by at this point."

"But Len, don't you see? If she's been blackmailing Foster, she's not the one behind the thefts, and there's no reason for her to threaten Charlotte Carlyle, or to kidnap her—unless Miss Carlyle discovered the blackmail and threatened to turn her in, but there was no hint of such a thing in the letter to Gwen, only worry over the thefts. And she can't be our murderer, either! We've uncovered a crime, yes, but not the one we need. And now what are we going to do about Miss Carlyle?"

"Not to mention, what are we going to do about this?" Len said, closing the book. "I know we ought to take it to Dale and let him sort it, but that would undoubtedly result in Foster losing his job at the very least. Not that there's anything wrong with having married a German during the War, but plenty of people would consider it unpatriotic, or even treacherous. After all, he wouldn't be paying out the blackmail if his conscience was clear. On the other hand, if we do nothing, Miss Pelham is free to continue her blackmail, and I'm reluctant to allow her to do that. But ultimately none of this is our business, so ought we really to poke our noses into it?"

"I'm glad to hear you ask that," said Mr. Foster himself, speaking softly from the front door.

Len spun on his heel, instinctively placing himself between Maia and the perceived threat, even before he saw the snub-nosed gun in Foster's hand.

"Now look here," he began, hoping he could bluff the fellow

into yielding. In a small space like this, it was hardly likely Foster could miss if he fired at them. "There's no need for violence."

"I agree," Foster said, entering further into the room and closing the door behind him. "If you just hand over that notebook and pretend you never saw any of this, we can all go our separate ways and no one needs to get hurt."

"What about Miss Pelham?" Maia asked, moving from behind Len to stand beside him. Inwardly, Len groaned. Of course she wouldn't stand back and let him protect her! Her willingness to face danger shoulder-to-shoulder with him was both one of the things he loved her for, and one of things that caused him the greatest agony.

Foster's smile was chilling. "As Mr. Davies said—that is none of your business."

Len caught the stubborn set of Maia's shoulders. As much as she might dislike Miss Pelham, and blackmailing in general, she would never stand by and let the woman be harmed.

There were only so many ways this situation could end, and none of them looked good.

Chapter 14

"You are pointing a gun at us, Mr. Foster," Maia stated. "I believe that makes it our business."

"Tell us about Hilde," Len said suddenly beside her. Maia spared him a glance. Was he really that curious, that he needed to know about Foster's German wife here and now? Or was he up to something else?

"Don't say her name!" Foster spat, his grip tightening on the revolver.

Len held his hands out away from his body, palms up. "I only thought, if we knew more about the situation, it might make it easier for us to hold our tongues. We'd like to understand your point of view."

This was not the time to insist on righteousness and truth at all costs, though Maia's lips tightened all the same.

"I couldn't fight, you know," Foster said in a rush. "I wanted to, but my eyes—they wouldn't take me. I have to take a healer's potion regularly or I wouldn't be able to see a thing, and the rules against using magic to aid in the war effort meant I wasn't allowed to do that. When I tried to enlist, the board rejected me as being mostly blind—which I am, without the potion. But since in everyday life I can take the potion and get by with only spectacles, it looked to the average person like I was a shirker. Most people thought of me as a conchie and treated me like dirt. I even had some ladies send me white feathers. My fiancée broke things off with me, said she couldn't be seen with someone who looked like a coward." He stopped and pushed his spectacles up his nose with the forefinger of his free hand.

Despite herself, Maia felt a pang of sympathy for him. What a dreadful situation to find oneself in, and to be unable to explain!

"Finally, I volunteered as an ambulance driver, as the powers that be in the Circle determined that wouldn't be as likely to upset the balance of the war as much as a magic-using soldier might. That's where I met Hilde."

"In France?" Len's voice was skeptical; Maia couldn't blame him. What would a German woman be doing in war-torn France?

"She was—fleeing. From her own people. I couldn't understand everything—she only spoke German, and I only spoke English and French, but I gathered that her family was trying to marry her off to a wealthy man much older than herself, and she was afraid ..." Foster trailed off. "I know it sounds impossible, something out of the Middle Ages! Whether you believe it or not is irrelevant; the point is that I believed her. I fell in love at once, and offered to marry her for her own safety. She agreed, and we found an old French priest who was mostly daft and didn't care who either of us were."

"And?" Len prompted. "What happened then?"

Foster laughed bitterly. "Nothing. She got ill the night after we married and was dead by the end of the week. I never knew whether she had been telling me the truth or if she was a German spy and I merely the dupe who fell for her lies. What did it matter? I loved her, and she was dead."

The words hung in the air, weighted with desolation.

I loved her, and she was dead. Not all the poets together could fathom a lament more tragic.

Foster sighed. Through the entire tale, despite his emotion, his hand had not wavered.

Maia had not been idle during the story either, though. She had not yet mastered the 12th century spell she and Len had spoken of earlier, but she was certain that by implementing Len's advice she could make it work, and was setting it up in her head even now..

"How did Miss Pelham get a hold of the information?" Len asked. Maia didn't know if he guessed what she was doing and was buying her time to prepare, or if he was planning something of his own. She knew him to be perfectly capable of throwing himself in the path of a bullet if by doing so he could save another person's life. She didn't intend to give him the chance.

"I don't know," Foster said, his shoulders slumped. "She went to France last year on holiday, and when she came back she began holding the information over my head. I had to pay! I would have lost everything if the story had come out. The sneers and scorn were bad enough when people thought I was a conchie; imagine what it would have been like if the world learned I had refused to fight *and* had married a German woman while we were at war. Nobody would have believed her story, they would either think I was a traitor or a fool. I would have lost my job, people's respect, everything. What could I do but pay?

"Then you lot came, poking and prying into everybody's business. I thought that the Carlyle business was a ruse. I assumed Pelham was blackmailing others as well and one of them had come to you for help. I was both hopeful that you would stop her, and terrified you would discover my secret. Then Appleby died and I didn't know what to think. Pelham may be many things, but she's no murderer."

He pushed his spectacles back up his nose again.

"I tried breaking in here a couple of days ago, but couldn't get the lock undone. I was coming back to try my luck again today when I saw you two sneak in. I waited until you came up and into the flat—I saw you through the curtains—and then came up after you to see if you'd found the book. And you did. And now I want it."

"What if I say no?" Len asked, still holding the little book securely in his hand.

Foster's face hardened. "I don't want to shoot you," he said. "But I will if I have to. Not to kill—I'm no murderer, either. But it will hurt, I promise you that, and I will get that book."

Len glanced at Maia. She nodded, hoping he understood what she meant. He returned the gesture and turned back to Foster.

"No."

There was a moment of blank shock from Foster, just time enough for Maia to gather her magic and thoughts together in one fierce rush. Then, as Foster's finger pressed the trigger, Maia shouted,

"*Conjunctim contexere!*"

The air before her and Len shimmered and hardened into a barrier in an instant. Len flung out a hand and rumbled a hurried spell; the bullet struck the shield, ricocheted off, altered its path mid-flight, and buried itself in Foster's leg.

The mathematician shrieked and crumpled to the floor,

dropping the gun. Maia ended the shield spell, breathing heavily, and darted forward to scoop up the weapon, training it on Foster.

"I doubt he'll try anything else," she said. "But I'll keep an eye on him while you phone Inspector Dale."

"Must we phone him?" Len grumbled.

Maia didn't want to take her eyes off Foster even long enough to throw an exasperated glare at Len, so she settled for letting the exasperation fill her voice. "I know you don't like him, but honestly Len, what else can we do? We can't just let him go. He tried to shoot us. And we have to stop Miss Pelham from blackmailing anyone else, even if it means exposing Mr. Foster's secret. This isn't a matter of principle, it's simply practical at this point."

"I agree," Len said, surprising her. "I just wish I didn't have to speak to Dale."

Maia huffed a faint laugh.

"You'll ruin me," Foster snarled between clenched teeth, his hands wrapped around his bleeding leg. Maia thought she ought to get him a towel to stem the bleeding, but that would have to wait until Len was done with the telephone.

"You made your choices, Mr. Foster," she said now. "You have no business complaining when you reap the consequences of those choices."

This glib response, as easily as it came to her lips, though, didn't sound as right to her ears as usual. Did they have the right to drag his secrets into the light? What was their responsibility?

This was what Len had been trying to get at before, only she had misunderstood him. Of course! He wasn't dismissing Miss Carlyle's claims on justice because she was drab and unlikeable.

He wasn't questioning the need for justice—only asking what their role in it ought to be.

Maia didn't have the answers to that problem, but she felt much lighter all at once now that she understood what Len had been getting at.

Still, as she had told him, it was a matter of practicality at this point. Perhaps she and Len could wrangle the matter out over tea and crumpets by his fireplace when they were back in London. In the meantime, they could only keep moving forward on this path as best they could.

She still wished he hadn't brought Miss Carlyle's personality into the argument, but that was hardly relevant at this moment.

Len came back into the sitting room, carrying a towel without her even needing to ask for it. He knelt by Foster, avoiding the man's weak swing, and wrapped the towel around the wounded leg. Maia wondered if she ought to offer to switch places, given her VAD training, but Len had enough practical experience with injuries that he managed to stem the bleeding just fine on his own.

"You could have let the bullet hit a wall," Foster wheezed.

"That would have left you free to shoot again. While I was certain Miss Whitney's shield was up to however many bullets you cared to fire at us, I did not wish to put her to the trouble of maintaining it that long. This was the simplest way of forcing you to yield. I won't apologize—it's no worse than what you intended for us." Len met and held the other man's eyes. "Don't think I didn't notice you were aiming for Miss Whitney, not me. You should be thankful I directed the bullet toward your leg and nowhere worse."

* * *

"We can arrest Foster on the charge of attempted violence against Miss Whitney, and we might be able to arrest Miss Pelham under the Larceny Act of 1916, but that's considerably trickier," Inspector Dale told them. "If Foster continues to refuse to press charges, we won't be able to do much of anything to her, I'm afraid."

"I, however, can," said the Magistra. "And you may be certain that I will." Her face was set like stone.

Inspector Dale and his team had arrived quickly in response to Len's phone call. They bandaged Foster's leg properly and took him into custody, after which Dale returned to the college and took Miss Pelham into custody as well. Maia hadn't seen the woman escorted off the grounds, but the rumors were already spreading about how she attempted to curse everyone around her until the Magistra put a magic-dampening spell on her. Maia was taking that one with several grains of salt.

Now Maia, Len, Inspector Dale, and the Magistra were seated in the latter's study discussing the events of the morning. Maia rather wished they could move on from it—she and Len still had Miss Linton's home to search, not to mention the need to search the river—but she understood the Magistra's need to know exactly what sort of viper she had inadvertently nursed in her bosom here.

"The blackmail was appalling enough," she went on. "But what you have told me about her attempt to utterly dominate the secretarial staff! The way she interfered even with the other staff! Utterly shocking. I hold myself partially to blame, of course. I ought to have known more of what was happening in my domain."

"A leader has to trust that the people under him or her will be doing their job properly, and not constantly checking," Len said. "Unless someone were to tell you specifically that there was a problem, you had no way of knowing."

It sounded as though he were speaking from personal experience. Maia wondered what that story was.

"Nonetheless, a leader must also accept responsibility for acts done under their leadership," the Magistra replied. "It seems clear to me now that even if Miss Pelham was not directly responsible for Charlotte's disappearance and Appleby's death, the atmosphere of repression and secrecy that she spread amongst the staff had a hand in it. Had Charlotte felt herself able to come to me about the thefts and the threatening letters she received, none of this might have happened." She drank from her teacup and then continued.

"Miss Pelham will of course be sacked without a reference, and furthermore I intend to use whatever influence I have to see to it she is shunned from all respectable magical work. Let her spread her poison in other communities, if they will have her. I will keep her out of ours."

Seated across from Maia, Len opened his mouth, closed it again, and silently drank his tea.

Inspector Dale nodded. "Quite right. And we will keep an eye on her as well. If she tries her tricks again, she'll be caught." He shifted in his seat to face Maia. "I wish I had been there to see your shield spell, Miss Whitney! A thoroughly tricky piece of magic working, and from what Mr. Davies tells us, you performed it magnificently."

For once, Maia didn't blush at his compliment; she was still distracted by thinking of Mr. Foster and Miss Pelham. "Thank you," she said. "I should tell you, though, Inspector, that I don't intend to press charges against Mr. Foster. He ought not to have fired, of course, but he was driven to desperation. He has been punished enough; let it rest."

"As you wish," Dale said, looking disappointed. Len, however, sent her a pleased smile across the table. Only then did Maia realize she had just done the exact same thing on a smaller scale that Len had wanted to do with Tom Wright. She excused Mr. Foster's wrongdoing because of what had driven him to that place, and decided his punishment was sufficient even though strict justice ought perhaps to demand more.

Oh, why was everything so complicated? What had happened to simply solving mysteries and leaving the consequences up to the authorities? She hated this constant questioning of her motives and actions.

Maia had always known her duty, from the time she was young. Had she been born fifty years earlier, she likely would have accepted a dull but socially acceptable marriage without question, knowing it was what was expected of the eldest daughter of an English gentleman.

Thankfully, she'd been born in more modern times. Her duty had instead consisted of keeping the family home running smoothly despite her mother's tendencies toward hysterics and dramatic scenes, and her sisters' uncanny abilities to alienate the staff. It wasn't until her discovery of magic that she escaped the net of familial responsibilities. Even that hadn't changed her sense of duty, merely redirected it.

Only since arriving at Cambridge, duty hadn't seemed so clear-cut, nor was it as reassuring as it used to be. Even justice seemed to be getting muddled. It wasn't because of Len's struggles, either; those had perhaps been the catalyst for Maia's unrest, but she certainly had plenty of experience in knowing her own mind even when her nearest and dearest stood against her. No, this tumult was her own, shared with Len, but not caused by him.

"If Foster is not to be charged, that leaves it up to me whether I keep him on here or not," Dr. Bingham said with a sigh. "He is an excellent mathematics tutor, and I don't wish to hold it against him that he was blackmailed, but the act of violence cannot be condoned, nor do I feel entirely comfortable not knowing what it is Miss Pelham was holding against him, and if it is something with which I should be concerned." She looked from Len to Maia. "Neither of you feel inclined to share still?"

"No," Maia said firmly.

"But I give you my word of honor it was nothing that would give you cause to ask him to leave your employ," Len added. He had kept Miss Pelham's book in his possession, refusing to turn it over to the police unless they absolutely needed it—which was unlikely, since Foster refused to press charges. Neither he nor Maia felt inclined to expose not only Foster, but Miss Pelham's other victims, to public censure and disgrace.

"I shall have to think it over," the Magistra said.

Anything more that she might have said was lost when the door to the study was flung open, revealing a disheveled Gwen with Betsy peeping over her shoulder with scandalized eyes.

"Apologies, Magistra, I couldn't stop her," Betsy blurted while Gwen was still catching her breath.

Maia was on her feet without being aware of it. Something had to be dreadfully wrong for Gwen to look so wild.

"Never mind, Betsy. Gwen, what is it?" the Magistra asked.

Gwen gulped in a few breaths of air, and finally managed to speak.

"I was—searching the college for any hidden rooms or magically-created hiding spots—and I was in Miss Linton's supervision room—there's a cupboard tucked in the wall that I thought might have been magically enhanced to be made larger, large enough to hide Lottie—so I opened it—started pulling things out—and I found—I found—"

Inspector Dale was on his feet now as well. "What?" he barked. "Did you find Miss Carlyle's body?"

Gwen shook her head. Len came over to her and put a gentle hand on her arm. "Easy does it," he said, his deep voice a comforting rumble. "Go ahead and tell us in your own words."

Gwen closed her eyes, then reopened them and faced everyone with restored calm. "I found Appleby's walking stick, hidden deep in the back of the cupboard. His heavy blackthorn that he never went anywhere without? It was there—and the top of it was smeared with what looks like dried blood."

Dale was out of the study in a flash, shouting for his men and running for the nearest door to the outside.

Maia sat back down, stunned.

Miss Linton?

She hadn't taken Len seriously when he said he suspected the irascible teacher. Apparently she should have.

Len had left the room when Dale did, but returned now with a tumbler of water for Gwen. After handing it to her and making sure her hands were steady enough to hold it without it falling to the floor, he sat down in the chair next to Maia's.

"I suppose that solves the case," he said.

"The murder case, at any rate," Maia answered. "We still don't know where Miss Carlyle is."

"True." Len drummed his fingers on the table. "I don't like it. It feels too convenient."

"Convenient? We've been running about chasing our tails for three days now!"

"I know, but …" Len shook his head. "It doesn't feel right."

"It must have been Miss Linton, though," Gwen said, her voice calmer now but still subdued. "The Inspector dashed out too quickly for me to say anything, but wrapped around the stick was Miss Archer's scarf, the one that went missing. It was torn and stained, but I recognized it."

"Torn?" Maia asked. "A hole at one end? Is the scarf orange and brown, with geometric patterns?"

"Yes—how did you know?"

Maia looked at Len. "I don't understand," she said. "I *saw* that scarf—that's the one that was hanging in Miss Carlyle's room the day we investigated it."

While they stared in mutual incomprehension at each other, Betsy came back into the room. Len automatically rose to his feet as she neared. She bobbed a quick curtsey.

"Begging your pardon, sir and miss, but a messenger brought you a note earlier. They gave it to young Tom, but he gave it to me because he thought I'd be more likely to see you before he did." She pulled a crumpled piece of paper out of her apron pocket and passed it to Len.

"Thank you, Betsy," he said. He checked the signature, and his eyebrows raised. "It's from Mrs. Hawkins, Miss Carlyle's landlady. I wonder how she knew where to send it?"

"There's an address most folk connected to the college use to collect post, and then a messenger who knows about us gathers it up and brings it to us," Betsy piped up.

"Well?" said Maia. Normally she would have been fascinated by these details, but now she was more impatient to know what the note said. Wouldn't it be wonderful to find out that all their worry and fear for Miss Carlyle had been for nothing, that she had merely hidden herself away and was now back safely?

It wasn't likely, but it would be lovely.

Len handed her the note, his brow furrowed. "Read it for yourself."

Dear Miss Whitney and Mr. Davies,

A most peculiar thing happened yesterday evening. I went to get down my favorite cookery book from the top shelf where it belongs, except it wasn't there. I always keep it there, always, but I searched around my entire kitchen, and even looked in the sitting room and all the bedrooms in case someone borrowed it without asking, but it isn't anywhere to be found. I know it isn't anywhere near as important as Miss Carlyle being missing and all, but it is peculiar, and I thought I ought to mention it.

Yours truly,

Layla Hawkins.

"How strange!" Maia exclaimed.

"She's probably just misplaced it, except from the sounds of it, that's not plausible," Len said.

"And she's probably right that it has nothing to do with Miss Carlyle, but it is still an odd coincidence that a missing book should show up—or rather not show up—at the same time as a missing person," Maia agreed. "Especially on top of the scarf having been there, and now here."

Even if Miss Linton were the murderer, this case was still far from over.

Chapter 15

"One of us should go back to visit Mrs. Hawkins and see what we can find out about her missing book," Maia said. "Someone else should stay here and see if Inspector Dale can persuade Miss Linton to tell us what she did with Miss Carlyle. And don't you think you ought to check in on Becket? I haven't seen him since he brought me supper while we were working on the bloodhound spell."

Len hadn't realized his manservant had done that, but it didn't surprise him. Becket was always thoughtful, and he was especially conscientious toward Maia.

"Jolly good," he said. "I'll find Becket. Do you want to go to Mrs. Hawkins'?"

Maia lowered her voice, glancing toward where Gwen still sat with glassy eyes and a horrified expression. "I do, but I'm not sure it's fair to leave Gwen here with all this. She was so shaken by the discovery of Mr. Appleby's walking stick ... I think it might be better for her to get away from the college for a bit."

Len nodded. "Good thinking."

He still felt a small pinprick of jealousy when thinking about Maia and Dale working cheek by jowl, so to speak, but it didn't gnaw anywhere near so deeply as it had earlier that morning.

He wasn't entirely certain if that was because he and Maia seemed to be regaining their old rapport, or if his better self was getting the upper hand, but either way, he was pleased.

He was going to need to tell Maia soon about his estate difficulties. He would have done it already, except events kept getting out of hand and taking away any opportunity to talk about personal affairs. She deserved to know that he was going to have to leave London, leave *them*, for an undetermined period of time.

He hated feeling that he was letting her down. Though she would understand and even applaud his devotion to his responsibilities, he still felt like a cad, promising to stand by her side and make something worthwhile of their detective business, only to bow out after a mere six months. He intended to return, naturally, but who knew what would happen in the time he was gone? She might decide she needed a new partner, or even decide she preferred to work alone.

No matter what happened in the future, their idyllic interlude of these last few months was going to be gone forever.

And that was enough of *that* line of thinking, or he'd grow impossibly maudlin.

Maia had already begun to walk back toward the door. Len hastened to follow her, then stopped, realizing one of them had to tell Gwen what was happening now, and what they wanted her to do. He retraced his steps and sat down in the chair next to the one their junior partner was occupying.

"Better?" he asked sympathetically.

Gwen glanced quickly at him, then looked back out the window. "I'm sorry for falling to pieces like that," she said stiffly. "I'll be fine if you want to go with Maia to be there when they—when they arrest her."

Despite the misleading pronoun, Len understood that she was referring to the arrest of Miss Linton, not of Maia. He knew firsthand how difficult it could be to speak someone's name after they had betrayed everything one once believed about them.

Even if Gwen hadn't been particularly fond of Miss Linton, she would still have naturally held the woman in high regard by virtue of her position in the college, if nothing else. Accepting that she was capable of murder would take some time.

"Actually I'm going to see if I can pry Becket away from the library," he said now. No sense in probing at Gwen's fresh wound by showing too much sympathy. "I wondered if you'd be willing to pay a visit to Mrs. Hawkins for us. We had a rather odd note from her just now, and we could use some more information." He carefully did not add, "if you're up to it," as that would sound dreadfully condescending. Far better to behave as though he assumed naturally Gwen would be up for anything, despite the blow that had fallen.

Her forehead creased as she finally looked away from the window and met his eyes. "What sort of an odd note?" she asked, with suspicion in her voice, as though she thought he was making it up to give her something to do.

Which he might have done, if he thought it necessary, but thankfully that was not the case. He silently handed over the note, and waited while she read it. When she finished, she looked back at him with her eyebrows raised.

"I don't understand," she said.

"Exactly," Len said. "All the other thefts took place here at the college, and before your friend, er, vanished. Why would something go missing from Miss Carlyle's boarding house, and why now?"

"Can't you just ask Miss Linton?" Gwen asked, and she managed the name with only the slightest of hitches. Len was proud of the effort she was making.

"Possibly. No guarantee Dale will allow us to question her ourselves, though, or that he will think a missing cookery book of enough importance to ask her himself. Plus, to be honest with you … something about this still doesn't seem right. I still feel as though we're looking at things the wrong way around, only I don't know how. You finding the stick seems to point clearly to Miss Linton, and goodness knows I had my suspicions of her from the beginning, but all the same …" Len trailed off, not entirely sure what he was attempting to say. "I think we need more information," he finished more firmly.

It was the same thing they had all been saying throughout this entire case, and yet it was as true now as it had been the moment they alighted at the Cambridge station. How could they have learned so much and yet still know so little?

Gwen shook her head. "I doubt it will make a difference, but I'll go," she said. "After all, you're the boss," she added in her best attempt at a hard-boiled American accent.

Len laughed, wondering where on earth she had learned such a thing. "Maia's the boss, not I, and heaven help anyone who forgets that."

That task accomplished, he left the room to pursue his original goal: hunt down his mysteriously missing manservant and discover what clues he had dug up while the rest of them were having adventures.

"So long as he hasn't vanished as well," Len muttered to himself as he began his search.

He had reason to be thankful the college grounds were so

small; it didn't take him long before he found Becket holed up in the library, still.

"Great Scott," Len began in a subdued undertone, looking at the books spread across the small wooden table Becket was sitting at. Becket himself was as disheveled as Len had ever seen him, his eyes rimmed with red, his hair sticking up on end, his tie crooked and his cuffs askew.

"I was about to come find you, sir," Becket interrupted, also most unusually. Len gathered that this was serious, and forbore to ask any questions.

"The stolen items," Becket continued, pulling the list out from where it was buried underneath three books and several sheets of scribbled notes. "They were to create a memory potion."

"What?" Len said, forgetting to modulate his voice. Across the room, Gardiner raised his head from his work at the front desk and sent a mild glare in Len's direction. Len bobbed his head apologetically and turned back to Becket.

"What did you say?" he repeated, taking care to keep his voice barely above a whisper.

"Look." Becket handed him the list of stolen items, now annotated in his handwriting.

Red lipstick (Lily Jamison, secretary) **-carmine**
  Linen handkerchief (Marjorie Cooper, secretary) **-linen thread**
  Fountain pen (Gerald Foster, mathematics) **-silver**
  Powder compact (Sally Linton, student) **-talc**
  Silk scarf (Dolly Archer, chemistry) **-silk threads**
  Carved wooden bear (Robert Robertson, student) **-pear wood**
  Umbrella (Elaine Green, secretary) **-ivory (handle)**
  Garnet and gold bracelet (Leah Fischer, secretary) **-garnet**

Ink bottle (Stephen Gardiner, librarian). **–copper oxide**

Len looked up from the paper to meet Becket's eyes. This was a tremendous discovery. "I say, old man, however did you hit on this?"

"Something about the stolen items rang a bell for me," answered Becket. "But I couldn't put my finger on it. I studied potions extensively before coming to work with you for MI, as my spell-casting abilities even then were better suited to household spells, nothing bigger. Thanks to that background I did begin to wonder if there was a potion one could make from the various items on the list. I tried many different combinations," waving diffidently at the notes covering the table, "but it wasn't until I started thinking like an agent again that it came to me."

"Of course!" It wasn't that long that Len had been telling Maia about memory potions, and how all MI agents were trained in how to recognize them by smell—in Miss Carlyle's rooms, in fact, as he was sniffing her sleep potion.

Len sucked air in through his teeth. A sleep potion? Or …

He gripped his head with both hands, as though he could physically wrestle his thoughts into submission.

"Nothing about this case has made sense from the start," he muttered. "What if that was deliberate, not us being obtuse?"

"Sir?"

Len didn't respond. He closed his eyes, trying to fit the pieces together properly, seeing things as they really were, not as they seemed to be.

Two plus two equaling five. That's what this case had felt like. But two plus two *had* to equal four; it was an incontrovertible fact of the universe. They'd been looking at this case upside down and inside out from the beginning.

"It's not quite there," he said. "There's still one thread missing. The cookery book. Why the cookery book?"

It was Becket's turn to gasp. Len opened his eyes.

"What's that?"

"What cookery book, sir?"

Len explained about the missing book. Becket's voice shook when he replied, his hand stretched out over the tomes on the table.

"That was the other part of what I wanted to tell you, sir. When I thought of the memory potion, I wanted to double-check my memory of the ingredients, as it had been such a scant part of our training. There are so few books containing that information, though, that I wasn't sure if I would be able to do so without contacting the old potion master from MI—you remember him, of course."

Roger Bellamy, short of stature and of patience. He'd had little time for Len's slapdash way of learning potions, but likely would have gotten along far better with the careful and neat-fingered Becket.

"Then I thought of the Merriman Collection, and I thought that if the potion recipe was written anywhere, it would be in one of those books. I gained permission from Mr. Gardiner to inspect the books, and found this."

He pointed to a book bound in red, just like the ones Gardiner had shown Len the other day. Dull gold leaf lettering spelled out the words *Potions and Philters*.

"And that's where you found the recipe?" Len asked, unsure of how this connected to the missing cookery book.

Becket shook his head. "Pick it up, sir."

Wondering, Len did so, and frowned. Something about it

didn't sit right in his hand … as though it wasn't actually the size or weight it seemed like it ought to be.

"Open it," Becket said.

Len did so—and the final piece fell into place.

For on the frontspiece before him were the words:

A Practical Dictionary of Cookery.

"It's a glamour spell." Becket's voice sounded as though it was coming from a long way off. "I showed it to Mr. Gardiner, and he said it was likely a prank by one of the students, and he would give them what-for when he found out who had done it. But it didn't seem likely to me to have been a prank, not when combined with everything else that has happened."

"No," Len said, his own voice thick. "It's not a prank. It's the answer."

"The answer to what, sir?"

"To everything," Len replied. "Becket, you didn't hide Mr. Appleby's mugs, did you?"

"The mugs, sir? No. I never even saw them. Why?"

Appleby's misplaced mugs—the potion—everyone's insistence that nobody would want to harm Charlotte, because nobody cared enough about her to do so—the missing logbook—the clues pointing to Miss Pelham—the walking stick hidden in a place pointing to Miss Linton—the timing of the thefts—the lack of physical evidence left on the bridge after the attack on Miss Carlyle—the result from Maia's bloodhound spell—Tom's story—by Jove, yes, of course, *Tom's story*, that was where it had all begun, only he was too much of a fool to see it!

"It was all right there in front of us the entire time," he said at last into Becket's expectant silence. "But we couldn't see it because we only saw what we expected to see."

"Yes, sir," Becket answered. "Would you care to elaborate on that, sir?"

"Yes, but it's only fair to collect Maia and Gwen first—oh, Gwen's not going to like this, and neither is Maia, come to think of it—" Len winced, remembering the argument he and Maia had had. No, Maia wasn't going to be happy about this at all.

His fingertips suddenly tingled. "Wait!"

His voice was too loud again, and this time Gardiner actually left the desk and approached them. Len paid him no attention.

"No, there's no time," he said, standing up in a hurry. "We've got to move, *now*."

"Really, Mr. Davies, this is a library, you know," Gardiner said in a threatening whisper, looming over Len. "People are trying to study! We can't have all this disturbance."

Len whirled on him. "You—can you take orders? Even if they don't make sense? Even if it goes against your sense of chivalry?"

"What—?" Gardiner began.

Len pinned him in place with his gaze. "No dithering, man. Can you?"

"Yes," Gardiner answered. "I was a soldier, after all. What's all this about?"

"I'll explain on the way," he said, turning and leading the way out of the library.

"On the way where?" Gardiner complained, following through the glass-fronted doors. "I can't just leave my post!"

"You can if you want to help me stop a murderer," Len said grimly. "Becket—find Inspector Dale and Maia, tell them to follow us to the train station as fast as they can. There's no time to lose."

"Very good, sir," Becket said, and slipped away without

another word.

"I don't understand any of this," Gardiner muttered, but he followed after Len anyway, out the gate and onto the streets of Cambridge.

"A little over a mile and a half," Len said. "We'd better run."

"I'm better at rugger than running," Gardiner warned, but he began a heavy jog that kept him at Len's heel all the same.

Len's mind raced faster than his feet. The stick—of course, it was planted to distract attention! If it hadn't been Miss Linton it would have been someone else; it wasn't about her, it was about getting away. While everyone's focus was on the supposed murderer, the real murderer intended to slip away and escape. Not in an automobile, no—too easy to trace, plus he doubted the murderer could drive. No, far simpler to go by train, ending up who-knew-where. London first, most likely, and from there, anywhere.

At least Gardiner had stopped talking. Len could check over his conclusions and make sure they were solid. He turned them all over and over in his mind, trying to see if there was any other way he could make everything fit.

Nothing else made sense of every piece. His solution was the only thing that turned the kaleidoscope of jumbled shapes and colors into an actual picture. He wished he liked the picture better, but wishing didn't change the way things were.

Perhaps it was just as well he was going to have to take a leave of absence from the detective agency. After this, Maia would likely never want to speak to him again.

Still, it had to be done.

Coe Fen passed in a blur. Len's legs began to feel heavy, his breathing labored. Dash it, he ought to be in better training than this! What was a mile and a half to run, even if he was wearing the wrong shoes?

A screech of tires on the road—he glanced up at the shout.

"Get in, Davies!"

Len blinked, and the image became clear. It was the college's auto, with Tom at the wheel, Dale, his sergeant, Maia, and Becket piled in.

"Thank goodness," huffed Gardiner, and threw himself into the rear seat. Len followed, still bemused.

"Motorcar," he managed, as Tom threw it into the right gear and they tore off again. "I didn't think of that."

"You know who the murderer is?" Maia shouted in his ear.

Len nodded, still trying to catch his breath.

"Who is it?" Dale yelled over his shoulder.

Len shook his head. "You won't believe me—have to see it for yourself. Maia! Can you cast the bloodhound spell again as soon as we reach the station?"

Maia looked started. "Yes, of course: now that the parameters have been set it's an easy matter to recast. But why? It's useless."

"I'm not so sure about that," Len answered.

"*What?*" Maia asked, but there was no time to answer: they were at the station.

Tom put the auto into park, and the rest of them disembarked in a flurry of limbs.

"What are we looking for, Davies?" Dale demanded. "And don't give me any nonsense about not believing you!"

Len's eyes flickered over the crowds of people waiting for the next train to London, but he couldn't see the form he was looking for.

"The spell, Maia," he urged.

"*Idem inveniet,*" Maia said. She blinked suddenly. "Oh!"

"What is it?" Dale asked, at the same time that Len asked, "Where is it?"

"There," Maia said, answering Len and pointing to a tall, stately woman dressed peculiarly for this time of year in a mink coat. "She's surrounded by a mauve cloud." She caught her breath, clearly coming to the same realization Len had. "Oh no," she said. "On Len, surely not."

"I'm sorry," he told her, then nodded at Gardiner. "She'll do anything in her power to escape, both magical and non," he said. "We'll take her together."

Gardiner opened his mouth, then closed it again, perhaps recalling his promise to follow orders without question.

"Right," he said.

"What on earth—" Dale began. Len ignored him.

It wasn't that he didn't think he could trust Dale, or was trying to steal the glory of the capture for himself—it was more that if there was the slightest chance still that he was mistaken, he didn't want to have the blame fall on the police's shoulders. Far better he should be taken for a delusional fool than that the police should bear the charge of having harassed an innocent woman.

He and Gardiner wove through the crowd, splitting up so they could approach the woman from both sides. Her eyes passed calmly over Len—of course, she'd never seen him before—but when she saw Gardiner, she gasped, and took to her heels.

"Now!" roared Len, and he and Gardiner leapt forward as one and pinned the woman in place, holding her arms fast even as she squirmed and writhed to escape.

"How dare you!" she shrieked. "Unhand me!"

Len, assisted ably by Gardiner, dragged her out of the crowd, many of whom were beginning to cast dark glances his way, and some of whom even began to move as though they would stop them.

"Help, help!" the woman shouted. "They're assaulting me!"

Before things could turn ugly—or uglier—Maia stepped up to the rescue, even as Becket joined Len and Gardiner and, with an apologetic look, cast a silencing spell around her, so that her voice was inaudible to anyone but herself.

"I am so sorry," Maia said to the crowd in general in her clear, well-bred voice. "My sister, you know. I'm afraid she's had a brain fever. We're trying to get her back home so the doctor can help."

Maia's air of command, as well as her obvious status as an upper class woman, turned matters. The people who had been about to pull Gardiner and Len off the woman now sent them sympathetic glances, while everyone else turned aside, embarrassed to be witnessing such an unpleasant incident.

The men dragged the woman to the motorcar despite her kicking, clawing, and thrashing, and held her in place against its side. Dale was red-faced with suppressed fury.

"Who is this?" he demanded. "Are you trying to tell me that this stranger is behind everything? Impossible!"

"Not a stranger," Len said. "This is Charlotte Carlyle."

With his words, the glamour she had been using to disguise her true face fell apart, and she stood revealed before them all at last: a dowdy, dumpy young woman Len wouldn't have looked twice at if he had passed her in the street.

She threw one wild glance around and began to cry. Len nodded at Becket, who reluctantly released the silencing spell.

"Oh, help me, officer!" Miss Carlyle wailed at Dale, her nose turning red and blotchy as if on cue. "I've been in terror of my life! I know I shouldn't have tried to hide and run away, but I was so frightened! Once I managed to escape from Miss Linton, I only wanted to get away so I could feel safe! I was going to write once I was someplace secure and tell you everything. I know it was wrong of me, but please, don't be angry! Haven't you ever been afraid for your life? No, I can tell you haven't been, but that's because you're so big and strong. Imagine what it would be like to be little old me, though? I'm no match for Miss Linton in either magic or physical strength. What else could I do but try to escape?"

Dale blinked, as though stunned. "Is that true?" he asked, seemingly of all them together. "Is that why you brought us here, Davies, to stop her so we could have a witness against the Linton woman? But why make it sound like we were after the murderer?"

"A murderer!" Miss Carlyle's voice rose to a shrill scream. Len saw Maia sigh and wave a hand while murmuring in Latin, and realized that she'd encased them in a bubble of not-noticing. Their conversation would sound like a barely audible murmur to anyone outside their little group now. He thought about it for a moment, and then joined a modified version of his chameleon spell to hers.

Now not only would their voices be indistinct, their appearance would be vague as well. Unless someone had a reason to look directly at them, a person's eyes would slide right over them and onto something else as he or she passed by.

It was trickier to maintain a spell of this sort on a larger number of people than one or two, and Len had to keep most of his attention on maintaining it, meaning he couldn't focus on answering Dale's question plainly.

"Could we talk about this back at the college?" he gritted

out.

Miss Carlyle's voice rose in a wail again. "Oh, don't make me go back there, Inspector Dale! Not until that horrible woman is in jail and I know I'm safe! And maybe not even then—I spent so long in that cupboard, hoping for someone to find me, but no one ever did, until I was finally able to slip out and get away. I don't want to go back there, please don't make me!"

Dale scratched the back of his neck. "Well …" he began helplessly.

"Miss Carlyle," Maia said, her voice cold and clear, like ice on a winter's pond. "You were in that cupboard the entire time you were missing?"

Miss Carlyle pouted. "Yes, and not one of you found me! Didn't care enough to look, I suppose." Her voice sharpened with spite.

"And being in that cupboard, you naturally were not aware of anything that was happening in the rest of the college?"

A wary look flashed into Miss Carlyle's watery brown eyes, so brief that Len would have missed it if he hadn't been half expecting it to appear. "I knew when Miss Linton killed poor Mr. Appleby," she said. "She thrust that horrible stick she'd used to do the deed into the cupboard with me and gloated about it. She said she was going to do the same to me just as soon as she had the chance."

"There's our eyewitness statement," Dale said, but Maia overrode his voice.

"Then *how did you know this man was Inspector Dale?*"

Fear flickered back into Miss Carlyle's face. "I—I—one of you said it," she stammered. "Or Miss Linton used his name when she came to gloat. Or—I don't know, stop trying to confuse me!"

"You know it," Maia said, her voice quieter now but no less ruthless, "because you were never in that cupboard. You were never kidnapped. Your life was never in danger." She looked at Inspector Dale. "Miss Linton isn't the murderer. Miss Carlyle is."

"What?" Dale gasped, in unison with his sergeant and Gardiner.

Faced with the strength of Maia's character, Charlotte Carlyle couldn't maintain her charade. Her eyes narrowed, her false tears vanished, and her mouth screwed up into a point.

"It wasn't my fault!" she burst out. "Nobody would listen to me. Nobody would trust me. The Magistra ignored me. All I ever wanted was what was best for the college, but did she care? I told her about Tom's negligence—yes, yours, you foul little boy," she hissed, her glare falling on Tom, sitting as though frozen still in the driver's seat of the motorcar. "But did she dismiss him? No, instead she chided me for tale-telling! As though I were a child! And then Jenny—I'll not call her *Miss* Pelham, she's no better than me despite what she wants to think—kept being given more and more responsibility, and I knew she was using it to hurt others, but what would be the point of telling the Magistra when she wouldn't listen to me even when I had proof about Tom's carelessness? I had to do something."

"So you started stealing things to try to make it look like Miss Pelham was a thief." Maia's voice was still cold, still steady.

"I knew if I encouraged people to report the thefts to the Magistra, Jenny would contradict me, simply for the sake of trying to keep me in my 'proper' place. I knew that if I could start small with the thefts and work my way toward something larger, something big enough the person *had* to tell the Magistra, it would come out that I'd been telling them to take it to her and Jenny had been forcing them to keep quiet. Then Jenny would be sacked and I'd finally be recognized and appreciated." Her face twisted. "I even had planned to give her the memory potion at just the right moment, so that she'd forget where she'd been and what she'd been doing at the time of the final theft, and she wouldn't have an alibi. Oh, everybody thinks of me as useless little Lottie, but I was clever! Cleverer than they could have imagined!"

"But something went wrong," Maia prompted.

Charlotte's face crumpled. "Nobody cared at all about the thefts. Jenny even managed to convince most of them their things hadn't been stolen at all, just lost or misplaced! Even the garnet and gold bracelet wasn't enough. I wrote threatening letters to myself, and even made it look like I'd been attacked on the bridge, but it still wasn't enough. So I wrote to Gwen, because I knew she would believe me." She sneered. "Stupid little Gwen, the darling of the Magistra, always ready to be the champion of the downtrodden. If she told the Magistra the matter was serious, the Magistra would listen to *her*."

"But then Gwen said she was coming to help you, instead of taking it to the Magistra."

"Interfering! She was always interfering. If it's anyone's fault about Appleby, it's hers. If she'd just stayed in London like she was supposed to, instead of coming all the way out here ..."

Len thought he might be ill, and he could only thank the heavens that Gwen was still at the boarding house and not here having to listen to this.

"I had to make the potion in a hurry, so I stole my landlady's cookery book—she deserved to lose it, she never treated me with respect, either—and swapped it with the potion book from the Merriman Collection. I wrote one final letter to myself and left it in my room so that it would be obvious that I was kidnapped. I was going to leave it in an envelope, but I remembered it would look odd if there wasn't a postmark, so I left the letter as was. Then I vanished, so that finally, people would believe that I knew something important, and would trace it back to Jenny, and she would get her comeuppance and I would be a hero!"

"But what about the porter?" Dale said. "I don't understand that."

Charlotte cast him a glance of utter scorn. "Of course you don't, you stupid little man. You didn't understand anything, not the entire time. I gave him the memory potion, of course, when I left the college after swapping the books. I came into his lodge and offered to share one of his disgusting cups of tea, and I put the potion in the tea so that he'd forget I was there and that I had left through the front gate. And it worked, too—no matter how much Miss Linton said I was a failure at potions, that one worked!" Her eyes shone with vindictive glee.

"Then why kill him, later?" Dale demanded.

Charlotte rolled her eyes. "Nobody was blaming Jenny. I had set up listening spells all over the college so that I would be able to hear when she was blamed, and could figure out the best time to stage my dramatic re-appearance, having rescued myself from her dastardly clutches."

"That's why I saw all the traces of your magic all over the college," Maia said. "It was your listening spells."

"Yes, and very rude and intrusive that was of you, too!" Charlotte glared at her. "You and Gwen, and these other two—you all mucked things up royally between you. Couldn't even tell that Jenny was to blame! You left me with no choice but to come back into the college and plant Archer's scarf in Jenny's desk. I'd intended to keep it for myself—I hadn't needed much of the silk for the potion, so I knew I could mend it and wear it once I was away from this place where someone might recognize it—but you forced me to use it against Jenny instead. I tried using a chameleon spell so no one would notice me, but somehow, I couldn't get it quite right. It's not my fault! But Appleby saw me coming through the gate, and then he started to remember our tea together—that shouldn't have happened, either! The potion was supposed to make his memory loss permanent! It's not my fault, I know I did everything right. That Merriman must have written it down wrong. But once Appleby started to remember, I had to kill him, don't you understand? I had to, or he would have ruined everything!"

"And the stick?" Maia asked.

"I held onto it, thinking I could still use it to blame Jenny. Then I heard that you'd found out she'd been blackmailing Foster—that's one decent thing you did, I suppose, though you might have been a bit quicker about it. So then I took advantage of the gate being left unguarded while the police were dealing with all that rubbish, and came back to hide it in Miss Linton's cupboard. That would teach her to always sneer at me! But then I realized I'd better get away while I still could, because I couldn't think of a way to make it look like I'd been kidnapped and hidden by Miss Linton—the plan had been aimed at Jenny, you understand. Anyway, Jenny was done for, so what did I need to stick around for anymore?" She turned her head to scowl at Len. "I still don't know how you caught me. You're none of you clever enough to have figured it all out. My plan was perfect! It should have worked! If everyone else had just done what they were supposed to, it would have all been fine. I even remembered to steal Appleby's ledger, to make it look like that was the motive for his death." She drew a shuddering breath and began to cry again, this time for real.

"I didn't want to kill Appleby," she wailed. "Why didn't the old fool just stay forgetful? Why does nothing ever go the way I want it to? All I ever wanted was for people to appreciate me! Why couldn't they have just seen all my hard work and how much I tried? Why did everyone force me to do this? It wasn't my fault!"

Dale cleared his throat and nodded at the sergeant. "Better take her in custody, sergeant," he said.

Len had never been so happy to hand a prisoner off to someone in higher authority in his entire life.

Chapter 16

The aftermath of a case was always unpleasant. This one was worse than usual.

Maia felt—detached, somehow, from her body, and from the scenes that followed upon their arrival back at Saint Dorothea's. She seemed to see it all from the side and above, everything that happened.

Len, laying out the pieces of the case and connecting them logically for the Magistra and other staff.

The Magistra's face as she realized just how far Charlotte had gone to try to gain her approval.

Miss Linton's rage at having been arrested for murder and what she felt was the lack of support from the Magistra and her fellow staff members, and her resignation on the spot of her position at Saint Dot's in retaliation for the slight.

Miss Archer's gently grieved expression through the entire tale and beyond.

Gwen, returning from the boarding house in time to hear of Charlotte's arrest, and her refusal to believe it until Becket took her aside and spoke to her privately, after which she left abruptly for a long walk.

Len's haunted expression as he explained it over and over again, until finally everyone seemed to understand it all.

The frightened students, scurrying past Maia and Len on the grounds and in the corridors, as though they were carriers of some highly contagious disease.

Nathan Quirke, bowing courteously to the Magistra and thanking her for allowing him to observe how the English put together a magical college, but he thought they'd follow a different path in Boston.

(*So that was what he was doing here*, Maia's brain whispered, but even that didn't seem to matter anymore.)

Foster handing his resignation in to the Magistra, saying he couldn't work in a place where he was not trusted.

Inspector Dale, returning from the police station to tell them his team was working on a way of handling this that wouldn't reveal magic to the university or larger police force, and to congratulate Whitney and Davies on solving the case for him.

"I will, of course, see to it you are credited," he said.

"No need for that," Len answered wearily.

Sally Linton's staunch declaration to the college at large that she didn't care what had happened or what her aunt or that stupid Mr. Quirke thought, *she* was going to stand by Saint Dot's.

And all the while, Maia didn't feel or think anything, merely observed dispassionately.

In fact, Maia didn't come back to herself until Len abruptly drew her aside as everyone filed toward the dining hall for a meal nobody really wanted, and said,

"I think our Gwen had the right idea. Come along."

Maia blinked and felt a small amount of life return to her numbed limbs and brain.

"Yes," she said, and didn't even ask where they were going to go. She simply wanted out—away from these walls, these buildings that had held so much promise when she had first arrived and had delivered only death and ugliness.

She fetched her coat and hat, eschewing gloves despite the impropriety of it, and rejoined Len at the gate, walking away from Saint Dorothea's with a quick twist of her shoulders, sloughing it from her back as a snake shed its skin.

She didn't pay much attention to where they were going at first, only that they were not heading toward the station—thank heaven—nor the part of Cambridge where Mrs. Hawkins kept her boarding house, nor toward Miss Pelham's flat. So long as they were headed elsewhere, Maia didn't care if they walked all night.

In fact, it was only about ten minutes before Len paused and touched her arm, and Maia came out of her trance to see a complex wooden footbridge spanning the Cam about fifty feet down from the road where they stood.

"The Mathematical Bridge," Len said. "I thought you ought to see it at least once before we left Cambridge."

"Ah," said Maia. She thought for a moment. "Is it true that it was originally designed without any nuts or bolts holding it together?"

Len shrugged. "Who knows? That's the story, at any rate. They also say it was designed by Sir Isaac Newton, but I doubt that part of the story as well. Perhaps a magician built it."

"Perhaps," Maia answered. She spoke a little bitterly. "I wonder if he ever regretted taking up magic."

She felt more than saw Len's look, but he spoke lightly enough when he responded. "Most likely. I don't think any of us get through life without some regrets for our choices, magicians or not. Part of being human, I suspect."

Maia did not respond, but the hard knot that had built itself around her heart began to ease ever so slightly.

They strolled into the center of the city, both of them looking and admiring now. King's Parade was bustling with students and visitors, the towers of King's College Chapel with their filigreed turrets dominating the view, practically glowing in the setting sun that was breaking through the clouds only now, at the end of the day, as it sank toward the horizon. While Maia admired the impressive buildings, she was happier when Len led her down a side street, where things were less busy, though no less beautiful.

When she saw the old stone church building—St. Bene't's was the name on the front—a sense of longing settled over her.

"Do you mind?" she asked Len, indicating the building.

His face lightened as he followed her motion. "Ah. Jolly good thought."

Maia had a brief moment of ruefully wishing she'd worn gloves after all as she entered through the peaked archway, but as she stepped inside all her discomfort melted away, leaving her with nothing but peace. Not the emptiness and numbness she'd felt earlier, but genuine peace, giving her the space to look squarely at what had happened and why it had hit so painfully.

No one else was in there at the moment, and Len strolled up and down the aisles, seemingly happy to wander until she was ready to move on. Maia sank down into a pew and allowed herself to *think*.

What had made the ending to this case so much worse than any of the others?

It wasn't just the pain that it had caused Gwen, though that was clearly a part of it. Coming to help a person who ended up not only not needing their help, but had caused the trouble in the first place—that was another part. Seeing the scholars she had come to respect so stricken by the loss of five of their members played another part.

But none of those got to the heart of the matter.

Which was, in short, that Maia could all too easily see herself in Charlotte Carlyle.

She had from the beginning, she realized that now. From the start of the case, with Gwen's description of Lottie as plodding and dull, Maia had leapt to her defense, feeling all the sting of those words thrown at her by her sisters, her enemies, and even sometimes her friends over the years.

"Oh yes, Maia is a lovely person, so conscientious ... but really rather dull, I'm afraid," was the refrain of her life. *"Not much spark to her."*

It was why she had reacted so strongly to it appearing as though Len cared more for Tom than for Charlotte when he had thought Tom the murderer, and why she had castigated herself so thoroughly for letting herself get caught up in the joy of spell-creation when she felt she ought to have been focusing on saving Charlotte.

And even at the end, as Charlotte Carlyle had raved and blamed everyone around her for her actions rather than accepting responsibility for what she had done ... Maia could still see a frightening resemblance.

She didn't think she'd ever fall so low as to lie, plot, and murder. But that intense desire to be appreciated, to be valued even though she wasn't charming, exciting, or any of those other traits that made people admired and loved? Oh yes, she knew that all too well.

She didn't want to change who she was. She didn't want to be charming, like her sister Ellie, or passionate, like her other sister Merry. She wanted to be herself still, to be *Maia*, but to have the world somehow suddenly see her personality as just as desirable as theirs.

That desire had already started to twist itself into resentment, as evidenced by this case and how prickly she had been toward her friends through it, taking everything they said as a personal slight or dig. Was she going to let herself continue down that path, turning into someone as bitter and self-pitying as Lottie?

She was not. She didn't know how she would prevent it, not yet, but she vowed then and there—or perhaps it was a prayer—that she would put aside resentment and bitterness, and find a way to reconcile who she was with how she wanted to be seen.

She had thought, when she first started pursuing magic, that this was her chance to finally be valued. Her abilities were strong, even Aunt Amelia said that. And perhaps, if she had followed her aunt's path, she would have gained admiration and respect from her peers.

But that wasn't Maia. Aunt Amelia was ambitious, and she enjoyed power. Maia helped people. It was what she had always done. And she wasn't willing to give that up.

Was there a way to continue helping others that didn't involve making herself small, turning herself into a doormat for others to trample over, living in a constant state of seething rebellion without ever being able to do anything about it? She had thought this detective business would be the key, but it had proven just as confining as all her old ways of life so far.

So where did that leave her?

Maia wasn't sure. But she was certain now that she would find a way, somehow, even if it took her the next ten years—

though she also freely admitted to herself she hoped it wouldn't.

She drew a deep breath and rose, feeling lighter than she had in—well, months. Len looked over at her, a smile crooking his mouth.

"Better?"

"Nearly," Maia said. "Thank you for your patience."

He shook his head. "I needed this too, though I don't know that I would have thought of it on my own. So I think I should be thanking you."

Now that she was calmer, Maia was conscious of a burning emptiness in her middle.

"Good gracious," she said all at once. "We missed dinner and tea, and left the college in the middle of supper!"

No wonder she had felt so odd before—she had been attempting to deal with deep emotional turmoil on an empty stomach.

Len chuckled. "Luckily for us, there's a pub right across the way—it's where I was headed when you spotted this place. While you were fetching your things earlier, I told Becket to find Gwen and meet us there. There's ... something I need to tell you all."

That sounded rather ominous. Maia's new sense of peace ruffled on the surface, like water disturbed by a heron taking flight.

Still, there was no sense in fretting on an empty stomach.

"I hope they do a steak and kidney pie," she said. "I'm ravenous."

* * *

The Eagle pub *did* do a steak and kidney pie, and it was splendid.

Gwen and Becket were waiting for them and had secured a table when Maia and Len entered the building with the low, dark ceilings and cozy atmosphere. Becket placed the order for everyone and brought back four pints of cider.

Len held up his pint. "To …" he began, and fell silent.

Maia understood his dilemma. How to toast the end of the case when Gwen was so heavy-eyed with grief and betrayal still?

"To faithful friends," Len finished, surprisingly.

"Hear, hear," Maia and Becket murmured. Gwen didn't speak, but she touched her frosted glass to theirs and drank with the rest of them.

They didn't speak much throughout the meal, focusing more on the good food and letting the troubles of the day melt into the background. Not until they were finished eating and on their second round of cider did Len clear his throat and speak again.

"I have some sad news, I'm afraid—well, sad for me, at least, and I hope sad for you. Though not too sad, as I'd rather not see you all gloomy and what-not. But a little sad, that would be good."

"Len, you're playing your foolish Englishman role again," Maia said.

He blinked. "Right. Sorry. Habit, y'know. Well. The truth of the matter is—that is, I have no choice but to—or rather, circumstances are such that—well, the long and the short of it is, I have to go home."

It was so unexpected that none of them reacted at first. Then Maia said, cautiously,

"I see. Now?"

"As soon as I get back to London."

Oh. *Oh.* He meant to the family estate on the Welsh border, not his flat in London.

"Is your mother well?" Gwen asked quickly.

"Oh yes, the mater is always in the peak of health. It's the estate that's not well. Dashed unwell, as it turns out. My tenant's been robbing me blind, by the looks of things, and making a mess of the estate in the process. Firing the steward, turning the tenants out so he can put his own cronies in place, threatening them with his solicitor pal when they complain, cutting down trees … it's a devil of a tangle, and it's going to take all my best efforts—and Becket's, which will more than likely be to the point—to make it smooth."

Realization hit Maia like a horse's hoof to the chest. "You're not talking of a brief weekend visit."

He met her eyes. "No."

"You mean to stay."

"I have to. As long as it takes to make this right. Which could be months … or even years, if the worst is true."

No more Len in London. No more morning coffee or afternoon tea together, no more chats by his fireside, no more experimenting together with magic, no more working together to solve the ills of the world, no more … no more *Len.*

Maia felt desolate in a way she hadn't even when she had realized the truth about Charlotte Carlyle. What was she going to do without Len?

"Oh," said Gwen in a small voice. "That means you won't be part of the detective agency any more."

That was a fresh blow. Maia hadn't even thought of that yet. How could they have Whitney and Davies without the Davies?

"You could consider us the Herefordshire branch, I suppose, but in reality—no. I am sorry. I only just found out myself yesterday, and there hasn't been a chance yet to tell you all. Dashed bad timing, I know."

"No, it's just—I was going to tell you both that I'm coming back here," Gwen said.

"Here to Cambridge?" Maia asked, stunned under this fresh revelation.

"Here to Saint Dot's," she clarified. "With all that's happened, I feel I owe it to Dr. Bingham and the rest to come help them through. It's going to be difficult, what with the losses, and the rumors that will spread even though Inspector Dale said he would do his best to keep this quiet. And—and to be honest, I'm not sure I want to be a detective anymore. It—I know it's important, but somehow justice doesn't feel like enough anymore. There needs to be something more. I don't know what, but I don't think I can go back to solving cases as though nothing had changed after—after having been *inside* this one, so to speak." She looked miserably at Maia. "But I don't want to abandon you, Maia. I thought—I thought it would be fine for me to leave, with you and Len and Becket still working together, but it—it doesn't feel right to leave you all on your own."

"No," Maia said, for once speaking without even thinking it through first. "No, Gwen, you must of course follow your conscience. And Len, of course you and Becket must go straighten things out on the estate, however long it takes. This isn't about me. Please, don't any of you feel guilty for a moment about it."

"But what will you do?" Len asked, looking dazed. He clearly hadn't been expecting Gwen's defection on the heels of his own need to depart.

Maia thought about it as she drank more of her cider. It was odd, but after feeling so unappreciated by her friends throughout this entire case, as though they didn't value her because she wasn't bright and brilliant, she didn't feel abandoned or resentful at all now that they were all leaving her. She *knew*, down to her very bones, that Len would rather stay in London, and was only leaving of necessity. She *knew* that Gwen was not leaving because she didn't care about Maia, but rather because she needed to find her own path forward. She *knew* that Becket was leaving because of loyalty to Len, not because he wished to depart.

This knowledge wasn't based on logic. Perhaps some of Len's intuition was rubbing off on her.

"What will I do?" she said at last. "Do you know, I haven't the faintest idea."

But she was looking forward to finding out.

THE END

About the Author

A storyteller from the time she could talk, as soon as E.L. Bates learned to write she began putting her stories down on paper and inflicting them on the general public. Stories of magic and derring-do have been her favorites from almost as young. She is a firm believer in Lloyd Alexander's maxim that "fantasy is not an escape from reality; it is a way of understanding reality." Also, it's a lot of fun both to write and to read.

When not writing, Bates works as a freelance editor and an office admin, and recently returned to school for Information and Library Science. In her spare time (what's that?) she enjoys knitting, reading, and hiking with her family.

You can find out more about E.L. Bates via her website, where you can also sign up for her newsletter for exclusive looks at new books and upcoming sales.

You can connect with me on:

🌐 http://www.stardancepress.com

Also by E.L. Bates

Whitney and Davies
  Magic Most Deadly
  Glamours and Gunshots
  Death by Disguise
  Magic & Mayhem (short story collection)
  While Shepherds Watch (a Christmas novella)

From the Shadows (a cozy space adventure)

Writing as Louise Bates
  Pauline Gray Investigates